James Maidment, William Hugh Logan, John Tatham

The Dramatic Works of John Tatham

James Maidment, William Hugh Logan, John Tatham

The Dramatic Works of John Tatham

ISBN/EAN: 9783337337735

Printed in Europe, USA, Canada, Australia, Japan

Cover: Foto ©Andreas Hilbeck / pixelio.de

More available books at **www.hansebooks.com**

DRAMATISTS OF THE RESTORATION.

TATHAM.

THE DRAMATIC

WORKS OF JOHN TATHAM.

WITH INTRODUCTIONS AND NOTES.

THIS VOLUME IS DEDICATED,

IN ALL SINCERITY AND AFFECTION,

TO

THEODORE MARTIN, ESQ., C.B.,
ETC. ETC. ETC.

BY

THE EARLIEST FRIENDS OF HIS YOUTH,

THE EDITORS.

CONTENTS.

———◆———

INTRODUCTORY NOTICE.

OF John Tatham, the author of the present plays, etc., very little is known. He is characterised in the *Biographia Dramatica* as City Poet, and undoubtedly was the author of the *Lord Mayor's Pageants* from 1657 until 1664.

Granger, however, in his *Biographical History of England*, vol. iv. (a work of immense literary value, although seemingly not yet recognised), remarks thus in reference to the engraved portrait of our poet :—

" ' John Tatham,' says Winstanley, 'was one whose muse began to bud with his youth, which produced early blossoms of not altogether contemptible poetry,' of which he has given us 'a taste' in the following lines. The author addresses himself in the person of Momus—

> ' How now, presumptuous lad ! think'st thou that we
> Will be disturb'd with this thy infancy
> Of wit ?
> Or *does* thy amorous thoughts beget a flame
> (Beyond its merits) for to court the name
> Of poet ? Or is't common now-a-days
> Such slender wits dare claim such things as bays ?'

" However strange it may seem, it is certain that he *did* ' claim such things ;' and, what is more strange, his claim was readily admitted. He has been erroneously called *City Poet*, and was deemed a worthy forerunner of Settle. He undoubtedly wrote panegyrics upon two Lord Mayors (in the reign of Charles II.), in whose estimation they were as *good rhymes*, and probably pleased as much, as if they had been written by Waller himself. He was author of several plays, most of which were published before the Restoration."

This short notice, by "W. Richardson," is referable to the engraved portrait mentioned in Granger thus :—

" JOHN TATHAM, poet ; *an anonymous head, over which*

b

two Cupids hold a crown of laurel. Underneath are these verses—

> ' Here is noe schisme, the judging eye may see
> In every line a perfect harmony,
> And love and beauty, for soe great a grace
> Joy in theire lovely Reconciler's face.—C. R.' "

This engraved portrait is by no means "an anonymous head," as the copy in our possession distinctly announces it as "John Tatham."

Mr. Fairholt, in his *Lord Mayor's Pageants*, printed for the Percy Society in 1843, says : "As I have set myself the task of compiling this book, I have endeavoured to do it worthily ; and I have visited every accessible library to get together extracts from all the pageant-pamphlets that were published, but their great rarity, and the impossibility of getting at all, has foiled my attempt at thorough completeness."

The same may be said of Tatham's Pageants. With the exception of that which we now reprint, *London's Triumph*, celebrated October 29, 1659, and of which Mr. Fairholt observes, "I have not been able to see a copy," they are difficult to assemble together, if copies of all exist.

He wrote the City Pageants for eight years, all of which were, with one exception, named *London's Triumph*.

The pageant of 1657 was in honour of Sir Richard Chiverton, of the Skinners' Company, who was mayor. That of 1658 was produced for the mayoralty of Sir John Ireton, of the Clothworkers' Company. The Lord Mayor of 1659 was Thomas Aleyn.

The year 1660 was that of the Restoration of Charles the Second, when Tatham, in accordance with the subject of the times, produced his pageant of *The Royal Oak*, which Mr. Fairholt has reprinted in his book.

The *London's Triumph* of 1661 was the complimentary pageant of the mayor, Sir John Frederick, of the Grocers' Company. His Majesty, who had been enrolled as a member of this Company, was present at the show, and one of the characters, Galatea, thanked him in their name, wishing he might "outrun a century of years."

In 1662 *London's Triumph*, "presented in severall delightful scenes, both on water and land," was produced for the mayoralty of Sir John Robinson, of the Clothworkers' Company.

Londinum Triumphans, or *London's Triumph*, for Sir Anthony Bateman, of the Skinners' Company, was the pageant of 1663.

The last of Tatham's productions—that of 1664—was invented to do honour to "the truly deserving of honour, Sir John Laurence, Knight," of the Haberdashers' Company. A speech was addressed to the King, who was present, beginning:

> " Pardon, not praise, great Monarch, we implore,
> For showing you no better sights, nor more.
> We hope your Majesty will not suppose
> You're with your Jonsons or your Inigoes ;
> And though you make a court, you're in the city,
> Whose vein is to be humble, though not witty."

Evelyn has recorded that on this occasion "he din'd at Guildhall, at the upper table. My Lord Mayor came twice up to us, first drinking in the golden goblet his Majesty's health, then the French King's, as a compliment to the Embassador [Commines, who was present] ; then we return'd my Lord Mayor's health, trumpets and drums sounding. The cheer was not to be imagined for the plenty and raritie, with an infinite number of persons at the rest of the tables in that ample hall."

The great fire and the plague for the five years following caused the accustomed pageantry to be in some degree abandoned.

Thomas Jordan, who was a comedian of some popularity, succeeded Tatham as City Poet.

Mr. Fairholt, in the introduction to his reprint of the pageant of *The Royal Oak*, remarks of Tatham : "From a perusal of his plays, he appears to be chiefly remarkable for his loyalty, and his hatred of the Scotch." He further says in his notes, quoting the word "pentioners" (in the original this is misprinted petitioners), "I may here notice that the pageant seems to have been carelessly printed throughout, which, added to Tatham's incompetency as a writer or grammarian, occasionally makes such havoc of the 'King's English' that his meaning is sometimes obscured." Of this "incompetency" our readers are left to judge for themselves.

Such of Tatham's works as are in the British Museum are as follows :—

Fancies Theatre, 1640.

Mirrour of Fancies (another edition of the same), 1657.
Ostella, 1650.
The Distracted State, 1651.
Scots Figgaries, 1652.
London's Triumph (Richard Chiverton, Lord Mayor), 1657.
London's Triumph (Sir John Ireton, Lord Mayor), 1658.
London's Glory—Entertainment of Charles II., 1660.
The Royal Oak (Sir Robert Brown, Lord Mayor), 1660.
The Rump, 1660.
    Do. 2d edition, 1661.
London's Triumphs (Sir John Frederick, Lord Mayor), 1661.
Aqua Triumphalis, 1662.
London's Triumph (Sir John Laurence, Lord Mayor), 1664.

Knavery in all Trades is ranked among Tatham's dramatic pieces, both in Rhode's *Catalogue* and the *Bibliographer's Manual*, but it is exceedingly questionable whether he had any hand in it, after his long experience, it being a very feeble production. The *Biographia Dramatica* thus notices it :—

"*Knavery in all Trades*, or *The Coffee House.* Com. Anon. 4to, 1664. This play was acted by a company of London apprentices in the Christmas holidays, and, as it is said in the title page, with great applause. This applause, however, was probably no more than their own self-approbation, it being a very indifferent performance, and not entitled to success in any one of the regular theatres."

The pageant we now reprint, which appears to be the rarest of them all, is from a copy preserved at Edinburgh in the library of the Faculty of Advocates.

JAMES MAIDMENT.
W. H. LOGAN.

25 ROYAL CIRCUS,
EDINBURGH, *30th Nov.* 1878.

LOVE CROWNS THE END.

A

Love Crownes the End. A Pastorall presented by the Scholleea [sic] of Bingham, in the County of Notingham, in the yeare 1632. Written by Jo. Tatham, Gent. "Sed opus docere virtus." London : Printed by I. N. for Richard Best, and are to be sold at his shop, neere Grayes-Inne-Gate in Holborne. 1640.

THIS pastoral is not of itself inscribed to any one. Bibliographically, *Love Crowns the End*, although with a separate title-page, is continuous of Tatham's *Fancie's Theatre*, of the same date, 1640, which is dedicated to Sir John Winter. This is followed by the author's verses "to the honor'd patron of his book," "Fancie to the Reader," and verses to the author, severally signed by R. Brome, Tho. Nabbes, C. G., Geo. Lynn, Robert Chamberlaine, H. Davison, James Jones, William Barnes, Tho. Rawlins, An. Newport, R. Pynder, and W. Ling.

Fancie's Theatre ends with signature I, and *Love Crowns the End* begins at K ; but there is no pagination to either.

It is thus titled : "*The Fancie's Theater*, by John Tatham, Gent. Horat. :

"' Quod si me Lyricis vatibus inseris,
Sublimi feriam sidera vertice.'

London : Printed by John Norton, for Richard Best, and are to be sold at his shop, neere Grayes-Inne Gate in Holbourn. 1640."

This piece is thus entered in Langbaine's list : "*Love Crowns the End*, a tragic comedy acted by the scholars of Bingham, in the county of Nottingham. This play is not divided into acts, and is much shorter than most usually are ; being fitted purposely, as I suppose, for those youths that acted it. 'Tis printed with his poems, called *The Mirror of Fancies*, in 8vo (London, 1657), and dedicated to Sir John Winter, Secretary of State to His Majesty in exile."

It will be observed that Langbaine here notices the second edition of these poems.

Sir John Winter, to whom Tatham also dedicated the first edition of his poems in 1640, does not at that date appear to have been generally known as having received the honour of knighthood from Charles I.; for in 1642, when the unfortunate monarch had yielded to the demands of his enemies by the process of "squeezing,"—so very effective when the rulers of a kingdom give evidence of weakness of

purpose,—among those for whose removal from his own presence and that of the Queen there were specially named
" Mr. William Murray, Mr. Porter" (Endymion Porter, it is
presumed), " Mr. John Winter, and Mr. William Crofts,
being all persons of evil fame, and disaffection to the public
peace and prosperity of the kingdom, and instruments
of jealousy and discontent between the King and the Parliament." *

That the King would assent to this demand cannot be
doubted ; for if he could sacrifice Strafford, he could have
no scruples in banishing his attached servants from his
presence.

The office of " Secretary of State," which Sir John Winter
held, was to the Queen and not to her husband, as is thus
evidenced in the dedication of the *Fancie's Theatre* in 1640:—

" To the Honorable and the most worthy Mecænas Sir
    JOHN WINTER, Knight, Secretary of State and Master
    of Requests to the Queenes most excellent Majestie.

" HONOR'D SIR,—The confidence I have of your native
goodnesse (of which the world is sufficient dilater) has
prompt mee to this audacious presumption, which with some
would have beene held a crime insufferable.   But I know
your Honor is so farre from a censurer, that you had rather
cherish endeavours than destroy 'em : Besides, there's a
certaine sect of selfe-affecters, that will (unlesse some judi-
cious Patron be fixt to the fronts-peece, as the beames of the
sunne, to correct their sawsie peering with blindnesse) not
only disgorge their envie, but wrest the sense to be succinct ;
I (knowing your name to be such, as among the discerning
spirits deserves the highest attributes of worth ; and of such
singular power, 'twill extirp the malevolent thoughts that
raigne in the vulgar and most infectious traducers) tender
this, as my first sacrifice, at the altar of your mercy.   And
if it may obtaine the reflection of your acceptance, 'twill so
much encourage your poore admirer, that I shall be ambitious
in the continuance of your favours.   These are the mayden
blosomes of my muse, which (without your protection) may
(in their infancie) be destroyed by the breath of Zoilus ; but,
shelter'd by your Honor, they shall live, and dare the
criticks' rancour, retorting to their owne shame.   Sir, the
fostering this orphan will make you famous for charity, and

* Clarendon, vol. ii. p. 187.   Oxford, 1826.   8vo.

impose an obligation beyond expression upon your Honor's
truly devoted, JO. TATHAM."

It may also be as well to give Tatham's verses :—

"To the Honor'd PATRON of his Book.

"SIR,

"As my service binds me and my love
(May your fair self so of the same approve),
As your deservings, I have plac'd you here
Equal with Phœbus in his hemisphere,
Where your refulgent brightness casts a light
Into these twinkling lamps, and gives them sight.
Minerva bade me tell you she is proud
Of those deserts which in your breast do crowd
As in a throng, which our capacity,
Not able to find out, leaves to her eye.
Thrice worthy Hero, may your halcyon days
Be ne'er extinct till crazy Time decays.

"JO. TATHAM."

Clarendon is silent as to Winter's future fortunes ; but
from the dedication of the second edition of *Fancie's Theatre*,
it would seem that he had followed Charles the Second to the
Court of France ; and, from the following note in Evelyn's
Diary, 11th July 1656, had returned to England, no doubt
encouraged by the countenance afforded by Cromwell for
the return of such exiles as could bring with them from
abroad such inventions as might be deemed serviceable to
the interest of England.

"Came home by Greenwich Ferry, where I saw Sir J.
Winter's project of charring sea-coal, to burn out the sulphur,
and render it sweet. He did it by burning the coal in such
earthen pots as the glass-men melt their metal ; so firing
them without consuming them—using a bar of iron in each
crucible or pot, which bar has a hook at one end—that so
the coals, being melted in a furnace with other sea-coals
under them, may be drawn out of the pots sticking to the
iron, whence they are beaten off in great half-exhausted
cinders, which, being rekindled, make a clear, pleasant
chamber-fire, deprived of their sulphur and arsenic malig-
nity. What success it may have, time will discover."—
Evelyn's *Diary* (edited by Bray). London, 1854. Vol. i. p.
316. "Many years ago, Lord Dundonald, a Scotch noble-

man, revived the project, but with the proposed improvement of extracting and saving the tar. Unfortunately his lordship did not profit by it. The gas companies sell the coal thus charred by the name of *coke*, as fuel for many purposes."

It is surmised that Winter died before the Restoration, as, from the office he had occupied, it is to be presumed he would have been preferred by Charles to the Peerage. The family of Winter was an old family in England; and Crofts, who is mentioned with him, was created a Baron.

The merits of the piece itself are rather humble, but it bears the impress of having been a juvenile effort, and on that account ought not to be too severely criticised. The printer, besides, takes some blame to himself for imperfections, for he appends this note :—

"*Gentle Reader, there are some faults which (through the obscurity of the Coppie, and absence of the Author) have passed the Presse; To particularize them were needlesse; But favourably looke o're them, and with thy Pen courteously correct such defects as thou shall finde, not condemning the Presse or injuring the Author.*"

THE PROLOGUE.

You stars of honour, brighter than the day,
Or new-rais'd Phœbus in his morning ray !
As rich in wisdom as in virtues rare,
Accept the choicest dish our wits prepare
As a third course to please your eye, which still
Covets to have of novelties its fill.
We have not bundled up some kickshaws here
To bid you welcome ; we do hate such gear.
Our brain's the kitchen, and our wit's the meat,
Preparative to which we bid you eat
If like't, if not, refrain't ; you judges sit
To damn or save our not yet ripen'd wit.
So rest upon your goodness ; if you frown,
Our poor endeavours then are trodden down.

DRAMATIS PERSONÆ.

ALEXIS.
CLITON.
LUSTFUL SHEPHERD.
LYSANDER.
DAPHNES.
LEON.
FRANCISCO.
SCRUB.

FLORIDA.
CLOE.
CLAUDIA.
GLORIANA.

THE DESTINIES, A HEAVENLY MESSENGER,
NYMPHS, ETC.

LOVE CROWNS THE END.

———

A grove discovered, and in an obscure corner thereof
CLITON, *as being asleep.   To him* ALEXIS.

Al. How still the morning is ! as if it meant
To steal upon us without Time's consent,
And pry into our errors.   I have been
Searching in every thicket, wood, and green,
To find my lamb, and many doleful cries
Enter'd my ears ere day.   What's this that lies
In such an obscure place, where none scarce tread,
Unless the ghosts of the disturbed dead ?
Bless me, great Pan ! I see it's Cliton's face,—
With a sword drawn.   How happy was my chase
This way !   I hope his folly has not made
Himself a beast, as butcher'd with this blade.
'T may be he sleeps.   I'll speak to him, and try !
Yet I half doubt him, 'cause he here doth lie.—
Cliton, awake ! the night's dislodg'd, and now
Bright morn is trimming her fair virgin brow
To court the sun, when, from the eastern deep
And Thetis' lap, his glimmering beams up peep
To gild his glorious car.   Cliton, awake !
And, with thy sleep, all dreams of horror shake
That may affright thee.

Cli.   Kind Alexis, thanks !
How found you me ?
    Al.   Walking those flow'ry banks,
'Twixt the green valley and the place which we
Have consecrated to love's deity,
A stray'd lamb seeking, I did hear sad moans
Proceed from some, like peals of parting groans;
Which I pursued, but in my search I found
None but yourself—you resting on this ground.
I wonder'd much to see you !
    Cli.   So you might ;
But when you've heard the cause on't, 'twill affright
Your easy breast.   Do you observe this hand ?
This fatal hand, at my unjust command,
Did— Oh ! I could destroy't !
    Al.   For what offence ?
    Cli. This hand has spilt the blood of innocence,
My Florida's.   Yes !
    Al.   How ?
    Cli.   And when I'd done—
As I might well—did hide me from the sun,
Fearing his eye would be the only cause
To find me out ; and here, from men and laws,
I have obscur'd myself, and could not say
'Twas justly night when night, nor day when day.
My fact hath sullied both and stunn'd my sense,
Hurl'd to confusion all my confidence.
    Al. What urg'd thee to such inhumanity ?   Oh !
        say.
    Cli. Suspicion of her loyalty.   One day,
Dreaming Lysander had enjoy'd her love,
My jealousy to cruelty did move.
I slew her three days past, and since have been
Each night at that place I stain'd with my sin
To seek the body ; but some power divine—
For none else durst approach her vestal shrine—

Surely has render'd her immortal, and
Convey'd the body to some holier land.
   Al. The body gone ?
   Cli.   Or else my eyes deny
Their help to such an abject wretch as I.
   Al. Thy crime requires contrition ; to that
   end
Thou shalt with me, thy days to come shalt
   spend
In holy uses. I'll prepare for thee,
In the best form I can, each property
Belonging to a pensive man. You must
Forget all youthful pleasures, think on dust
And penitence, the only means to bring
Thy soul to rest after this wandering.
Will you with me ?
   Cli.   To death, or otherwise ;
Since Florida is dead, life I despise.   [*Exeunt.*

   CLOE *pursued by a* LUSTFUL SHEPHERD.

   Lust. Oh ! stay, my darling, do not fly ;
This place is private, here's none nigh.
Fear not, wench, I'll do no harm,
But embrace thee in my arm ;
Cull and kiss, and do the thing
Shepherds do at wrasteling.
   Cloe. Oh, help ! If any shepherd's near,
Hear my laments !
   Lust.   Nay, do not fear.
But if you, with coy disdain,
Think thus to leave me in my pain,
I'll force these golden locks of thine
To lie beneath these feet of mine.
Then yield, and here enjoy such sweet
As with our embraces meet.
   Cloe. Oh ! hapless maid, no aid will come.

LYSANDER *steps forth.*

Lys. Fear not, virgin !   Here is some
Nature's monster.   Villain ! why
Does thy flame now burn so high ?
Will no other serve thy turn,
To quench the heats that in thee burn,
But so fair a soul as she ?
Villain ! hence, or else I'll be
Thy butcher !   Beast, away, away !
And shun the searching eye of day.

LUSTFUL SHEPHERD *gazeth on him, then runs in.*

Cloe. Kind youth, to whom am I
Bound for this fair courtesy ?
      Lys. First unto heaven, fair creature; next to me,
A poor unworthy shepherd, as you see.
      Cloe. May your sweetest, whom you love,
Ever constant to you prove.
Be she brighter than the sun,
Pleasing as our day at noon ;
Fresher than the morning dew,
Sweeter than a new-kill'd ewe ;
Like Aurora deckt with flowers,
Or the welcome April showers !
May she love you, and you be
The mirror for true constancy.
Go, gentle youth, and this day prosperous be
Amongst our swains in your activity.   [*Exit.*
      Lys. A thousand thanks are yours.   Pan, be my
            guide !
And thou, fair Gloriana, my soul's pride,
Whose beauty has encinder'd my poor heart
Almost to nothing, and, by some strange art,
Exerts a spell to charm all men, shalt find
Thou hast a power above mere human kind. [*Exit.*

Enter DAPHNES.

Daph. Bright sun, why dost thou shine on me?
  Ah, why?
Is it to mock me? Keep thy light, for I
Had rather live in darkness, and so die.
Or dost thou show thy lustre in disdain,
Because I have so oft, with speech profane,
Blasphem'd against thy goodness, and in praise
Of a poor earthly creature spent my days?
Dost thou yet smile? Forgive me, and I'll be
No more her servant, but will honour thee.
Keep thou thy brightness, Phœbus, and this day
From all our swains I'll bring the prize away.
                             [Exit.

LEON, GLORIANA, *and* FRANCISCO.

Fran. Fairest, this day be pleased to smile on me,
  And let those hidden favours, yet unshewn,
Flow in abundance, that the swains may see
  None e'er can conquer me but you alone.
Glor. My favours, friend, are past; and you
  have tasted
So much of my poor bounty, that 'tis wasted.
Leon. We stay too long, son; pray make haste,
Let us not spend time in waste.
Daughter, you shall go with me
Where their pastime we may see.
Hark! I hear them with their noise. *[A noise within.*
Oh, my hearts! my bonny boys!
Play your parts. Would I were young,
To make one in your joyous throng!
Fran. Dearest, I must depart; this calls me hence.
Father, I leave you.—*[To Glor.]* Farewell, Inno-
  cence.   *[Exit* FRAN.
Glor. I hope for ever! Would I could foreknow
And guide the future, 'twould indeed be so.

Leon. Daughter, this way let us hie!
I am old, I'll not come nigh ;
Nor shalt thou, my dapper girl,
Lest those staves, that often whirl,
Hit thy face.   What ! again ?   [*Shout again.*
Nay, then, I fear we go in vain.
 Glor. Yet, father, let us go, that we
May learn who gain'd the victory.   [*Exeunt.*

  Enter the LUSTFUL SHEPHERD *like a* SATYR.

 Lust. Because Dame Nature—pox of all her
  tricks !—
Has not dealt so well with me as she ought,
Making me but a lump of rough-hewn stuff,
The pettish wenches will not play with me,
Nor tick, nor toy ; and, 'cause I'm apt for sport,
Howe'er I'm form'd, I've put on this disguise
To fright the baggages, when, getting some
'Twixt these my arms, I'll force them to my will,
Yet pass unknown.   Thus I my senses fill.
   [SCRUB, *within.* So ho ! so ho ! so ho !
What noise is yon ?

    Enter SCRUB.

 Scrub. Through the woods and through the
woods have I run after the runaway, my master.—
What art thou, in the devil's name ?
 Lust. Sirrah, I am—
 Scrub. A devil? I knew 't before. Thou should'st
be a lecherous devil by thy hairy hide ; but I am
no Succubus, goodman devil.
 Lust. Dost thou fear me ?
 Scrub. O Lord ! me, sir ?   I have met such
another devil as thou art in my porridge-dish.
 Lust. And didst thou know him ?
 Scrub. Know him ?   How do you mean know

him ? I should be loth to know him or thee, or he thee, or thy grand master me, for any ill ; for I have defied the devil and his works ever since the general earthquake, and that time my mother's cat miscarried in the horse-pond.

Lust. Was thy mother a witch ?

Scrub. How ! a witch, you devil ? I'll witch you !

[*Offers to strike.*

Lust. Hold, man ! she was an honest woman.

Scrub. Nay, now thou liest, and thou be'st the devil's devil ; for I have heard her soberly say, she had six bastards by a sow-gelder before she pig'd me. [*Offers again.*

Lust. Hold, hold, man !

Scrub. The devil afraid of blows ? I'll make you spit fire. [*Runs after him.*

A great shout. LYSANDER *enters, with a garland on his head, and scarfs on his arms,* CLOE *following him.*

Cloe. Friendly swain, the day is yours. You see
My prayer, it seems, successful was to thee.
Pity my maiden tears ; till now I ne'er
Sued to a shepherd, they my suitors were.
Nor deem me light because my love is such ;
I love indeed, and fear I love too much.
You sav'd my life, my chastity ! What more ?
Take me as one that was your own before.

Lys. How much I grieve, fair shepherdess, my fate
Will not permit me to apportionate
So just a mede as I ought render thee,
And thy deserts have merited from me.

Cloe. I'll be your servant, and will tend your
sheep,
Nightly watch o'er you while you sweetly sleep ;
In early morn, when you arise from bed,
You'll find for you the welcome board bespread.

And, against noon, when you from toil return,
Again fond woman's tender care you'll learn.
All these and more, when your approval's won,
Crave but your kindly smile, and say, " Well done."
   Lys. To starve your hopes from further prosecu-
     tion,
Know I've already fixed my resolution
To love but Gloriana ; she
Commands my life, my fortunes, liberty.
So much I pity you, that, I declare,
If I'd two hearts, one you should gladly share
As recompense for your love, though 'tis vain.
But why do I this language entertain?
May you live happy, and enjoy as rare
And constant shepherd as yourself is fair !   [*Exit.*
   Cloe. Is my face withered? or has nature so
Deformed me lately that I am not Cloe?
For thee, poor Cloe, shepherds have pitched the
     bar,
Wrestled, and leaped, and shown the feats of war.
For thee—each strove to gain thee as his dove,
But thou didst slight and scorn their simple love.
How many verses have the shepherds made
In praises of thy beauty, whilst thou laid
Thy heart on him that cannot hear thee nam'd,
Though thy delight is still to have him fam'd !
Many the rings and gloves thou hast receiv'd
From the poor swains thou ofttimes hast deceiv'd.
For thee on holidays, with step so bold,
They'd to the heath, next to the pinder's fold,
Where they, with music and such sweet content,
Would spend their time to make thee merriment.
Since, then, my love is not one mite rewarded,
But worse, my beauty is no more regarded,
I'll tear these golden locks, that shepherds may
Leave off their sports, and make no holiday.

Sings.

I will follow through yon grove,
Where I soon shall meet my love ;
Then with warm embraces we
Will clip and cull while none shall see.
A willow garland will I make,
And sweetly wear it for his sake.
Then through the thickets, woods, and plains,
I will hide me from the swains.
Hy da ! hy da ! what art thou ?
Come, thy name and state avow !
　　　　[*As she is running in*, DAPHNES *meets her.*
Daph. You were not wont to question thus of
　　old.
How fares my dear ?　What ! has thy love grown
　　cold ?
Cloe. Hence ! thou coward, hence from me !
Blush at thy disloyalty.
Did'st not tell me that thy fame
Would throw a lustre on my name ?
Yet suffer'st now a stranger bear
The prize, and thou to have no share ?
Daph. Your frowns, my fairest, and not he
Gain'd the victory from me.
Had you smil'd as you did frown,
All his strength I'd manger'd down.
What has disturbed thee, lovely one ?
Who injury to thy person done ?
Cloe. Ha, ha ! fool, fool ! see'st naught amiss ?
A very fool ! ha ! kiss ! kiss ! kiss !　　　[*Exit.*
Daph. What fickle things are women !　Though
　　we flout them,
It is confessed we men can't do without them.
Our too much doting, though, makes them elate ;
For, loving them, ourselves they'd make us hate.

B

This bad distemper in her, I suspect,
Proceeds from overweening self-will check'd ;
From some denial, if we only knew 't,
Lysander may have given to her suit,
Knowing my love to her.   Ah, yes ! 'tis so.
I must not let her suffer too intensely, though.

[Exit.

*A place discovered all green myrtles, adorned with
roses, a title written over it thus :*

' LOVERS' VALLEY.'

LYSANDER *and* GLORIANA.

Lys. My dearest love, fair as the eastern morn
As it breaks o'er the plains when summer's born,
Hanging bright liquid pearls on every tree,
New life and hope imparting, as to me
Thy presence brings delight, so fresh and rare
As May's first breath, dispensing such sweet air
The Phœnix does expire in ; sit, while I play
The cunning thief, and steal thy heart away,
And thou shalt stand as judge to censure me.
To recompense thy loss I must agree
To give my heart, a course we may define
As mere exchange,—I keep your heart, you mine.
    Glor. Content, my love ; thus would she court,
        sweetheart,
And thus and thus she'd play the wanton's part.

[Kisses him.

Do I not blush, Adonis ?
    Lys.   Wherefore blush ?
You spoil the jest on't.   Nay, no words—soft—
    hush !
I'll span thy waist ; now do as wantons use :
I'll be Adonis, yet will not refuse.
    Glor. Nay, fie ! you stray beyond your limits.

Lys.   Kiss !
Modesty denies not such sweet joy as this.   [*Kiss.*

To them FRANCISCO.

Fran. Where are my eyes ?   What curst unruly
    wind
Has blown them out, and left false orbs behind ?
Ye gods ! to suffer this you are unjust !
If these eyes be my own, I fondly trust
They may be more subservient to me,
Than, without leave, such objects dare to see.
But yet, let passion bend to Reason's will,
For wherefore on myself should I wish ill ?
Her oft-repeated nescios avow,
And the continual scorn upon her brow
When love I've proffered,—my suspicion was
Not wholly conjured up without some cause.
Were I prepared to combat for her charms,
I'd rush upon them, tear her from his arms ;
And— No ! Securely here I'll watch awhile,
And listen to a tale of mutual guile. [*Stands aside.*
    Glor. Now must we part, we've dallied time too
      long ;
Wilt walk ?
    Lys.   Does Gloriana think aught wrong ?
Or that time's lost that's with Lysander pass'd ?
    Fran. Deluding devil !
    Glor. That time runs so fast,
I would, Lysander, if 'twere not the stain
Would rest upon my maiden years, remain
For ever gazing on thy beauty.
    Lys.   Nay !
You mock me, Gloriana ; but the day
Is not far distant when we shall acquire,
With more security, what our hearts desire.
Where shall we meet again ?

Glor.   In yonder vale
To-morrow—early, dear.
    Lys.   I will not fail!   [*Exeunt.*
    Fran. [*Aside.*] Nor I to meet you both.   Oh,
      my best star !
Witness how just the avenging powers are !
For mischief, ye kind gods ! ye've stampt my
      brain,
Which on them I shall execute amain ;
And none shall pry into my faults within.
Revenge has coverts fit to hide his sin.   [*Exit.*

Enter CLOE, *mad.*

Sings.

Hey down a down derry,
And shall not we be merry ?
A fire on thy hole,
'Tis as black as a coal,
And thy nose is as brown as a berry.

Hi ho ! what a thing this love is !

She sings.

When love did act a woman's part,
She could have died with all her heart ;
It swell'd her so in every part,
She swore 'twas wind, and then did—

Hi ! hi ! hi ! hi !

NYMPHS *to her.   Sing about her.*

Love cannot choose but pity yield !
He never lived in tented field,
'Mongst iron-hearted men !

He knows both how and when
    Thee to restore
To what thou wert before.
He has a tender breast, which knows
Your wants by the tormenting woes
    He's subject to intense.
Then do not you despair,
That are both young and fair :
    Thus we convey you hence.

                  [*Take* CLOE *with them.*

Cloe. Where do you lead me ?   [*Exeunt.*

Enter LYSANDER *and* GLORIANA, *meeting.*

Lys. How blest are we, that Fortune hath so
  soon
Again accorded us this gracious boon !
  Glor. A favour we in duty must avow,
And to the gods in all that's grateful bow.

                  [*She sits down.*

  Lys. So sits the pride of Nature ! all things
  gay,
Each beauty that the chequer'd fields display,
In Flora's richest wardrobe, far above.
  Glor. Long practised in the flatt'ring rules ·of
  love,
Say, for such compliments, what reward you claim ?
  Lys. A kiss is more than I can merit.

                  [*Kisses her.*

  Glor.   Shame !
You are too free.
  Lys.   Pray sing !
  Glor.   And what my gains ?
You'll give me such another for my pains !
  Lys. Just put it to the trial, lovely one,
You shall not lose your labour when all's done.

Song.

Glor. Sit ! while I do gather flowers,
     And depopulate the bowers.
       Here's a kiss will come to thee !
Lys.   Give me one, I'll give thee three !
Both. Thus in harmless sport we may
     Pass all the idle hours away.
Glor.   Hark ! hark, how fine
       The birds do chime !
       And pretty Philomel
       Her moan doth tell.
Both. Then pity, pity love, and all is well.
Glor. Here's the violet, pink, and rose,
     The sweetest breathings for the nose !
Lys. Yet thy breath to me doth yield
     More fragrant scents than all the field.
Glor. Love cares not for flowers or toys,
     Play-games for your apish boys.
       Nor superstition,
       For his condition
       Is for to know—
Lys. If you love or no ?
Glor. Then answer, love ! ay or no ?
     But yet methinks that face should be
     The model of true constancy :
       Therefore no reason have I
       To suspect thy loyalty.
       Here's another kiss for thee !
Lys.   Give me one, I'll give thee three !
Both. Thus in harmless sport we may
     Pass all idle hours away.
Glor.   Hark ! hark, how fine
       The birds do chime !
       And pretty Philomel
       Her moan doth tell.
Both. Then pity, pity love, and all is well.

Lys. You've sung me 'most asleep, my eyes feel
    queer ;
I needs must make thy lap my pillow, dear.
   Glor. Repose thy gentle head on't.   Alas, ah me !
I'm heavy too, and yield to destiny.   [*Sleep.*

The DESTINIES *Sing.*

Sleep on, sleep on !
For we have so decreed
That thou must bleed.
  Sleep on, sleep on !
And may'st thou never rise,
For blood the shepherd cries.
  Sleep on ! sleep on !   [*Exeunt.*

A HEAVENLY MESSENGER *in white.*
Song.

Rise ! rise, Lysander, to prevent
  What the Destinies decreed !
Thou art constant, permanent,
  And must not bleed :
  Thy constant seed
Shall be the shepherd's joy.
    No annoy
    Shall attend
    Such a friend
As the lasses need.
    Rise ! rise ! awake !
    And sleep offshake !
The heavens are pleased thy part to take,
    For thy love's sake.   [*Exit—they stir.*

Glor. Lord, how my fancy's troubled !
Lysander ! where art thou ?

Lys. Gloriana ! I've had now
Strange thoughts, that me of sleep had dispossest
If on thy lap I had not ta'en my rest.

FRANCISCO, *disguised, with others.*

Fran. That is the man ! Upon him instantly,
While I attack his mistress.
Glor. Gracious me !
What means this outrage ?
    1*st Vil.* We'd have life and death !
Glor. What ! both ? How can that be ? Both,
    too, in one breath ?
Fran. Thy life, and thy Lysander's death !
Glor.   I'll swear
I've heard that voice ere now. Villain, beware !
Afford some milder language.
Fran.   Lest she teach
And charm my heart to pity, stop her speech !
Lys. Are you but men, and dare do this ?
1*st Vil.*   We dare !
Glor. Oh, sheathe your swords in me ! Lysander
    spare !
Fran. We'll not expostulate ;—take that !
2*d Vil.* And this ! [*They stab* LYSANDER, *who falls.*
Glor. Lysander ! Oh, my all ! my earthly bliss !
                    [*They take her with them.*
    Lys. Stay, stay ! let me but breathe my last
Upon her lips, and I'll forgive what's past. [*Rises.*
Cowards and miscreants, do you leave me thus ?
And oh, my fairest, wherefore upon us
Should light such dire misfortune ? Tell me where,
Sweet Echo, my beloved breathes the air ?
I'll follow her : they shall not dare to taint
The least hem of her garments. But I faint,
And must surrender up to earth that part

I took from her. Gloriana! oh, my heart!
[Falls fainting.

Enter CLAUDIA *and* FLORIDA.

Clau. We may for recreation walk,
And use some pretty harmless talk.
Religion does not tie us to
A stricter course than we can do.
Flor. 'Tis dangerous walking,—every field
Doth naught but sounds of horror yield;
And, to my fancy, there appear
Poor slaughtered maids : the butchers bear
The name of lovers, and can find
A way in killing to be kind.   *[Lysander.* Oh !
Ah me ! whence came that groan ?
I dread this walking here alone.
Clau. It is a shepherd, wounded sore !
Flor. Sure, I have seen this face before !
Lysander 'tis ! the truest swain
That ever pressed the verdant plain.
Clau. What ! is he mark'd for present death ?
Flor. No ; there are hopes of life : his breath,
I feel, comes coldly.
Clau.   Help him in !
Pan, be just: reward this sin. *[Take him with 'em.*
[Exeunt.

Enter SCRUB.

The devil and his dam, I think, have carried away
my master. I cannot find him in never a wench's
placuit (pocket, I should say), and yet I have been
in a simple many since I came among these mut-
ton-mongers—these sheep-eaters—unless they have
hid him amongst their wool. I cannot imagine
where he can be. I will wear my shoes to pieces
but I'll find him. *[Exit.*

Enter LYSANDER, CLAUDIA, FLORIDA, *and* CLOE.

Lys. Religious matron, from your hand divine
I have received this weary life of mine.
My wounds were not so desperate, or sure
Some angel did afford a sovereign cure,
As instantly to heal them.   Howsoe'er,
I must ascribe it to your pious care ;
For which I owe you more than I can pay,
Unless it be my life itself, which—
   Clau.   Nay !
The surgery I use is sent from heaven ;
'Tis to the gods you owe that life now given.
   Lys. Say, Florida, have you aught heard of Cliton,
     since
You tried in vain his reason to convince
Against his base suspicions, when, as dead,
In rage he left you, and unpitying fled.
   Flor. Never ! Yet gladly would I see him, friend,
Did I but know how to achieve that end.
   Cloe. Dear friend, the stories of us both, if weigh'd
In equal balance, would be equal made.
[*Aside to* LYS.]—To test her love your message I
     will bear.
   Lys. Thou wilt endear me to thee, then, sweet fair.
                         [*Exit* CLOE.
   Flor. You heard how Cloe came to our happy aid ?
   Lys. Never.
   Flor. Amid the beech groves—whither she had
     stray'd—
The wood nymphs found her, brought her to our cell,
And with these kindly spirits wrought this miracle.
   Lys. Good !   Now I can promise, if you will
     with me,
You shall ere long the reckless Cliton see.
   Flor. Oh, joy !   Have with you, then.

Clau. Say ! Whither now ?
Flor. I go no farther than you will allow.

[*Exeunt.*

Enter GLORIANA *distracted.*

Sings.

I know Lysander's dead :
Then farewell maidenhead ;
    Thou art but one
    When I am gone :
It never shall be said—hy ho, ho.
    Oh, Lysander !

Enter CLITON *like a hermit.*

Cli. Save you, fair maid ; I wish you joy,
Free from aught that may annoy
Your quiet, or disturb your sense ;
Send you health and penitence.
    Glor. Ha, ha, ha ! What—are you Lysander ?
    what—with that beard ?
There's a great beard, indeed. Hark you, Friar
    Tuck ; do
You see yon handsome shepherd Lysander ?
Why did you say he was dead ?
    Cli. You are mista'en. A hermit, I can cure
All wounds but what sin makes impure ;
And those are cur'd by One above.
I can help those ills that move
Man to distraction : jealous fears
In man or woman. I have years—
Have gain'd experience to apply
For all sorts a safe remedy.

GLORIANA *sings.*

Do you see where he doth stand,
With a cross-bow in his hand ?

I will follow thee, my dear,
Though the goblins keep watch there.
                                        [*Offers to go.*

Cli. Oh, stay, pure maid!
Glor. Old man, why do you hold me so?
In sooth you shall not! Let me go!
Cli. If you will be ruled by me,
You shall your Lysander see.
Glor. Shall I, indeed, now?
Cli. Come with me, and you shall know
More, if you'll but patient grow.   [*Exeunt.*
Leon, jun. Good father, calm this grief!
Leon, sen.   My only daughter!
Is not my daughter lost? In vain we've sought her,
The only staff whereon my age did rest,
And earthly joy with which my heart was bless'd?
Oh! I am miserable.
Leon, jun.   Do not so take on;
We yet may find her. Hope is not quite gone.
Leon, sen. Never! Some savage has laid hands
    upon her,
Having deflower'd her of her virgin honour.
Talk not of patience : 'tis the only course
To cure a bad distemper, to grow worse,
And fire it out of him.

Enter ALEXIS.

Al.   ·   Courage, dear sir!
Again let's try! I'm lost in losing her.
Leon, sen. I'll take thy counsel, goodness guide
    me still;
Sometimes are parents cross against their will.
                                        [*Exeunt.*

LYSANDER, CLAUDIA, *and* FLORIDA.

Lys. We're almost at his cell, where he does waste

Himself with grief, thinking you are graced
A citizen in heaven ; and that foul wrong
He did you smells so rank and strong,
Has so defil'd his soul, that the offence
Cannot be purg'd but by such penitence.

    Flor. Y'ave mov'd my heart, that 'midst my
        trembling fears
I feel my life-blood may well out in tears.
For me that strictness here he has undergone,
Will call my grateful thoughts to dwell upon.

Enter CLOE *and* DAPHNES.

    Cloe. I'm glad I've chanced upon you : do you see
We're coupl'd as true lovers ought to be ?
But, out alas ! your Gloriana's lost
Beyond recovery.

    Lys.   How my soul is cross'd !

    Daph. She, hearing you were dead, frantic be-
        came ;
Nor have these groves since echoed with her name.

    Lys. Let us put wings to our pursuit, to find
The best, the fairest, truest of her kind.
And first we'll search his cell.

    Clau. Great Pan, send all things well.   [*Exeunt.*

    Fran. Why, conscience, wilt thou buzz into my ears
That word " despair," to fright me with dark fears ?
The thing attends my guilt,—Gloriana fled !
For whom I heap'd new sins upon my head.
What has my fury purchas'd ?   Nothing ?   Yes !
Hell and perdition crown such wickedness.
And these perforce shall be my utter fate
When this earth's weary coil shall terminate.

Enter SCRUB.

    Scrub. You, sirrah madcap, that creeps like a crab
there ! hark you, do not you know one Francisco

and Pisander,—two vagabonds, that cannot live in peace with poultry, but they must fly after sheep?

Fran. I owe that wretched name Francisco.

Scrub.   Who?
You with that face! pray where's Pisander, too?

Fran. I left him at the Court when I came thence,
Debating matters of much consequence.

Scrub. I see you shepherds will lie abominably; he has been from the Court ever since seven years before he was born.

LYSANDER, LEON, GLORIANA, CLAUDIA, FLORIDA, CLOE, CLITON, DAPHNES, *and* ALEXIS.

Lys. Friends, we are rendered happy,—fortune,
    love
Are ours, to crown the end—joys from above.

Cli. Oh, Florida! it glads my heart to hear
How this celestial matron did appear
So opportunely, and, with balsams rare,
Under her guidance and her tender care,
Did so restore you—and my peace restore;
I not deserv'd nor did I hope for more.

Lys. I'm blest in Gloriana!

Daph.   I in Cloe!

Cli. And I in Florida!

Leon, Al., Clau., and Flor. We to see you so!

Fran. Protect me, ye blest powers! Keep farther off. I am not yet reconcil'd with heaven. I do confess I kill'd you! Oh, be merciful for their sweet sakes, whose innocence cannot see or be disturbed by thee! Ay, here they are by thee, thy once dear Gloriana!

Lys. What a distemper's this?

Fran. What will appease thy Ghostship? Give me but time to ask forgiveness of those sacred powers I've most offended, by depriving thee of life and being, and thou shalt have my life for thy just sacrifice.

Lys. I apprehend his guilt. Your hate grew not
To the effects so desperate as you sought.
Shepherd, fear not ; feel that I live and breathe !

Fran. Delude me not, it is impossible.

Lys. These here shall witness it.

Omnes. We do !

Fran. Can you forgive, then, my attempt ?

Lys. With a true heart and hand.

Omnes. Lysander's still himself, noble and wise.

Fran. And can you, fairest, wipe that ignominy off I deserv'd from you ?

Glor.   In troth !
Lysander's word sufficeth for us both.

Fran. Then may you both live happy many years :
May your joys never be disturb'd by fears !

Scrub. Hark you, sir, now all my talk is over,
I would know one thing of you ?

Lys. And what's that ?

Scrub. Have you met with one Pisander, Leon,
and Francisco in your travels ? The duke is dead
that banished good old Leon, and, could I find
him, his lands shall be restor'd.

Leon. I am that Leon ! With my children dear
I've liv'd e'er since in rural quiet here.

Omnes. Blessings do follow blessings.

Lys. Then I am that Pisander, that left the Court
to gain thy daughter's love by the name of Lysander. Scrub, dost thou know me now ?

Scrub. A pestilence on't, you are he indeed !

Fran. Pisander, embrace thy friend Francisco.

Lys. Francisco, thou cloy'st me with joy !
                                        [*Embrace.*

Fran. I left the Court for the same end that you
did.

Lys. She's mine now, sir, is she not?
Leon. As fast as th' priest can make her;
Fortune has made all happy.   Yet 'tis fit,
If they will wed, your hands shall license it.

Amor finem coronat.

THE DISTRACTED STATE.

C

The Distracted State. A Tragedy. Written in the year 1641, by J. T., Gent. "Seditiosi sunt reipublicæ ruina." London: Printed by W. H. for John Tey, and are to be sold at his shop at the Sign of the White Lion, in the Strand, near the New Exchange. 1651.

INTRODUCTORY NOTICE.

The *Biographia Dramatica*, in noticing this piece, observes : "This author was a strong party man, and wrote for the distracted times he lived in, to which his present work was extremely suitable. His hatred to the Scots is apparent throughout this play, wherein he introduces a Scotch mountebank undertaking to poison Archias, the elected king, at the instigation of Cleander. The scene lies in Sicily. It is the best of our author's pieces."

As Cromwell, in 1651, had attained the object of his ambition, by becoming the ruler of England, Scotland, and Ireland, Tatham might naturally be supposed to have run a great risk in publishing a play so obviously calculated to illustrate the serious consequences arising from any attempt to disturb the legitimate succession of monarchy by the intrigues of ambitious and designing persons, who, representing to the populace abuses, which perhaps had some foundation, as sufficient to authorize popular disaffection, gave rise to consequences much more prejudicial to the commonwealth than the abuses they pretended to redress. It is evident that Tatham was an uncompromising zealot of charles I., and that in his drama he intended to exhibit to his countrymen the fatal effects of giving over to the exaggerated statements of factious men, who, under pretence of putting down this Government, were anxious only to aggrandize themselves ; and it certainly is remarkable that, with an object so thinly veiled, the Protector allowed *The Distracted State* to be sold, without, as he might have done, causing its suppression. There is one marked feature in it, that, although there was no occasion for Tatham availing himself of Cleander's employing a Scotchman to poison Archias, he shows his bitter detestation of the Scotch nation,—a dislike which is still more manifest in the comic piece which follows, called *Scotch Figgaries*. There can be no doubt that the Scotch were deservedly unpopular in England at the time, not so much for their Puritanical religious assumptions, as for the fact that they had sold their monarch to his opponents for filthy lucre :—a prejudicial feeling, from an act that cannot be justified, long dwelling in the recollection of the English, who, although they did not object to the purchase, held the sellers in profound contempt, and judged the entire nation accordingly for a sin perpetrated by a small section of its community.

The introduction of what is supposed to be the Scotch language is curious, more especially as, at a later date, Tatham's specimens, as occurring in his dramas, seem to have been recognised in England as the ordinary dialect of the North. In the reign of Charles II., the same peculiar mode of pronunciation, as indicated by the spelling, occurs in Lacy's play of *Sauney the Scot*, as well as in many songs alleged to be Scotch, which seem to have then come into vogue, and which were printed in *The Westminster Drollery*, and subsequently in Durfey's *Pills to Purge Melancholy*, and other ballad-books of the time. It may be noticed, however, that the Scotch airs have been preserved and introduced into English dramatic pieces. Thus the very beautiful air of "Gilderoy" was made use of by Sir Charles Sedley in his comedy of the *Mulberry Garden*, wedded to words beginning, "Ah! Chloris, could I now but tell," which, by the way, were for a number of years accredited to President Forbes of Culloden. The original air, with the Scotch words, will be found in *The Westminster Drollery*.

Of the merits of *The Distracted State* as a drama, we are not prepared to speak very highly, although there are no inconsiderable portions of it, both in regard to poetry and action, which are worthy of commendation. The plot commences well, but its termination is far from satisfactory. The interest is kept up till the death of the usurper by his own hand, towards the end of the third act, after which the succession of kings and the several contentions for the throne become tedious. The character of Cleander, though somewhat original, is very offensive ; and had the play ever been acted, which it does not appear to have been, it could scarcely have met with much toleration. Agathocles, who at the outset impresses the reader favourably, at the close indicates how little reliance can be placed upon the protestations of patriots, whose assumed purity of principle yields whenever an opportunity occurs for bettering their position.

Among the *dramatis personæ*—nineteen in number— great havoc is made, twelve of them being killed by different means : one is decapitated, one commits suicide, one is poisoned, some are killed in hand-to-hand combat, the heroine becomes a prey to the assassin, who in turn meets his death by falling through a trap-door. Neither Hamlet nor Tom Thumb can equal this.

Sir William Sidley, Baronet, to whom the play is dedicated, was grandfather of Sir Charles Sidley or Sedley, one of the gay wits of the Court of Charles II. Sir William was the founder of the Sedleian Lecture of Natural Philosophy at Oxford. His son, Sir John Sidley, married Elizabeth, daughter and heir of Sir Henry Saville, Knight, the learned Warden of Merton College, in Oxford, and Provost of Eton. His grandson, Sir Charles, became a great favourite of Charles II. Shadwell says that "he has heard Sedley *speak* more wit at a supper than all his (Shadwell's) adversaries, putting their heads together, could *write* in a year." He was the author of several plays and some amorous poems, in which the softness of the verses was so exquisite as to be called by the Duke of Buckingham "Sedley's Witchcraft." The *Biographia Britannica* says: "There were no marks of genius or true poetry to be descried ; the art wholly consisted in raising loose thoughts and lewd desires without giving any alarm, and so the poison worked gently and irresistibly. Our author, we may be sure, did not escape the infection of his own art, or, rather, was first tainted himself before he spread the infection to others." Sir Charles' daughter—though by no means handsome— attracted the notice of the Duke of York, who, on his accession to the crown, created her Baroness of Darlington and Countess of Dorchester. By him she had a son who died early, and a daughter who married James, Earl of Anglesey. The Countess subsequently married Sir David Collyear, Baronet, who was created Baron by King William III., and afterwards, in 1703, Earl of Portmore by Queen Anne, both Scotch peerages. The issue of this marriage was two sons, the eldest of whom, Lord Milsington, married Bridget, a daughter of John Noel of Walcot, in the county of Northampton, by whom he had several children, all of whom, as well as he, died before the Earl. The title thereafter devolved upon his second son, Charles, who died in 1785. He also had married and left sons, all of whom also died, and the titles being limited to males, this peerage became extinct. Sir Charles Sedley was so displeased with the King at this connection with his daughter, that he became a partizan of the Prince of Orange, and assisted in placing the King's daughter in her father's seat.

The complimentary verses to Tatham bear the signatures

of I. R., R. D., and G. Lynn. The author of the first set is presumed to have been Joseph Rutter, translator of the *Cid*, from Corneille, in two parts, 1637 and 1640, and of the *Shepherd's Holiday, a Pastoral Tragi-Comedy*, acted before their Majesties at Whitehall in 1635, and published the same year, bearing the author's initials only on the title-page. He was tutor to the son of Edward, Earl of Dorset, Lord Chamberlain to the Queen. The *Shepherd's Holiday* was recommended by two copies of verses, one from Ben Jonson, the other from Thomas May. It was included in the original edition of Dodsley's *Old Plays*, and again appears in the twelfth volume of the reprint of that collection, presently passing through the press under the able superintendence of W. Carew Hazlitt.

R. D. is evidently Robert Daborne, Master of Arts, who was in holy orders, and, it is believed, had a living in Ireland, as there is a sermon by him, published in 1618, on Zech. ii. 7, which he preached at Waterford. He wrote two plays: *The Christian turned Turk*, T., 4to, 1612; and *The Poor Man's Comfort*, T. C., 4to, 1655.

G. Lynn is otherwise unknown as a poet.

TO THE TRULY NOBLE SIR WILLIAM SIDLEY, BARONET.

LIKE to a young student in necromancy, whose itch to rarity makes him attempt the raising what he wants skill to lay, I have adventured, in this little commonwealth of poetry, to beget some distractions that cannot be reconciled without your patronage. Sir, you have the fame for piety and love to your country, and have so equally balanced your actions in these distempered times, that you have not only merited the title Apollo gave to Socrates, but drawn all men's eyes, loves, and admiration upon you. Amongst the number of which your honourers, a stranger tenders his offering; and though it is naked of worth, yet the property of your acceptance will be shelter sufficient to it and him, who, next to your pardon, shall endeavour to deserve the title of, Sir, your most humble and faithful servant,

J. TATHAM.

MR. JOHN TATHAM,

ON HIS EXCELLENT PLAY "THE DISTRACTED STATE."

I DO not write in confidence my fame
May lift you up, or hoist you to a name.
I of my own defects too knowing am,
To hope support you while myself am lame ;
And th' world so well your merits understand,
They do not need advancement by my hand.
Nor do I labour to be thought a wit
Because in you I do approve of it.
What makes you shine does make me not despair
To hope a glimmering in the selfsame air.
To love I'm vow'd, too—not that wayward toy
That for these thousand years writes himself boy ;
Who makes the lord and lady still to meet,
As sure as in a country dance we see 't.
'Tis motley, just like cheeses where I've been,
Chequer'd, one square of white and one of green.
'Tis at the best imperfect, such a pair
Like doublets in the middle joined are ;
While masculine affections, such as mine,
Like diamonds entire and clearly shine.
To womankind awhile I bid adieu,
And only now enamour'd am of you ;
And, certain, 'tis no miracle in me,
T' whom civil war hath been a nursery,
That I, in strict obedience to my fate,
Do fall in love with your *Distracted State*.

I. R.

MR. JOHN TATHAM,

ON HIS EXCELLENT TRAGEDY "THE DISTRACTED STATE."

GOOD wine does need no bush, nor does thy wit
Want our supporting. This thy play is writ
With so much judgment, and so firm a hand,
It shall against the storms of envy stand
A monument to thy fame. For if we may
Conclude language and plot do make a play,
Here they are met, each scene and act so well
Follow'd, that one the other doth excel;
And their contention does so neatly end,
As though thou didst a second rape intend
Upon our sense, drawing our greedy eyes
To read till they themselves do sacrifice;
For he that loves to feast on a good line
Will never think he has enough of thine.

R. D.

WHEN I that sweet elixir of thy lines
Tasted, and found within those golden mines
That rare refin'd delight, in which 'tis sin
Not to be lost or catch'd in fancy's gin,
I did thy worth so clear a victor see,
The laurel could be due to none but thee.
I cannot offer hecatombs of praise,
Nor altars to thy lofty fancy raise ;
This well-meant tribute I can only pay,—
Wit's high meridian glorifies thy play.

G. LYNN.

THE PERSONS.

EVANDER, . . *The vanquished King.*

MAZARES, . . *His Brother.*

ARCHIAS, . . . *A noble Lord, their kinsman.*

MISSELLUS, . . { *Provinciall of Vallis de Noto, friend to the King.*

AGATHOCLES,
EPECIDES, . . } *Two high-spirited Lords.*

PLANETIUS, . . { *Provinciall of Mona, made by Mazares.*

The ARCHBISHOP of *Monreall.*

CLEANDER, . . *A high Politician.*

PHILISTUS, . . *A young Lord, minion to Mazares.*

ADULANTER, . . *A base fawning Lord, a Buffoon.*

HERMOCRATES, . *General to Mazares.*

THIMISTIUS, . . *A Colonel.*

ANTANTER, . . *A noble Commander.*

PHILANDER, . . *An Officer in war.*

ICETIS, . . . *Governor of a castle in Palermo.*

HIPPARINUS, . *A Magistrate of Palermo.*

A SCOTCH MOUNTEBANK.

TWO PHYSICIANS.

HARMONIA, . . { *Daughter to* Cleander, *and Mistress to* Archias.

A CAPTAIN, SOLDIERS, GUARD, ATTENDANTS.

Scene—SICILY.

THE DISTRACTED STATE.

ACT I.—SCENE I.

Loud music.

Enter MAZARES, *the* ARCHBISHOP *of Monreall*,
CLEANDER, AGATHOCLES, EPECIDES, PHILIS-
TUS, ADULANTER, *etc.*

MAZARES *ascends the Chair of State, the* ARCHBISHOP
puts the crown on his head, then all but AGA-
THOCLES *cry,* "Long live Mazares, lawfully
King of Sicily!"

Aga. Heaven! where's thy vengeance?
Canst thou endure this mockery?
                    [AGATHOCLES *kneels with his back towards*
                        them, aside.
Maz. We thank you all.   But why, Agathocles,
Appears such trouble on thy brows?   Are we
Unwelcome to thy wishes?
    Aga. How, sir?   Pardon me;
Who dares say you are?
You are my King.   Is it not so, gentlemen?
The rays that from your brother's diadem
Gilded this kingdom are put out, and now

From you, our rising sun, we must expect
A virtual fervour.   Obedience is my safety ;
My wishes, trifles.   What may you not command ?
If you but will, my life is not my own ;
One frown may rivet me.   I am design'd
To be but what you please, and when—no longer.
I am your poor submissive.
    Maz,   You misconstrue
The power of Kings ; they dare not but be just.
That crown can ne'er sit fast that takes its rise
From others' ruin.
    Aga.   Out, imposture !   [*Aside.*
    Maz. My lords, I could have wished
The people's and your loves had spared this
      solemnity
Until another time,—a time that might
Have prov'd more fit for triumph ; for though
      heaven
Hath wreath'd our brows with victory, our thoughts
Are not at peace.
    Aga.   Nor ever will be, till,
By their continual motion, they have brought
All into public ruin.   [*Aside.*
    Maz.   The care of th' common safety
O'erwhelms our joy, and makes it seem un-
      seasonable.
Repose, after so long a toil of war, would be
Perfume unto our senses ; but we must not
Prefer our own before the people's quiet.
    Aga. Machiavel, thou art an ass, a very ass to
      him !   [*Aside.*
    Maz. My lords, you are my witnesses,
The public wrong, and not ambitious hopes
Of government, oblig'd me to this quarrel—
The people's, and not mine—against my brother ;
The justice of which cause gave us success.

Heaven knows, had he not been their enemy,
I should have emptied ev'ry vein I have
T' have serv'd him ! Nature and duty held
Strong conflicts in my blood,—nature promoting
Onewhile my brother's right, until my duty
Unto my country, with diviner reason,
O'ercame me, and discover'd the sad scene
Of a sinking people and a rising tyrant.

 Aga. Does Heaven hear this, and punisheth not ?
             [Aside.

 Maz. For my part, my lords,
Though the affection of the people circles
My temples with a crown, I shall not wear it
Longer than they esteem me worthy.

 Cle. Most singular prince !
 Aga.   Most singular devil !
             [Aside.

 Maz. My Lord Archbishop,
You are the Church's vine, and we the elm
Of th' commonwealth ; our flourishing estates
Depend on one another. By Heaven's hand
We are contracted, and must share all fortunes,
Or good or bad. The jewels of a crown
Retain not lustre longer than they have
Virtue from th' Church, and that she's glorious :
Nor can she be so longer than we are so ;
Her strength and welfare doth consist in ours.
Let not this sudden change
Possess her with a fear of her eclipse :
Sh'as a protector now that will expose
His life a sacrifice to preserve her purity.
We shall not be remiss to satisfy
What lies on our part towards her ; and what
From her belongs to us we need not intimate ;
You have a sense, my lord, can reach at things
And their necessities.

Arch. My duty shall not be wanting, my gracious
 lord.

Aga. The churchman will turn pander to him.
            [Aside.

Maz. My lords,
We're not insensible of the people's burthen
By keeping up our armies ; but necessity,
That makes men act what they would not, compels it.
We are not yet secur'd against the malice
Of our late vanquished brother ; there's a faction
That waits an opportunity to befriend him,
Beside his hopes in Italy.   Those clouds over,
We doubt not but a fair day will give birth
Unto the people's happiness and ours.
In the meantime, my lords, be it your care
To stop the current of their cries, and keep
Us fair in their opinion.

Aga. [*Aside to* EPECIDES.] As hell's projector.
Down, down, big heart ! thou'lt hang me else.

Epe. [*To* AGATHOCLES, *aside.*] My lord,
Let reason moderate your passions ;
They are too violent, and may prove your enemies.
Mazares wants not hands.

Aga. [*Aside to* EPECIDES.] Nor I a heart
To dare his worst.   Oh, Epecides,
I have liv'd too long to see this day !

Maz. My lords, we know
Crowns are but glorious burthens, and the weight
Requires more heads than one to bear it up.
You are th' approved pilots of the State,
Acquainted with all creeks and rocks where danger
Hides his destroying head, and wisely can
Steer her should th' malice of a foreign foe
Swell to a tempest, or malignant breaths
At home threaten her ruin.   On your faiths
Depend ours and her safety.

Cle.   Most gracious sir,
You have outdone even expectation ; and
The beams of virtue that shoot from you
Outshine the glory of your diadem,
And bind our lives unto your fortunes.

  Phili. May we own our lives no longer
Than they perform those offices of duty
Your virtues do command them to !

  Maz. We owe much to your loves,
And shall engross a time to pay the debt
Your merits call upon us.   We'll divide
The happiness, if any wait upon
A crown, amongst you.

  Aga. [*Aside to* EPECIDES.] When he's warm in's
          seat,
They shall as little dare to claim his promise
As the poor crane his reward from the lion
When he had pulled the bone out of his throat.

  Epe. [*Aside to* AGATHOCLES.] Restrain yourself.
There's little revenge in words, but words may be
Revenged.   Be advised !

  Adul. May never care breed fevers in your blood,
Nor troubles raise a palsy in your sceptre ;
May still success attend your enterprises,
And conquests beget conquests, till you write
Yourself the world's great monarch !

  Arch. May Heaven's eye
Keep sentinel while you repose, that no
Traitorous attempts may reach your sacred person !

  Aga. [*Kneels aside.*] Now may the groans of dying
          men, the cries
Of widows, orphans, and deflowered virgins,
Together with his brother's wrongs, continually
Keep him awake, till, with distracted rage,
For want of rest, he doth become his own
Dire executioner !

D

Maz. What means this, Agathocles ?

Aga. I have been at my prayers too.

Maz. We thank you, and shall
Endeavour to deserve so far
You shall not have cause to repent them.

Aga. I believe no less.

Maz. Lead on, my lords !
With upright care we shall discharge our trust :
Kings are no longer kings than they are just.
       [*Exeunt.* AGATHOCLES *pulls* EPECIDES *back.*

Aga. My lord Epecides, a word ;
The King may spare us two.   I may presume
We are as little needed as regarded.
If that thy looks deceive me not, thou art
Yet free from this disease, this itch of honour
Which so transforms us into servile flattery.
Art swell'd with lofty thoughts ?

Epe.   They reach no higher
Than th' public good, which they devoutly wish,
Though want a power to compass.

Aga.   Th' art honesty itself ;
And to thy bosom, as my sanctuary,
My soul shall fly to ease itself of what
Would burst me to keep longer.

Epe.   My lord, you may
Be confident I have a soul as big
With grief as you, that fain would be deliver'd
If reason would turn midwife.

Aga.   False Cleander
Hath made the field drunk with his country's blood
To set up an usurper.

Epe.   It is pretended
The people's pressures and continual clamours
Enforc'd the war.

Aga.   Kindled by the fire
Broke from Mazares' bosom, whose ambitious

Desire of rule bred the ill humours in
The easily corrupted multitude ;
Who, led by their pernicious hopes that he
Would bring on better days, gave breath unto
Their monstrous fury, and like a deluge
Broke forth, and sank the fortunes of Evander ;
That he, poor Prince, having no other ark
Of preservation than his innocence,
And faith he had in's friends, did fly to them,
Whose shelter served him but for a short time,
For they, with him, at last were overwhelm'd.
But, Epecides, be thou confident !
Though hell hath further'd the usurper's plot,
And smooth'd it with success, vengeance will
    reach him.
Though Heaven be slow, its punishment is sure.
   Epe. Hear but Cleander,
Philistus, Adulanter, and the rest,
And they will tell you Providence and justice
Sat on their weapons' points to punish tyranny ;
And that our kingdom, by Mazares' wisdom,
Will flourish in a far better estate
Than in Evander's time.
   Aga. Ambition wants not snares
To catch vulgar credulity, and carry
On their designs clear to the end they aim at.
They are the canes and trunks through which th'
    usurper
Speaks to promote his purposes, and blast
All good in's brother, and eclipse his right.
Is not Planetius, the first bold traitor,
Of Mona made Provinciall ?   Is not Cleander
As big with hopes and expectation ?
Does not Philistus fawn and court to out
Missellus, the Provinciall of Vallis de Noto ?
Credit such sycophants !

Epe.   Missellus is noble ;
And if Mazares look not well about him,
Evander may have an after-game to play.
Missellus was his creature.
   Aga.   Where'er he be,
Though fortune left his party, he retains
A mind invincible.
   Epe.   No question but
The State was much distemper'd ; and Evander
Was not without his faults.
   Aga. People dispos'd for change
Survey the vices of their Prince through optics
That rather multiply than lessen them ;
And what is in themselves but criminal
Is in their Prince held horrid, as the symptom
To the disease of tyranny.
   Epe.   And dare correct
That in their Prince they would not in them-
      selves
Have taken notice of.
   Aga.   But allow there were
Some things might grieve the people, wise ex-
      perience
Gives us to know that in th' lopping of trees
The skilful hand prunes but the lower branches,
And leaves the top still growing, to extract
Sap from the root, as meaning to reform,
Not to destroy.   I tell thee, Epecides,
Th' excess of what was good in Prince Evander
Might stock the barren breast of the usurper.
   Epe. Men never rate their goods so highly
As when they're robb'd of them. It is some
      ease
To our afflictions that we can thus vent
Our griefs to one another, for we must
Despair of other remedy.

Aga.   Very true,
If we continue children, and adore
The rod corrects us, kiss it till we smart for 't,
Enthrone base fear in valour's royal seat,
Let it lord o'er our spirits till our blood
Forsake its heat and become ice ; but if
We do retain the glory of our ancestors,—
Whose ashes will rise up against our dulness,—
Shake off our tameness, and give way to courage,
We need not doubt, inspir'd with a just rage,
To break the necks of those that would yoke
  ours.
 Epe. Ay, but—
 Aga. Those "buts" destroy us. Are you
  willing
To sit in th' dark, and never see the sun ?
With a besotted patience see your goods
Rifled, and your inheritance ta'en from you ?
Unless you, to secure his quiet, will
Part with your own, and by compliance banish
The peace your conscience yet is happy in.
 Epe. You know my spirit's not so chill ;
But I would know a way. Prescribe you one
That's passable, I shall not only run
My fortunes with you, but make all the friends
And nearest allies I have as ready minded
To do you service.
 Aga.   To a resolved mind
Nothing seems difficult. Archias has a
Noble, gallant spirit.
 Epe.   What then ?
 Aga. He ever was a friend to virtue, and's of
Mazares' line, too.
 Epe. Unfold the mystery.
 Aga. What would you say if he's well belov'd
  and active ?

Enter a MESSENGER.

Epe. Do you suspect me?

Aga. No; but hold! here's some upon us.

Mess. Which is the Lord Philistus or Cleander? either will serve.

Aga. What is your business?

Mess. I've letters to the King.

Aga. Whence came you?

Mess. From Messina.

Epe. How fares the Lord Planetius?

Mess. His honour is in health. I'd fain be discharged.

Aga. What news, what news? We'll bring you to the King.

Mess. Extreme good, gentlemen. The late tyrant, after his defeat, going for Italy, was surprised by some of Tyche, in the province of Vallis de Noto, killed, and cast into the river—a death too good for him.

Aga. So, sir—

Epe. Oh, forbear! But hear me, friend; is this news certain?

Mess. My Lord Planetius, the Provinciall of Mona, had it so, sir, and he hath sent the same unto the King; I can say no more on't, sir. Please you to bring me to those gentlemen.

Aga. There's enough in Court to show you; you may walk thither, sir.

Mess. I could have done that without all this ado, sir.   [*Exit* MESSENGER.

Epe. Passion's too much your enemy.

Aga. Dog!—A death too good for him?

Epe. What think you now on the business you were upon?

Aga. I am beside myself; my courage leaves me,

And reason tells me now I must be tame.
The King—

    Enter MAZARES, CLEANDER, PHILISTUS,
      ADULANTER, *etc.*, MESSENGER.

  Maz. Were not the villains found?
  Mess. I do not know, an't please your Majesty.—
The King seems to be troubl'd at this news;
                                [*Aside.*
I'll change my note.—'Tis like they were,
For w' heard the Provinciall of Vallis de Noto had
Appointed the death of somebody.
  Maz. He did but justice, then. Oh, Philistus,
And you, my honoured lords, our griefs want
      utterance!
He was our brother, though our country's enemy,
And they have ta'en away a part of us
That sent him hence. It was a deed—though
      Heaven's
Just hand was in't—we cannot but lament.
Your pardon, supreme powers!
  Phili. Most pious Prince!
  Maz. Blame us not, my lords. We say again,
He was our brother, and we cannot stop
The course of nature.   [*Seems to weep.*
  Aga. Can this be real?
  Mess. He was a gracious Prince, there's the
      truth on't;
I could weep too for him.
  Adul. How, you villain?
  Mess. Why, the King is not offended with me, I
hope? Alas, I have nature in me too! Good,
virtuous Prince Evander!
  Adul. Hast thou a mind to be hanged?
  Mess. How? Is the wind at that door? No,
sir, not for e'er a dead prince in Christendom.

Your Majesty may spare your tears, for in truth
and verity he was but so so.

Maz. Friend, didst not say
That th' actors were punished by Missellus ?

Mess. So I heard, an't like your Highness.

Maz. 'Tis strange !
Planetius writes not so, but it's very likely.
Missellus has in many things been seen
Ready and active for him, and no doubt
Would now—

Cle. Come, come ! Missellus grows too popular ;
Your Majesty may think on some more faithful.

Maz. We guess your meaning.   Philistus,
We shall despatch you upon some affairs
As soon as we can shake this sadness off,
And our mind's fit for business.

Phili. It becomes my duty to wait your Highness'
pleasure.

Maz. Fellow, attend our secretary for confirmation
Of the Provinciallship of Mona to Planetius.
Come, my lords !   [*Exeunt.*

Enter ARCHIAS *and* HARMONIA.

Har. Begone so soon, my lord ?   Y'are hardly
entered
My father's house !   Though th' entertainment
comes
Short of your merits, my lord, believe 't, y'are
welcome
To poor Harmonia.

Ar.   Th' art rich in all that's good,
And that's a dower Queens would be glad to
boast of.
Since thy descent to love me, I'm exalted
Above a Monarch's happiness !

Har.   And part so soon ?

You have some other mistress, whose heaven
Depends upon your visit.
   Ar.   Pretty jealousy!
How sweetly it becomes her! Believe me, dearest,
By the blest hopes I have in thee, not any
Beauty in Sicily—if there can any be
Besides thyself, for in thee is the full
Perfection of all beauty met—has part
Of the least thought of mine!
   Har. You shall not go, though, yet.

Enter CLEANDER.

   Ar. Thy father! Wilt thou now license me
      to go?
I'll see thee ere the sun be six hours older.
                    [Offers to go off.
   Cle. My Lord Archias, you have honour'd me
Exceedingly by this your visit. I hope my coming
Does not remove you hence.
   Ar.   My good lord,
Excuse me, I beseech you. Did not business
Of much concernment call me hence, I should
Account that time well spent wherein I might
Serve you and your fair daughter.
   Cle. Pleasure yourself, my lord.
   Ar. I am your lordship's servant. Adieu, sweet!
                    [Exit.

   Cle. Harmonia,
I guess this young lord loves thee;
His often visits promise some such business.
But I'd not have you countenance it.
   Har. Why, I beseech you, sir?
You have been pleas'd to lavish forth his praises
Beyond the common character. I've heard you
     say,
With pardon, sir, he had much virtue in him.

Cle. And has so.   But he cannot bring his heart
T' affect this King, although he be his kinsman.
   Har. That is no crime worthy my notice, sir,
Much less my disrespect.   Pray, give me leave
To use him with but that civility
Becomes the education of your daughter.
   Cle. My intents
Fly higher to advance thee.   If I live,
And that the King perform his royal word,—
As that he dares not but do,—thou shalt stand
In competition with a Queen for greatness.
Mazares is too weak a politician
To think my vast soul can be hemm'd within
The circle of a province, when a Kingdom
Will scarce contain it.   No! I do but take
This as a spot of earth to what I aim at.
I mean to match thee, girl, unto some Prince,
By whose assistance I'll reach the ascendant,
The royal seat, Harmonia; and then,
We are thy princely father!   Does 't not noise
Rarely, my girl?   The very sound inspires
My soul with flames of Majesty!   Go on, Cleander,
Till neighbouring Princes, wond'ring at thy fate,
With trembling sceptres dread their own estate!
                                        [*Exeunt.*

ACT II.—SCENE I.

Enter MAZARES, PHILISTUS, ADULANTER, *and*
              ATTENDANTS.

   Maz. Philistus, sit;
Sit, Adulanter!   Who waits there?   [*Sit at table.*
   Guard. We, an't like your Grace.
   Maz. Bring us wine!

We are dispos'd to drown our brother's memory,
And its appendant sorrows, in a full
Bowl of rich wine.

    Phili. Done like your princely self!

    Maz. What should we
Contract our youth to cares for, waste the heat
Beats in our agile veins, and draw upon
Our head a snowy periwig before
Age claims it? We are resolv'd to make
Our blooming years no prey for melancholy.

    Phili. You are our sun, and we the infant plants
That take life from you. When your brow is
        clouded,
We droop and pine, as wanting heat. Your
        Highness
Now shows yourself in glory, and our heads,
That lately were press'd down with discontent,
Look up to bless the change.

    Adul. Your Highness put
Us all in fear you would convert your Court
Into a monastery.

    Maz. Ha, ha, ha! into a mouse-trap, rather!
Philistus, to thee! [*Drinks.*] Fellow, let not any
Enter the presence if thou regard'st thy safety!
'Tis hop'd our subjects will allow us a time
Of mirth after our toil for them.

    Phili. Whether they will or not,
Your Majesty has power to take it.

    Maz. Howe'er we seem'd to take our brother's
        death,
'T has brought on our security; for such
As durst before speak loud and big, now dare not
Be seen to whisper 'gainst us.

    Phili. 'Tis a point of policy,
High as your Highness' safety, to keep them
At such an awful distance. There's Epecides—

Maz. A close and cunning sophister. He carries
A fire within him scarce to be discerned.
  Phili. Agathocles comes not much short of him.
  Maz. He has a daring soul, and. does attract
The lewd, licentious people, as the fire
That draws ill vapours to't. But we're resolv'd
He and the rest of's insolent crew shall meet
Our justice if they submit not.
  Phili. Your Majesty's brow
Is too serene ; something of wrath there seated
Would seem far better.
  Maz. Where's our secretary ?
  Adul. Call the King's secretary !

Enter SECRETARY.

  Maz. Hast done the patent we gave order for ?
  Sec. 'Tis ready for your Majesty's signing.
  Maz. Give us ink ! so.—Philistus,
We have just cause to doubt Missellus' faith too,
And therefore will remove him, and on thee
Confer the honour. He is seated like
A thorn in th' heart of Sicily, and must be
Cut off, lest he spread farther and do gore us.
                              [*Gives him the patent.*
Take this as earnest of our love to thee,
Whose loyalty we are assured of.
  Phil.   Fame
Shall spread your royal bounty through the world,
And may I leave* to Be when I forget
To be your Highness' servant !
  Maz.   Cleander had
Our promise for't ; but we do know him one
Of an unconstant spirit, full of spleen,
A mind high and unbounded, and, to drive
On his own ends, will enter into league

                    * Cease.

With Turk or devil. Therefore 'tis not safe
For us to lay a trust of so high consequence
On such a frail foundation,—one whose faith
Complies with every wind, and strikes his sails
With every tide and change. But
You drink slowly. Come! to thy
Good journey! [CLEANDER *knocks*.
   Guard. The King is private.
   Cle. I must speak with him.
   Maz. Who's that so loud there?
   Guard. The Lord Cleander.
   Maz. Tell him 'tis not our pleasure to be spoke with.
   Guard. My lord, you hear the King?

CLEANDER *strives, and rushes in.*

   Cle. My business is of concernment;
I will enter! How's this? Surrounded
With his flatterers! 'Tis like to be
A State well governed.
   Maz. Sir, you are uncivil.
   Cle. What mean you, royal sir?
   Maz. You're saucy; we say again, you're saucy!
   Cle. How?
   Maz. How durst you be so insolent?
   Cle. I have deserv'd, sir, better language from you.
My anger is too strong for my obedience,
And will have th' upper hand. I come
To claim your royal word. I am Cleander, sir,
Whose hand did seat the crown upon your head, sir!
   Maz. Provoke us not!
   Phili. Good my lord, for your own safety—
You see the King is moved.
   Cle.   Moved? By Heaven,
I'll move him worse! Tell me I'm insolent!
   Maz. And we shall punish it, if you go not the
      sooner.

Cle. I will not hence, and you shall hear
    me !

Maz. Go ! you're impudent.

Cle.   Am I so, sir ?
You did not tell me so when I did waste
Whole nights, and spent my spirits, to seduce
The people t' your party, and lost my blood
To serve you.   I was not then—

Maz.   Stir not in me
An anger that will shake thee !

Cle. Whose head, whose heart, whose hand
    appear'd till mine,
To make you what you are ?

Maz. If we be King, sir, you shall feel there is
A power belonging to 't.   Where's our guard ?
Take him away !

Phili.   I beseech your Majesty !

Cle. Effeminate lord ! I scorn to own a life
At thy petitioning !   Tyrant, do thy worst !
Is this the reward for all my services ?
Sit with your crew of vaulters, and contrive
To turn your citadels to dancing schools,
Or stews fit for your purpose, till the soldiery,
Like to a sudden tempest, scour your follies
And whip you to repentance !

Maz. Away with him !

Guard. Come, my lord.

Cle. Yes, I shall go.   Ungrateful Prince !
May all thy brother's—   [*Drag him off.*

Maz. Stop 's mouth.   Away with him !
So we are rid of th' screech owl.   Did you e'er
Hear spleen better vented ?   All the physicians
Palermo holds could not discover his disease
Better than he has done 't himself.

Phili. And were I as your Majesty, I'd cure him
By th' head for 't.

Maz. 'Tis not safe yet; but if this tame him not,
We shall fly higher.

Phili. The serpent spat, too, at me.

Maz. We'll have the venom from him, or his
life for 't!

Adul. He has a daughter of that beauty rare
Would thaw a Stoic's bosom;
She carries the quintessence of youth about her.

Maz. Art thou acquainted with her?

Adul. Though I am not, I want not confidence,
If that may serve your Majesty.

Maz. Is she composed for mirth?

Adul. She bears a fame for virtue.

Maz. What should we do with her, then?
She is no match for us.

Adul. If your Majesty have a mind to her,
I'll batter all her virtues with your glories;
And, 'less a host of angels come to guard her,
She shall not pass my purchase.

Phili. When you storm her, let not a repulse or two
Make you draw off your siege; the third assault
Constrains her to surrender.

Adul.   I am not, my lord,
To learn the art of courtship; I have more
Designs than one upon her.

Maz.   We do like
The law Lycurgus made, and will ordain
The like amongst us.   Why should youth be
curtail'd
Of that delight nature intended it?
Men's wives shall have the liberty to choose
A friend to play the husband's part sometimes.

Phili. Does your Majesty intend to marry?

Maz. Marriage is but a church device, that would
Prefer sobriety amongst the virtues—
A stale, unsavoury thing; whenas variety

Gives life to every sense, and doth beget
An appetite when th' other smothers it!
Adulanter, try thy skill; we shall reward it.

   Adul. I warrant she's your Majesty's.

   Maz. Come, Philistus;
We'll bring thee on thy way.   And lest Missellus
Should   prove   stiff-necked,   and   not   yield   his
      obedience
To our commands, our General shall send
With thee five thousand men to force admittance.
Leontium, Tyche, and Neapolis
Stand fast to us, and will assist you if
The Syracusians should stand out.

   Phili. Your Majesty does enrich me with your
      bounty.

   Maz. Adulanter, we   shall   find   employment
      worthy
Thy liking in Palermo.   We will have
Thee near us.

   Adul.   Your Highness' vassal!

   Maz.   'Tis fit
Royalty should maintain them which uphold it.

                                        [Exeunt.

        Enter AGATHOCLES *and* EPECIDES.

   Aga. He is my King; his brother's death hath
      made
His title good, and I must bring my heart
Down to obedience.

   Epe.   Then you begin to cool?

   Aga. I'm not convinced in conscience that 'tis
      lawful
T' oppose the power now o'er us, since the hand
Of Heaven is in't, whose high decrees we ought
      not
To question or dispute.

Enter ARCHIAS.

Epe.   A happy morning
To th' noble Lord Archias !
    Ar.   The like to your honours !
You heard the news ?
    Epe.   What is't, my lord ?
    Ar. Philistus is made Provinciall of Vallis de
    Noto.
    Epe. How likes Cleander it ?
    Ar. He's otherwise provided for—committed,
Upon displeasure Mazares has ta'en against him.
    Epe. That's news indeed !
    Aga. What ! Cleander, the magazine of policy !
Is he blown up ? Mazares' only Atlas,
That shouldered him into the throne ?
    Epe. This is some State gin, some trick politic.
    Ar. Believe 't, 'tis true.
    Epe. How can Mazares be without him ?
    Ar. Oh, my lord,
Mazares used Cleander as the lame
Do their supporting crutches—that's no longer
Than as they need 'em ; when that they are able
To walk alone, they cast 'em from 'em.
    Aga. Ha, ha, ha ! I'm glad on't, with all my
        heart !
Mazares never acted a thing as yet
So near commendable justice : fair Astrea
May give it a just plaudit.
    Ar.   But consider,
If such who have ventured their part of heaven
To do him service are not free from 's tyranny,
Where rests our safety ?
    Epe.   It is high injustice
So to reward him.
    Aga.   In the survey of politics,
                    E

Dost find a traitor otherwise rewarded ?
Stands it with thy discretion to let loose
A tiger when th'ast moved him into anger ?
No ; 'tis a way both safe and full of justice
To chain such danger up. Had he done otherwise,
He had been fitter rather to have ruled
A sheephook than a sceptre.
 Ar. Come, you are too bitter.
Think on Cleander's age, and lend your aid.
 Aga. He should have known more virtue in his
   youth,
And then his age had now been tempest-proof.
 Ar. For my sake, good my lord, and for his
   daughter's !
 Aga. Ay,—now, my lord, you speak,—you are
   concern'd in't.
 Ar. Your own and all our freedoms are con-
   cern'd in't.
Shall we pay duty and obedience
To him who does instruct us to rebel
By his own precedent ? Are we to learn
How he obtained the sceptre ? Or want we
   sense
To feel how he employs it ? Was it not
His own insinuating tenet to
The people, 'gainst his brother, that the virtue
And justice of the Prince were th' only bonds
That bound the people to him, and when he
Should violate either they were tied no longer ?
Are we not freemen, then ?
 Epe.   Highly requisite.
 Ar. Where is the common right,
Our just inheritance, bought with the blood
Of our indulgent ancestors, whose valour
Bounded the royal power so, it durst not
Spread beyond th' acts of piety and justice ?

Enter ARCHBISHOP.

Aga. See what love and women can do!

Ar. My Lord Archbishop, you are happily come
To contribute your advice.

Arch.   My honoured lords,
The safety of your persons frees my soul,
That lately was a slave to fear and jealousy.

Aga. Ay, churchman; 'twas your fears and
       jealousies
Heaved first at our foundation. Sicily had been
Clear from infection had not your hot lungs
Spat the contagion. It was you gave reins
To the licentious people, that, like negroes,
Shot their envenom'd darts at th' rays of Majesty,
Whose careful heat did warm them.

Arch.   You mistake;
We aimed at no such thing, but to discharge
Our duties to our country.

Aga.   And y'ave proved
The most undutiful'st of all her children!
And finding now the end of your ambition
Of being Cardinal is clear laid open,
By which your pride is like to be obscured,
You do begin to belch forth fresh sedition,
And create new distempers, 'cause Mazares
Will not do what you'd have him.

Arch.   I come not, sir,
To bandy words. The world knows what I did
Was in relation to the Church's peace,
Howe'er you term it; but so full of poison
I find the gilded pills of his professions,
That plainly I must tell you, without fear,
I heartily do wish those hands, that were
Employed to seat him o'er us, had been used
To put him in his grave.

Ar.   Or been lopp'd off
Before they had contracted such an ill
Upon our country !
　Epe.   There's no time too late
To lance the ulcer, and give ease unto
The groaning people, if my Lord Agathocles
Will call to mind his death that whets the
　　　instrument,
Whose precious memory will give life to all
Our undertakings.
　Ar.   Come, my lord ! I'll have
The Bishop and you reconciled.　We'll to
Cleander's house, where the poor lady mourns
Her father's absence ; there we will consult
On some way to obtain his and our freedoms.
　Aga. Let not the churchman be in it, and
　　　then
Doubt not but we shall make all right again.
　　　　　　　　　　　　　　[Exeunt.

Enter ADULANTER *and three or four* SOLDIERS.

　Adul. This is her walk.　I hope you do not faint
At the design, now 'tis so near attempting ?
　1 Sol. Yes, I warrant you, as though she were
the first wench we have had occasion to make
use of !
　2 Sol. Why, what do you take us to be ?　Milk-
sops ?　I tell you, sir, we are gentlemen in the
first place, soldiers in the second, and men in the
last place.
　Adul. Good reason the last should take place of
the first, then ; but stay,
Yonder's the bird for which we wait !　I'll try

Enter HARMONIA.

If she will come to hand ; if not, your net

Shall noose her into tameness.   Stand close !—
Hail, madam ! heaven's epitome, on whose
Blest smiles the happiness of Kings depends !
Pleasure and health attend you !

Har. I thank you, sir ;
But here it is unseasonable, where sorrow
Has its predominance.

Adul.   I bring you comfort,
If you but please to honour the address
With kind acceptance.

Har.   Has my ruthless fortune
More miseries to heap on me, that she
Presents me with such shadows of her favour ?

Adul. The King, to whom your father's life is
          forfeit,
Throws both it and his own into your lap,
If you will be so wise as to receive 'em.

Har. Could I express a thankfulness beyond
The duty that I owe 'n my prayers for him,
It should fly to him.   Pray be pleased to teach me
The way to it.

Adul.   Fame has been busy
In giving to the King an estimate
Of your perfections, whose high value fills
Th' exchequer of his breast ; and 'tis your love
Must free the heart your bounty has subdued.

Har. I'm ignorant of your meaning.

Adul. To be his mistress.

Har. Or, in plainer terms, which shows the
          truth on't,
To be his whore?

Adul.   Fie ! that is too common.
Consider, madam, he that courts you is
Your King, who may compel where he entreats ;
And you will forfeit your allegiance if
You should deny him.

Har.   To the gods I should,
Durst I presume to grant it.   If my father
Must not enjoy his life but on the terms
Of my dishonour, th' duty that I owe
To heaven and goodness will implead against
The bonds of nature, which can challenge but
The life it gave ; and that I'll offer up
To ransom his.
Adul.   That will not serve the turn :
You must to Court.
      Har.   I'll first go to my grave.
Adul. Nay, then, adieu compliment, and to your
        business, fellows !
Har. What mean you ?
Adul. To hide your blushes, madam.
Har. Help, help, help !
          [*They throw a silk bag over her; she strives
              with them; they stop her mouth with a
              glove, and bind her hands and feet.*
Adul. Stop her mouth !

Enter AGATHOCLES, ARCHIAS, EPECIDES, *and*
              ARCHBISHOP.

Aga. I am o'ercome in reason, and do crave
Your lordship's pardon.
      Arch.   My lord, you have my heart
At your disposing.
      Ar.   This reconcilement's handsome.
Adul. So, the field's our own !   Take up your
Bag and baggage ; march fair and softly.
When we come to Court we'll share the booty.
          [*As they are carrying her away they meet the
              lords; they cast her down and run back.*
A plague upon't !   Down with your load, and
        make
An honourable retreat !   [*Exeunt.*

Ar. 'Twas Adulanter! What's this ? it moves !
[*Unbinds her ; takes the glove out of her mouth.*
Your help, my lords ! Ah, 'tis Harmonia !
 Arch. What monstrous stratagem had they upon
  her ?
 Har. Air is a blessing. Oh, let me have more
  on't !
 Ar. Dear madam, speak your wrongs, and we
  will right you,
If the best blood in Sicily can do 't.
 Har. My life and honour—far more precious—
  were
Designed for slaughter !
 Aga. How, madam ? By whom ?
 Har. By him who should protect the innocent,—
The lawless King, whose causeless wrath upon
My father nothing could appease, unless
I made sale of my virtue and my youth
To satisfy his lust.
 Ar.   Whose fire we'll quench
With his own blood ! Be confident, Harmonia,
Thy father shall outlive his power and cruelty.
 Aga. If we take not this edge off, we shall
  have
Our wives and daughters made the subjects of
Our scorn and shame, and be squeaked out in
  ballads
For honourable cuckolds, princely panders.
Whose soul is so besotted to his fear
He can contract it to a minute's patience ?
 Arch. Not I !
 Epe. Nor I ! Sure he does think the gods
Are all asleep, or have forgot to punish.
 Ar. Hence, patience ! thou fools' virtue ! I'll
  shake off
Thy coldness with the witchcraft of obedience,

Who have so long kept me in cells of slavery
I could not see the glory of my freedom.

Aga. We'll kindle all our vigour at thy flame,
And teach our knees to pay their homage to
No power but thine ! My lords, if that we be
All of one mind, cry, Long live Archias !

Ar. I wait not for that dignity, believe me.
All my ambition is to free this lady
From th' ghastly fears that haunt her, and give
    liberty
Unto her happiness by her father's freedom.

Arch. Which to achieve, my lord, receive the
    power
Heaven and we offer you. Monreall is
Your own already.

Aga.   And the Agrigentines
Proclaim you in my voice their lawful King.

Epe. And all the citizens in Palermo speak
The like in me. Long live Archias !

Omnes. Long live Archias !

Ar. My lords, forbear ! Mazares lives.

Arch. Abhorred of the gods, and 'tis but justice
To take him off !

Ar.   Heaven fit me for the trust
You throw on me ! And now, Harmonia,
Sweet empress of my soul, receive thy Archias,
Who must not know a joy but what thou shar'st of.
Cleander freed, we shall request your hand
To join our hearts, my lord.

Arch.   Where virtue keeps
Her Court, the gods are guests. Your choice is
    heavenly.

Har. I was ev'n now the wretched'st of all
    living,
And now am lifted to a happiness
That Queens would kneel to purchase.

My dear lord!

 Ar.   My heaven on earth!

 Aga. Think on your business, sir;

The perfecting of that gives length unto

Your amorous days.

 Epe.   Whose flourishing we wish.

 Ar. My lords, my thanks. With your advice I

  move;

No engine is so powerful as your love. [*Exeunt.*

   Enter MAZARES *and* ADULANTER.

 Adul. The finest, coming'st lady that your

  Highness

Could wish to meet withal, and rarely handsome.

 Maz. And did accept our proffer?

 Adul.   As greedily

As bees suck sweetness from the fragrant stock

Of Flora's early bounty!

 Maz.   I'm all aflame!

By Heaven, not one of them shall 'scape my fury!

 Adul. Nay, I think I had like to have maul'd

  two of them,

Had not the churchman, with his club-law

  precepts,

Beat down my resolutions.

 Maz.   Damn his daubing!

He is that knack religious mountebank,

A box of frenzied zeal, which he applies

On all occasions to all sorts of sores,

And racks the patient with more fear and torment

Than hell itself can put him to.

 Adul.   A coat

He wears that has been turned seven times!

 Maz. Which we will turn o'er's ears, and then

  turn them.

Oppose our pleasure? He, and all the rest

Of his confederates, shall know we wear
Our crown not for a cipher, and our sceptre
Shall prove a scourge to them. They have awak'd
A fury that no prayers can allay.
Haste to the Governor Icetis ; tell him
It is our will Cleander's spirit leave
The world with speed and privacy. Proclaim
Our cock-brain'd cousin and the piebald church-
　　　man,
Agathocles and Epecides, traitors ;
And such as shall take them, five thousand talents.
So violent I grow in my desire,
I must enjoy it, or set all on fire !　　　　[*Exeunt.*

ACT III.—SCENE I.

Enter EVANDER *and* MISSELLUS.

Eva. Pursued by my bad fate, whose cruelty
I knew would not admit of any mean
Should it once seize on me, I struck myself
Into disguise, by whose obscurity
I came to Tyche ; there gave out my hand
Had kill'd Evander, at which some that were
My enemies gave tokens of their sorrow ;
Others, who thought their rising not secure
'Less by my irrecoverable fall,
Highly applauded me. At last a remnant
Of my poor friends, resolved to pay their last
Service unto my memory, though with
The loss of their estates and lives, did lay
Plots to destroy me as the horrid murderer ;
And I, not daring to open myself
To them, for fear I should let in the fury

Of my stern adversaries, did steal away
With the night's silence.
    Mis.   Though the beginning of
This story melts my soul, yet Providence
Is seen in th' winding up, which did direct
Your Highness hither, where you're as secure
From danger as your thoughts are in your bosom.
    Eva. We doubt it not.
    Mis. You dead, what can Mazares
Pretend to keep his armies up ? This I'll
Possess the people with, and stir them to
Propose their straight disbanding, which if
       granted,
The course of fate is turned, and he left naked
And shelterless from any storm may happen.
On t' other side, if he denies it, then
Th' incensed people, like a sudden earthquake,
Removes him, were his pride more mountainous
Than are his vices monstrous. Thus on all sides
I'll hem him in, so he shall know no way
To 'scape your vengeance. Be but pleased to suffer
Under this cloud awhile, and you'll appear
More glorious to your people's eyes and hearts
When time presents a fitness for discovery.
    Eva. Thou art our faithful counsellor, and we,
Next to the gods, do owe ourself to thee.
                        [*Exeunt.*

Enter PHILISTUS, THIMISTIUS, PHILANDER, *and*
             SOLDIERS.

    Phili. We are not far from Syracuse; this
       passage
Is the direct line to 't, as the map speaks.
    Thi. My lord, I hope your honour will not show
Yourself so much a stranger to designs
Of war as to give them th' advantage of

A parley, but rush suddenly upon them,
And, like a torrent, we'll bear all before us.
There's soldier in 't.

Phili.   It is too rash advice,
And must be slighted.   Missellus is a person
That roughness will not work upon.

Thi.   My lord,
He is no coward, and his honour's linked
Unto his life.   He that will seek the one
Must venture for the other, or lose both.

Phili. If my desires effect but what they aim at,
I care not when or how 'tis purchased.
Haste you with the King's letter to Missellus ;
Tell him 'tis my desire to keep the league
Of friendship 'twixt us, and without a bustle—
Which may let forth some blood—have him
        surrender.
Tell him 'tis no displeasure that the King
Has ta'en against him that occasions this,
But to give ease unto his age, and draw
Him nearer him at Court, where he shall find
The service of his youth in 's latter days
Crowned with a peaceful laurel, and content
Add length unto his years.

Philan.   I go, my lord !
                            [*Exit* PHILANDER.

Phili. Thimistius, march fair and softly, we
        shall be
Too soon upon 'em else.   This cannot but
Insinuate a faith into him to
Give way to my admittance, since the offer
Carries so full a sense of fairness in 't.

Thi. My lord, he 's not to learn this principle—
Where Princes call back honours done, the life
Is the next thing in question.

Phili.   Let the Fates

Contrive their worst against it; if Antanter
Bring us supplies from the Provinciall
Of Mona, we will fire it but we'll have it.
    Thi. Well, my lord, the craft's in th' catching.
                                     [*Exeunt.*

  Enter MISSELLUS, PHILANDER, *and* ATTENDANTS.

    Mis. Dost come to dare me, fellow?
    Philan. I conceive,
With favour of your Excellence, the terms
Are very civil, and no danger in 'em.
    Mis. I shall reward his subtle modesty,
If I but get him here, as I will you,
The worthy messenger. Take's head off!
    Philan. You dare not!
    Mis. Thou art mistaken, friend. Away with
      him!
Oh that I could with as much ease destroy
All th' barbarous enemies of my wronged sovereign!
Make strong the gates and walls, and let the Fort
Hexapile be stoutly manned; we'll be
Prepared to whip the boy and's company.
                                     [*Exeunt.*

  Enter PHILISTUS, THIMISTIUS, *and* SOLDIERS.

    Phili. The gates are shut against us.
    Thi. What think you now on 't?
    Phili. Beat a parley.
        [*The head of* PHILANDER *is thrown over
           the wall.*
How's this?—Philander's head?
    Thi. Which you might have preserv'd upon his
      shoulders,
Had you given but regard unto my counsel.
But you are lordly wise, and, 'cause you can
Batter a lady's fort with your fine rhetoric,

You think the town's your own, and men are
    bound
To bend unto your compliment, or trust
The glass of your deceit.

    Phili.   'Tis fine ! affronted
By greasy buff and brisket !

    Thi.   Some strong water,
To keep the thing from fainting !   Poor young
    man,
How pale he looks upon 't !

    Phili.   Take thy reward !   .
                             [*Pistols him.*

    Sol. Our Colonel slain !

Enter ANTANTER.

    Phili. Were there more living of his saucy nature,
I'd send them after him.   Antanter, what
Says the Provinciall ?

    Ant.   He'll do nothing, sir,
Without a warrant from the King.   He says
He does believe there will be no such need ;
Missellus will resign upon fair terms.

    Phili. But you see how it is ?
                [ANTANTER *looks on* THIMISTIUS' *body.*

    Ant.   I do indeed,
And sorrow that I see 't.   How came Thimistius
By this his death ?

    Sol.   That lord's hand did it.

    Ant.   How ?

    Phili. Come, we will venture with the men we
    have
To scale the walls.

    Ant.   We will not scale, sir.

    Phili.   So !
You will not ?   Very good.   Do you see this head,
    sir ?

Ant. And that body too, sir.

Phili. Let me have better language, or, by Heaven,
I'll make you as tame as these !

Ant. You cannot, sir.

Phili. How ?

Ant. 'Tis not all
The strength you have in feather or perfume
Can fright me, sir. Your amber bracelets carry
Not half the terror of chained shot ; nor is
Your title lord a bulwark to defend you.

Phili. You're a rascal !
Come, soldiers, march with me !

Ant. Not a man stir !
There's satisfaction to be given for
The life of that brave man, which I will have,
Or pay my own.

Sol. Gallant major !

Phili. I shall not spare to give you, sir, your due.
[*Strikes him.*

Ant. I'll not be backward in rewarding it.
[*Returns it, and draws.*

Phili. You are pot-valiant, sir, it seems.

Ant. 'Tis past the art of man to make you so.
I am a soldier, sir. [*Draws, fights.*

Phili. And must be beat
Into civility. I'll make you know
There is a difference 'twixt us !

Ant. True, indeed ;
You can out-talk me.
How do you, sir ? [PHILISTUS *wounded.*

Phili. You shall know by and by, sir. I am
lost ! [*Dies.*

Ant. Farewell, thou tyrant over woman's flesh !
Take up Thimistius' body ; it shall have
An honourable burial. As for his,
Let it remain a sport for the Syracusians.

The King, I know, will run beside himself
To hear on's minion's loss; but you, I hope,
My friends and fellow-soldiers, will wade with me
Through all the lakes of danger?
   Sol. We'll never leave you!
   Ant. Bravely resolv'd! And I will die with
   you!   [*Exeunt.*

     Enter MISSELLUS *and* SOLDIERS.

   Mis. They're marched away! What's here?
   Philistus' body,
Our late competitor? Why, here's revenge
Strangely effected! See the fate of traitors!
How wonderfully Heaven does bring about
Their punishment, that, like to cannibals,
The one doth eat the other! Bring it in!
My hate ends with his life, and now my charity,
Though he deserv'd it not, will give him burial.
                          [*Exeunt.*
    [ARCHIAS, AGATHOCLES, EPECIDES, CLE-
      ANDER, *and* ICETIS *pass over the stage;*
      the people follow, crying, "An Archias!
      An Archias! An Archias!"

   Enter MAZARES, ADULANTER, *and* ATTENDANTS.

   Adul. Their envy is invincible, and the people—
Time's shuttlecocks—do bring unto your gates
The hideous shape of danger.
   Maz.   My deceit
Shall rock that monster into sleep, had it
More eyes than Argus!
   Adul.   'Tis impossible.
The Agrigentines have thrown off obedience;
Monreall is revolted; all your castles
And strongholds in Palermo are deliver'd
Into their hands; the magistrates join with them!

Maz. Go, use thy best endeavours, Adulanter,
To appease the people! Turn right courtier;
      promise,
And we'll perform at leisure.
    Adul.   Your Highness,
I hope, is not in earnest? I go amongst 'em!
Have you a mind to have my brains beat out?
I am your pimp, they say, sir; am so hated,
The very boys throw turap tops at me!
    Maz. Alas, poor Adulanter! We will blow
This storm away, ne'er fear it. Let our guard
Be doubled, till we can send t' Hermocrates
To bring his forces hither! If the traitors
Come not too suddenly upon us, we
Will turn the poisoned darts they'd throw at us
'Gainst their own bosoms. They do play with fire
Till it consume 'em.
    Adul. They, like moles, have worked
In darkness all this while to set the Kingdom
In such a flame that might both perish you
And all your friends.
    Maz.   Fire sooner may dissolve
The adamant!—the parched negroes strike
Through th' battlements of heaven! We are
      above
The reach of malice; fortune is obliged
To wait upon our merit, and our influence
Can in a breath disperse their proud designs,
As winds divest the trees of leaves. Let fear
Dwell among fools; 't shall have no harbour here!
                    [*Exeunt.*

   Enter ARCHIAS, ARCHBISHOP, AGATHOCLES,
      EPECIDES, *and* SOLDIERS.

    Ar. Leave it to me; I'll do the business,
    gentlemen.
        F

Arch. 'Tis not discretion to expose your person
So unconcern'd in this ; 'tis we, the people,
Whose wrongs infer the cause.
    Ar.   Which I must manage.
You've made me your protector and revenger,
Which I'll perform.   Did gloomy magic guard
    him,
Or were he wrapt in air, or hid in some
Dark cavern of the earth, my heart, grown big,
Like dire revenging thunder, would make through
The bodies of them both to find him out.
    Aga. Our lives shall wait on yours through
    danger's mouth.
    Sol. An Archias ! An Archias !   [*Exeunt.*

       Enter MAZARES *and* ADULANTER.

    Adul. They have surprised the guards, and are
    upon us !
    Maz. Haste to the winner ; leave us to our
    fortune.
Provide for thy own safety ; we are armed
With resolution to o'ercome the worst
The fates can throw upon us.   Leave us, leave us!
    Adul. They'll hang me, sir, and I've no mind at
    this time
To such a death.
    Maz.   Trifle not away
The time ; they will not.   Go, leave us !
    Adul. Well, if I chance to swing, pray Heaven
    I may
Have heart enough to bear it.   [*Exit.*
    Maz. Injurious fate! for all the pride thou tak'st
In my destruction, thus I will embrace thee !
        [*Takes the sword off the table ; kisses it.*
Mischiefs, like waves, tumble o'er one another
To beat themselves upon me, and they're welcome.

This passes me through all.   Poor, ignorant souls,
That start at death, and think him terrible ;
His shape appears to me worthy the courting,
And, like my friend, I kiss him.   On this point
                              [*Kisses the sword.*
He shows himself most lovely, decked with all
The ornaments of honour fame can give him.
Thus I salute thee, thus again I greet thee,
                              [*Opens his doublet.*
And thus I offer up a heart unto thee—
A heart thy terror cannot tame.   'Tis love
Of thy sweet fellowship o'ercomes me, not
A fear to meet thee that my soul disdains.
Mazares ! dwell not on delays ; be high
In thy resolves : as thou hast liv'd, so die !
                    [*Throws himself upon his sword.*
Oh, I have prevented you !   [*Falls.*
                          [*A great shout within.*

        Enter ARCHIAS, ARCHBISHOP, AGATHOCLES,
                EPECIDES, *and* SOLDIERS.

    Ar.   And I
Envy thy death, in that I lose
The glory of saving of thy life.
    Maz.   Which must have lasted
But, pageant-like, two days upon your triumphs,
And my shame been perpetual.
    Arch.   Do you find
Any remorse within you ?   Do the wrongs
You've offer'd to the gods, in pulling down
Their temples and their altars, work upon you
Any show of repentance ?
    Maz.   Thou church glow-worm, '
Who dost pretend a heat of zeal, yet art
Colder than th' Alps in charity if proved,
My enmity to thee gives strength unto me,

And I could— But oh! I fail. This my death
Shall prove a monument to my glory. Farewell!
                                        [*Dies.*

Enter a SOLDIER *with* ADULANTER.

Sol. Here is another of the crew!

Ar. Hang him up!

Adul. Who?—me, sir? I ne'er dreamt of ill
against you; have prayed as heartily for you as for
any man living; for I may speak a proud word,
I never prayed in my life. I hope my mother
brought me up better than so to be hanged.

Cle. Let me beseech your pardon for him. Alas!
He is not worth your justice, and may prove
Useful hereafter—to me.   [*Aside.*

Ar.   Noble father,
For so we must be taught to call you, you
Have greater power upon us than this grant;
'Tis yours as soon as asked.

Adul.   Heaven bless the King!

Ar. Take up Mazares' body. His rites over,
The next thing we shall do is to perform
Our vows made to the gods, and take Harmonia,
Your daughter, to our bed.

Cle.   And the next thing   [*Aside.*
That follows is thy death. I must be King!
                                    [*Exeunt.*

ACT IV.—SCENE I.

Enter ARCHIAS, HARMONIA, ARCHBISHOP, AGA-
THOCLES, CLEANDER, EPECIDES, *and* ADULANTER.

Ar. We'll have the temples of the gods repair'd,
And their neglected altars smoke with sacrifices.

Arch. A glorious piece of piety !
Ar.   The citizens,
Who for their duty to Evander were
Banished by the late tyrant, straight call home ;
And to Hermocrates, with his 'complices
Who did assist Mazares, a free pardon.
Aga. A blest beginning !
Ar.   We will have the burthen
The Kingdom now groans under by the soldiery
Be taken off.
Arch.   The gods will dwell amongst us !
Ar. My lords, I shall endeavour to reduce
This rude and discomposed soil into
A Tempe of delight, where sweet Harmonia
Shall be the only Queen.
Har.   It will become me
To be but then your servant.
Ar.   Sweet, thou knowest
I am beneath thy courtship, and the interest
I have in thee is holy.
Arch.   May you flourish
Together like the plants the sun gives life to !
Cle. Will your Highness
Think on Antanter ?
Ar.   Oh, his modesty
Works much upon us. We could chide ourself
In that we have abused it by neglect
Of his so just and reasonable a suit.
As for the other, his competitor,
A black cloud of debauchness and lewd vices
Eclipses his valour, and gives us occasion
To look upon Antanter as more worthy
Of such a charge, whose virtue is our warrant.
Kings, in bestowing favours, should be nice,
And rather punish than encourage vice.
                              [*Exeunt.*

Enter CLEANDER *and* ADULANTER.

Cle. Adulanter!
Adul. My lord?
Cle. Wilt tell me one thing, and be just?
Adul. Rip up my heart, my lord, if I dissemble.
Cle. How stands thy affection to this King?
Adul. As clear as—
Cle.   Mine is not.   Be free; I love thee,
And thou hast found I do.
      Adul.   I have indeed;
I owe my life unto you.   You may take it,
For that's the thing you aim at.
      Cle. Th' art deceived;
'Twill benefit me nothing.   Come, I know
Thou canst not love him.   Thou hast lost a master
As far beyond him as pure substance is
Beyond corruptible; and, though he did
Me some ill offices, his memory is
Still dear unto me.
      Adul.   Oh, my lord, my lord!
Cle. By all the gods, I lie not; and to be
More plain with thee, I could wish Archias
Were ready for the earth.
      Adul.   If that your lordship
Be real, I would it were no worse.
      Cle. If he were dead, my daughter I would
            govern,
And thou shouldst govern me.
      Adul.   Oh, fie, my lord!
Cle. I do protest we would divide the Kingdom
Betwixt us; she, poor thing! would think it
            happiness
Enough for her to eat, sit, and be quiet,
Whereas the managing of high affairs
Should pass through us—through us, Adulanter!

Adul. Hum, hum !

Cle. Whose knee dares own a stiffness ? Whose
    obeisance
To Adulanter dare be wanting ? When
Thou frown'st, who dares but tremble ?

Adul. When such a thing shall come to pass,
    quotha—

Cle. Dost make a question on't, when now it lies
Within thy power to compass ?

Adul.   How in mine ?

Cle. Art thou not by my means raised near his
    person—
One of the bed-chamber ? How easy 'tis
To cut his throat.

Adul.   The sight of my own blood
Has ever been a terror to me.

Cle.   True,
That's natural, and yet no courage wanting
To draw a sea of blood from any other.
The colour is most precious for the sight,
And sweetly cordial to the man that tastes it.

Adul. Nay, I confess I'd rather see, of th' two,
Another's blood than mine.

Cle.   'Tis justly spoken.
Would'st thou be King alone ?

Adul.   Hum ! I care not much.

Cle. Thou shalt be so. Be but thyself, and show
Thy courage in this enterprise, I'll marry
Thee to my daughter.

Adul.   She's a pretty thing :
By Heaven, I shall be damned for her !

Cle.   I'd rather
Thou shouldst possess her than the fool that has
    her ;
And I, thy fellow-servant once, will then
Become thy humblest servant, truly faithful.

Adul. You puff me up, sir ! Tell me how I shall
Contain myself.

Cle.   Not within any limit
Less than a Kingdom.

Adul.   How shall I obtain it ?

Cle. Why, as you'd kiss your hand, to kill the
        King.
It is but making the guard drunk, or so.

Adul. And I'm as good at that as any living.
My lord, I will be drunk to boot, for then
I have most courage.

Cle.   Backed with night and silence,
You cannot want it. When you have done the
        deed,
Strike towards the back stairs; there I will wait you
And shelter you a while, till the bright morn
Salutes your happiness.

Adul.   My lord, 'tis done !
I am as mad as a March hare upon't ;
Methinks I have him here and there already.
You will hear more to-morrow.   [*Exit.*

Cle.   Silly ass !
That only art employed to carry me
Unto my bliss, thyself unto destruction !
He's held an animal has no deceit
In these times to make his own fortunes great.
                                [*Exit.*

Enter ARCHIAS, HARMONIA, ARCHBISHOP, *and*
        ATTENDANTS.

Arch. Heaven and good angels guard you both !
                [*Exit* ARCHBISHOP.

Ar. Good rest
To you, my lord!
                [*Exeunt* ARCHIAS *and* HARMONIA.

1 *Guard.* Lights for the Lord Archbishop !

Enter ADULANTER.

Adul. Did the King call for me ?
2 Guard. Not in our hearing.
Adul. Come, praised be Heaven, there is no danger lurking ; what need we wait ? 'Tis better for the state of our bodies to fall down into the wine-cellar, and there bid defiance to the devil and all's works.
Guard. A match, a match !　　　　　　　*[Exeunt.*

Enter AGATHOCLES, EPECIDES, *and* ATTENDANTS.

Epe. The Mask did keep the King up longer than
His usual time.
Aga.　　　　　　It was a handsome thing,
And well performed.　All happiness wait on you !
　　　　　　　　　　　　　　　　[Exit.
Epe. Peace keep with your thoughts, my lord !
　　Good night!
Atten. Lights there !　　　　　　　　*[Exeunt.*

Enter ADULANTER.

Adul. I have encountered with most of the wines
In the King's cellar to beget me courage,
Yet I'm as cold to 't as a cucumber.*
I was not made for fighting ; one loud snort
Destroys me and my enterprise.　'Tis dark,
As is the act I go about ; were 't light,
I should not have the heart to kill a pig.
I must turn on my left hand, when 'tis done,
To the back stairs, where there is a trap-door
That will receive me.　I do not like
These backward doings.　Pray Heaven I be not
Transported so with fear I do mistake
　　　　　* In original, "cowcumer."

My right hand for my left, and so be trapp'd.

[*Pulls by the hangings.*

I cannot say in sober sadness, "But with your
    leave, sir."

He's fast, yet dreams not on't. Now that one
    blow

May do't; I dare not stand the second.

[*Kills* HARMONIA, *and runs to the trap-door,
    where he falls and breaks his neck.*

  Har. Oh, oh, oh!

  Ar. What disturbs thee, sweet ? Speak to me.

Oh, her breasts are cold as snow-balls!

She grows stiff! Lights there! Where's our
    guard ?

No attendants ? Not one man ?

Enter AGATHOCLES *and* EPECIDES *in their night-
gowns, and lights.*

Hear me, are you all—   [ARCHIAS *rises.*

  Aga. The King's disturbed!

  Epe. How fares your Highness ?

  Ar. Bring your lights this way. Ah!

The bed swims in a sea of blood! Harmonia!

Enter CLEANDER.

  Epe. The Queen is murdered.

  Cle. The King murdered! How ?

  Ar. Look here, Cleander; here's a sight! My
    senses

Wander I know not whither!

  Cle.   How! My daughter!

Harmonia, the essence of my life!

Enter SERVANT.

  Aga. Can no man find the murderer ? Where's
    the guard ?

Serv. Dead drunk in th' wine cellar.

Cle. This is the murderer, then ; seek no farther !
I will have justice !   Oh, my cursed fate !

                    [Exit, tearing his hair.

Epe. How 's grief transports him !

Aga. Can you blame him ?
He has lost a daughter this age cannot parallel.

Epe. The murderer not found yet ?

Enter with the body of ADULANTER.

1. This does appear like such a monster.

2. His hire is paid ; his neck is broke.

Aga. 'Tis Adulanter !   Where found you him ?

1. The trap-door near the back stairs we found
open, which has not been these ten years before,
and we, suspecting, searched the place and found
him.

Ar. And is he found ?   Let him be carbonadoed,
To breakfast his confederate the devil ;
Or pickle him in boiling lead, to get
The fiend a stomach !   Oh, you gods ! you devils !
Heaven, hell, I will call all of you to question !

                              [Exit.

Aga. Let's follow him with circumspective care ;
This is the first step to the hill despair.

                              [Exeunt.

Enter CLEANDER.

Cle. Thou shalt no longer insult o'er my
      faculties,
Unprofitable grief !   I'm not designed
To end my days with thee, but must unload
Myself of thy dull burden.   Were the whole
Stock of woman lost in my Harmonia,
'T should not exact or draw a tear from me.
Shall I retreat now, that have charg'd so fairly

At th' bosom of a King? No! On, Cleander!
Perfect thy work; dis-seat him; make thyself
Lord of his fortunes by thy glorious conquest!
My resolution's fix'd as is the centre,
Which fate cannot remove.   King, thou must
        down;
Two heads cannot be impal'd within one crown!

Enter AGATHOCLES *and* EPECIDES.

But to my former shape.   These are Court spies;
I must not trust 'em.—Good health to your lord-
        ships!
You now do show the sweetness of your natures:
In time of heaviness there's virtue in
A visit.
    Epe. Would ours might bring you comfort!
    Aga. The King is so infected with his sorrow,
Advice is lost to cure him.   All his study
Is to preserve the memory of your daughter;
Which, 'cause he will not lose, he makes her
        shadow
His idol, to the which he offers up
His morn and night oblations.
    Cle.   How should I
Behave myself, then?   My grief should as far
Exceed his as my loss transcended his.
    Epe. Your loss was great.
    Cle. Great, do you tell me?   Great?
    Aga. I cannot think the ill was meant to her;
Rather unto the King.
    Epe.   The guard,
Upon examination, said that Adulanter
Was drunk when he left them, but what—
    Cle. Pray, tell me no more on't; 'tis not pleasing.
I may be quiet in my own house, I hope?
    Epe.   We came not, sir,

With an intent to raise your anger, but
To allay your sorrow with our best advice.

Cle. You may go home, then, and advise upon 't.
Tell me of comfort and advice !

Aga. Nay, good my lord,
You may take pet and hang yourself if 't please you;
'Tis all one to us.

Cle. Teach me to tame a tiger, when his fierceness
Ranges for prey and forbids opposition !
Empty the ocean and fill it again !   [*Raves.*
To breathe life into clay ! Tell me of comfort ?

    Epe. Come, let's leave him.   Alas ! 'tis his
        torment
To hear her named ! We take our leaves, my
        lord.   [*Exeunt.*

Cle. Why, farewell, you.—So, they are gone ;
I had no better way than to rave them hence.

Enter a Scotch APOTHECARY.

Oh, are you come, sir ? Why so long, first ?

Apo. Guid faith, gif I had rid the deil, and
splut the weam o' the wund, I cud 'a mead na
mair heast.   Kym away, sir ; what's your wull, an
please your honour ?

Cle. They say you have great skill ?

Apo. Very muckle, sir ; I ha' not been a poles-
screamer this twenty years for naught.

Cle. I do not love the King.

Apo. Reight weel, sir, nor I, by my sau'.
What wud you toll him, sir ?

Cle. I would be rid of him.

Apo. Wull your honour be a hearse or a mare ?

Cle. Away ! I'd be quit of him.

Apo. Ah, sir, your honour wud be quite o' him ?
By my sau', ye sall ; but whilk way, me lord, an
please your honour ?

Cle. I'd have him poisoned.

Apo. Peysoned! By my sau', I can dew that brawly; I learn'd it frae Bough-wha-nan,* sir.

Cle. And he was an excellent King-killer!
He has a picture of my murdered daughter,
On which he pays his early and late kisses—
Not for the love he bears her memory,
But to deceive revenge.

Apo. Aw, sir, she sall buss him deed, o' me sau'!
Wull ye shaw me tull her, sir?

> [*Pulls him by the sleeve.*

Cle. I'm glad to see the spirit of a Scot
So resolute; it starts not at the murdering
Of the fool's idol, King.

Apo. Aw King, mon! Deil a' me sau', bet I
an' me countramen ha' peysoned three better Kingdoms as this; an gif I sud noo for aw King, the deil
au me faw lugs.

Cle. Thou art a brave fellow, and 'tis pity such
Desert should suffer. Come along with me!—
When thou hast done I'll make an end of thee.

> [*Aside. Exeunt.*

Enter AGATHOCLES *and* ANTANTER.

Ant. I thought it then high time to overtake
His mounting pride, and level 't with the earth,
And not to let him grow more fruitful in
His sin and overtopping insolence.

Aga. It was a deed, Antanter, that deserves
To live in th' mouth of fame, that after ages
From thence may learn not to fear bugbear
    greatness.

Ant. Thimistius' body I gave burial, and
Left th' other's to Missellus' disposal.

---

* Buchanan, pronounced in Scotland "Bughwhanan,"—the
first syllable guttural.

Aga. 'Twas no small sport to him; but it was strange
Planetius should deny assistance to him.

Ant. I do believe Missellus and he held
A correspondence, but for what end
I cannot reach.

Aga.   He is not to be trusted.
If this distemper once would leave the King,
Thou wouldst not think 't a miracle to see

Enter EPECIDES.

Me in Planetius seat ?   Now, Epecides,
How fares the King ?

Epe.   Oh, gentlemen, our hopes,
That promised a growing happiness
From his indulgent beams, one minute has
Destroyed for ever !

Aga. How do you mean, my lord ?

Epe. The King is poisoned.

Ant. How! Poisoned ? Poisoned ?

Aga. There is a secret devil lurks among us,
Who holds intelligence with hell, to blast
Our Kingdom's peace and comfort. See, they come !

Enter ARCHIAS *in a bed,* ARCHBISHOP, CLEANDER,
      PHYSICIANS, *and* ATTENDANTS.

Ar. The flames of Ætna are not fierce to mine ;
Each faculty conspires my torment. Oh,
I burn ! I burn !

Phys.   Great sir, be not an enemy
Unto your being; take this as—

Ar.   Away !
You may as well give physic to the dead
As to his heart whose agony exceeds
The sense of ease. I am resolved to take
No more of your vain helps. Leave me, I pray.—
Cleander !

Cle. My most gracious sovereign,
I have a heart too weak to bear the burden
Of so much woe ; your sufferings bear me down
Beneath the hope of comfort.
  Ar.   Spare thy grief.
Harmonia treads the Milky Way, and I
Must through this fire be purified to meet
Her and the joys she brings me.
  Aga.   Does none hear
By whom or how these miseries should come ?
  Ar. Trouble not yourself, my lord ; I freely
    pardon
And will reward the doer.   So declare it,
For he has taken pains to send me to
The place I so much longed for.   I do charge you,
If my last words may win obedience from you,
Straight to proclaim this.   Fain I would salute
Him, e'er I die, that was so kind unto me !
  Arch. Unheard-of charity !
  Ar.   My lord, from you
I have conceived in specie the joys
I must receive hereafter.   Those sweet odours
Perfume my spiritual sense, and strengthen that,
Although my temporal decay and perish.

 Enter SERVANT *with the Scotch* APOTHECARY.

 Ser. Here is a Scotch apothecary that confesses—
Cle. Art thou the villain ?
         [CLEANDER *kills him.*
 Apo. Au, the mickle deil !   God, gin the King
wud gie me bet aen hauf ooer toll live, I cud speak
—aw, death, thou limmer loon !   Aw, aw !   [*Dies.*
 Aga. My lord, 'twas rashly done !   We might
    have found
Where the ill vapour rests begets these mischiefs,
And who set him on work.

Cle.   The devil! who else?
And he has paid him's wages.
   Ar.   Cleander!
   Arch. The King calls, sir.
   Ar. I feel my vitals fail me.   Oh, Cleander,
I shall see my Harmonia, thy blest daughter,
Ere forty minutes pass!   I must bequeath
    thee
A legacy of care, this drooping Kingdom.
My lords, I hope the love you ever bore me,
Though Heaven denies me time to merit it,
Will now express itself in the approving
Him I present to you—a dying man,
Who has no ends upon you nor the Kingdom,
Further than your perpetual flourishing.
   Cle. I beseech your Grace!   Alas!—
   Ar. You hear me, lords?
   Arch. We do, sir, and accept the choice you've
    made
With more than willingness.
   Aga. You have not spoke for me.   [*Exit.*
   Epe. Nor me.   [*Exit.*
   Ar. I am at rest.   Farewell!   [*Dies.*
   Arch. He's dead.
   Cle. And I,
His weeping monument, remain, till fate
Translates my better part t' a better state.
                      [*Exeunt.*

   Ant. These are fine turning times.   I wonder
    when
'Twill come to my turn to be King!   I have
A heart as fit and large, and dare as far
Adventure for't, as any; but the fates
Of soldiers serve to promote others' ends,
Which done, they do forget we e'er were friends.
                      [*Exit.*
         G

Enter AGATHOCLES, EPECIDES, HIPPARINUS, *and*
    ICETIS.

Hip. Your words sound like the oracle's, as full
Of truth, and plainer to the intellect.
    Aga. How sweet and freely Rome enjoy'd her-
        self
Till she submitted to the power and pride
Of one man's rule !   Tell me, what good did
        ever
Kings bring unto our country that we might not
Have purchased without 'em ?   Ills they have
Almost incredible,—our coffers emptied
To fill their treasury and maintain their riot.
    Epe. And wedded to perpetual slavery ;
For when one tyrant falls, another rises
From his corrupted loins that proves far worse,
Perhaps, than did the former.   So that we
Must never hope for better, but be armed
With patience to endure the worst.
    Aga.   Suppose
We would allow of kingly power, where is
The man descended from that race ?   Cleander ?
He was but one of us the other day ;
And sure we are not of so tame a brood
But to think we deserve 't as well as he.
Why should not you, Icetis, or Hipparinus,
Rule, or thou, Epecides, or myself ?
We're of as good a mould, and have as much
T' elate us as his worship. ┆
    Epe.   Very right ;
And have as great an interest in the people
And commonwealth.   This of necessity
Must breed confusion 'mongst us ; this example
Kindles in every man desire of rule,
Which to achieve, how perilous soe'er

Th' attempt may prove, they'll leave no means
    unsought,
Till their irregular sense, spurning at order,
Turns all into a chaos.
   Aga.   Who can tell
But this intruder was th' efficient cause
Of his own daughter's ruin and the King's?
   Epe. It was a notable piece of policy
To kill the apothecary, and prevent confession.
   Ice. What's your advice?
   Aga.   To join with us,
And take th' people's yoke off from the tyranny
Of Kings hereafter.
   Epe.   And to have our country
Governed by three or ten, as did the Romans.
   Aga. Who shall continue but a year in power;
And then successive patriots be chosen,
Who shall have power to punish in their time
The crimes their predecessors did commit
During their time of rule.
   Epe.   So shall the people
Not be to seek for justice, but find ease
Unto their grievances, and the vile minds
Of avaricious and ambitious men
Be either punished or else rebated.
   Ice. It cannot but content the people highly,
'Tis copied from so fair a precedent.
   Hip. And with you and for you and them, we'll
    spend
Our lives and fortunes.
   Aga.   We will do the like
With you and for you, and, thus linked together,
                       [Embrace.
We dare contemn Cleander's power!
   Epe.   And blow
His glorious hopes into the air!

Aga.   Be sudden,
And we may take the serpent in his cell ;
But our delays may give the monster time
Of coming forth, and strength to overcome us.
    Hip. We will possess the people with the glory
Of their long hidden liberties, with promise
Of restoration if it lies within
The power of friends, money, or life to compass.
    Aga. He that's besotted to his fear or ease
Will make his patience prove his worst disease !
                                        [*Exeunt.*

            Enter PLANETIUS *and a* CAPTAIN.

    Pla. Return my obedience to the King Evander,
And this unto Missellus.   Tell him I,
                            [*Gives him a paper.*
With all the force that Mona can afford me,
Will wait upon his Highness and himself
At Erix.
    Cap. I shall, my lord !   [*Exit* CAPTAIN.
    Pla.   How am I
Bound to the gods for their superlative goodness,
That here an offering of mercy meets me
By their dictation !   I, whose treachery
Unto my King merits severest justice,
Am punished with a revengeless pardon,
Which is indeed my torment—that I should
Ever have been so wicked 'gainst a Prince
Deserves so much good from me !   But my soul
Henceforth shall cleave fast to this principle,—
" The longer growth diseases do endure,
The more the grief, more famous is the cure."
                                        [*Exit.*

Enter HIPPARINUS, ICETIS, *and the* PEOPLE, *casting*
    up their caps, crying, " Liberty ! Liberty !"
                                        [*Exeunt.*

ACT V.—SCENE I.

Enter AGATHOCLES, EPECIDES, HIPPARINUS,
ICETIS, ANTANTER, *and the* PEOPLE
hauling CLEANDER.

Cle. Traitors, hands off ! 'Tis sacrilege to use
The person of your King with such irreverence !
Omnes. Our King ! Ha, ha, ha !
People. We'll make you sing another song.
Cle. Have I deserved so ill that none will give
A death more honourable to me ?
Aga.   Thou hast liv'd
Base, and must basely die.
Cle.   Forgive me, Heaven !
And you, bright stars, whose lustre I eclipse
Here to shine brighter there, plead not against me,
But be as merciful as you are innocent !
Aga. Wert thou the death of Archias and thy
         daughter ?
Cle. Ambition was, to which I gave consent.
Aga. And now you see the pinnacle from which
You must be tumbled down. Away with him !
Cle. Yet hear me !
People. Confession's tied to destiny. You shall
         with us !   [*People drag him in.*
Aga. You see the desperate effects that wait
On this thing called Monarchy, because
It carries a continuance, and all
Men naturally have an ambition to
Make great their line and families by succession ;
When ours doth blunt the edge of such resolves,
And no man, were it not for th' common good,
Would entertain the office, being rather

A place of care than profit, in the which
Men must so square their actions, they may be
Able to stand the people's questioning
Whenas their time of government's expired.
  Epe. It is not so with Monarchy. Kings
   may
Commit what outrages they please upon
The people, and none dare so much as think
They have done ill.

Enter a FELLOW.

  Fell. If you please to walk that way,
You may see Cleander swinging for his life.
  Hip. Oh, by all means, let's go!
  Ant. It may be he may confess something
   more.   [*Exeunt.*

Enter EVANDER, MISSELLUS, *and* SOLDIERS.

  Eva. My people's troubles do afflict me more
Than all the wrongs and injuries they've done
  me!
  Mis. The gods had lost their attribute of just,
Had they not punished them with these convul-
  sions,
Whose fits direct their sense unto the ruin
They've brought upon themselves, now at their
  doors.
  Eva. Good Heaven, divert it! I shall be more
  chary
In spilling of their blood than of my own;
And I shall think it greater honour to me,
In purchasing my own, to have my temples
Surrounded with a peaceful garland, than
Obtain it by the victory and slaughter
Of my poor subjects!
  Mis.   'Tis your mercy, sir,

Enter PLANETIUS *and* SOLDIERS. PLANETIUS
kneels.

With which you overflow.   Here is Planetius !
  Pla. I offer, at your Highness' feet, a life
That has long since been forfeited.
  Eva.   The which
I give thee back.   Live to deserve my favour !
  Pla. I would I could recover so much time
As I have lost, to add unto the days
I'm yet to spend to serve you !   This your mercy
Does come so near the temper of the gods,
Fame cannot but record it !
  Eva.   Have our subjects
The knowledge that we live ?
  Pla.   I did disperse it
Through all the parts of Mona.
  Eva.   And how took they it ?
  Pla. Miraculously ; but so I might discover
Their joy was inexpressible.
  Eva.   We'll have
Our pardon, as we march, proclaimed to all
Will come in to us.   Clemency, not force,
Befits a King ; rigour makes people worse.
  Sol. Heaven bless the King ! March, gentle-
    men !   [*Exeunt.*

Enter ANTANTER, *and* SOLDIERS *pass over the stage ;
then enter* AGATHOCLES.

  Aga. 'Tis brave to be a King !   His spirit's low
And base as earth that knows not how to use
The power the Fates have put into his hands,
And will accept of less !   Damn annual rule !
Shall I, who dare do more than kill a thousand,
Be subject to the questioning of ten ?
The people have put me in power, and I

Will make my best advantage on't ; it is
But justice to break faith with faithless men.
Give me the nod that strikes a trembling in
The stiff-necked people, and does make 'em keep
A distance and a duty.　There's no glory
Like being singular.　Hence, idle honesty !
That sleep'st thy time away, and art adored
By none but empty skulls and tattered jerkins !
There's no such thing as virtue in thy rags.
That we prize to be virtuous and good
Merits its estimation. . Welcome greatness !
Virtue resides with thee.　My hopes by this
　　　　　　　　　　[*A shout within.*
Are by Antanter perfected.　He's here !

Enter ANTANTER *and* SOLDIERS.

Now, my best genius, tell me how much
I stand indebted to thee.　Is it done ?
　　Ant. Done to a hair, sir.　We surprised 'em
　　　　suddenly,
Trussed up the magistrates, to whom y'ad pro-
　　mised
Such glorious freedom, who did curse and swear
At death and destiny.　The forts and castles
Are all our own, and now we safely may
Cry with one voice, " Long live Agathocles !"
　　　　　　[SOLDIERS *cry*, " Long live Agathocles !"
　　Aga. How shall I make requital for this
　　　　project,
Which thou hast more than formed, performed so
　　bravely ?
I will create thee Archduke of Palermo,
And when I die will leave the kingdom to thee.
　　Ant. But give me leave, I pray, sir ; in whose
　　　　power
Lies it to make me Duke ?

Aga.   In mine ; whose else ?
Am I not thy King ?
  Ant.   Pray, who made you so ?
  Aga. The gods !
  Ant. Pray, which of them ?   Have I been idle ?
  Aga. No, dear Antanter, no !   It was thy hand,
Directed by the gods, that made me King.
  Ant. Then 'twas my hand, directed by the gods,
That made you King ?
  Aga.   Right, right, Antanter !
  Ant. And now my hand, directed by the gods,
Will you unking !—Take him into your charge !
  Aga. How ?
  Ant.   Very right, sir !   Charity begins
At home, and I'm not such an ass to stand
To your reward when I can pay myself !
  Aga. What dost thou mean ?
  Ant.   To be what you would be—
That is, a King.
  Aga.   A King !   Of what ?
  Ant. Of better men than thou art !   'Tis a
    wrong
Unto our honour to hold parley with thee.—
Off with his head !—It is a death more noble
Than you bestowed upon Cleander, sir,
Or ordered for Icetis or the magistrates !
  Aga. But do you hear, sir King ?
  Ant.   Obey our will.—
And, sir, say ye're well dealt with.
  Aga.   Hell take you
And your dealing too !   Heaven is thus just
With such as fall from virtue to their lust !
              [*Exeunt with* AGATHOCLES.
  Ant. So he is gone — fallen in the trap he
    laid
For th' magistrates, whom I have but secured

Till they allow my power or die by it.
The title King's indifferent to me :
Give me th' essential part, and let the shadow
Vanish and be forgot ! What had this lord
More in him of a man to draw obedience
Than I, except his title ? And that had not
Virtue enough to save him from my wrath.
It is not birth or blood, but thou, dear instrument,
                                        [*To his sword.*
That can defend, offend, raise, or dis-seat
High potentates, and make a beggar great.
Be thou auspicious, armed Mars, to me,
And I'll adore no other gods but thee !

Enter a CAPTAIN.

Cap. The General, hearing of these distractions,
Has drawn his army this way, and puts in
For title to the Kingdom.
Ant.   Though he was
My General once, I'll scourge him into duty,
And make him know his distance. We will meet
    him.
Leave what force you can possibly allow
Here, to secure the people and the garrisons
Now in our custody, lest they revolt
Or become mutineers. Hermocrates
Shall find as tough a business on't as e'er
The wars afforded him. Give double pay
To such as will come in to us and leave
His party. Since that I am in, I'll through,
Though th' Kingdom's treasury bleed for 't, and
    lean famine
Feed on the people till there scarce are left
The image of a man alive. 'Twere base
Now to retreat ! Fear gives a coward place !
                                        [*Exeunt.*

Enter HERMOCRATES, CAPTAIN, *and* SOLDIERS.

Her. Is't possible Antanter dares do this ?
Cap. Agathocles is beheaded ; Hipparinus,
With th' rest of th' magistrates of Palermo,
    and
The Governor Icetis, are secured ;
The forts and castles all are in his power ;
And h'as surprised the treasury.
Her.   A brave fellow !
How long thinks he to keep this ? I do wonder
Missellus or Planetius stir not 'bout it.
But they, indeed, are such known enemies
To one another, neither of them dare
Peep forth, lest th' other be upon his back.
Cap. I know your Excellency will be the man
Must make the soldier flourish and be happy !
Her. I and Antanter are the only men,
I see, must go to cudgels for 't.
Cap.   Alas !
Our force will scatter his as northern winds
Disperse the leaves in autumn !
Her.   But he has
The advantage by the treasury, and money
Will purchase men and friendship.
Cap.   Victory
Will draw them all to us. I hope there is not
A man amongst us so in love with 's life,
But he will sacrifice it for your Excellency.—
What say you, gentlemen ?
Sol.   Our lives are his !
Her. I thank you, fellow-soldiers ! Armed with
    you,
I dare oppose the destinies ! He down,
The guerdon of our conquest is a crown !
                          [*Exeunt.*

Enter EVANDER, MISSELLUS, PLANETIUS, *and*
            SOLDIERS.

Eva. How poor and bare 's this province made !
      We scarce
Can get provision for our men and horse.
    Pla. But we are near the city of Monreall,
And that was wont t' abound with all provision.
    Eva. Have you informed th' Archbishop and the
            magistrates
That we are drawing towards them ?
    Mis.   We have,
By your express, and wonder that we hear
No sooner from them.

Enter ARCHBISHOP, EPECIDES, *and* MAGISTRATES.

    Arch.   Disobedient guilt
Throws me thus low for mercy !
    Eva.   Here ; rise up !
                              [*Lends his hand.*
    Arch. Distracted shame so overcomes me, sir,
I cannot look your Highness in the face.
    Eva. Return unto your virtue, and we shall
Be happy in your friendship.   Epecides,
How dost thou relish us ?
    Epe.   As I would, sir,
The author of my being, peace, and happiness.
My soul has wandered all this while, and now,
With you, it is returned to its first station.
    Eva. But what hath brought thee to Monreall ?
            Tell me !
    Epe. After Cleander's death, my friend Aga-
            thocles,
Whose breast I thought had been so manned with
            virtue
Ambition could not batter it, complied

With th' soldiery, of which Antanter was
The chief, to put the magistrates to death.
No sooner that Antanter had secured
The forts and castles, and made all his own,
But he begins to fall off from his bargain
With the new King, and to himself does give
A law to take his head off.   And, indeed,
No man could promise to himself a safety
Unless he did submit unto his power;
To which I knew I could not bend my heart,
And therefore for self-preservation made
Bold with my Lord Archbishop.

 Eva.   What is that
Antanter, whose audaciousness is so
Destructive to our peace ?

 Pla.   He was an officer
Under Hermocrates, Mazares' general.

 Arch. And now they both are tugging to undo
The Kingdom, and from either's ruin to
Raise to the victor glory.

 Eva.   Ah, poor Sicily!
How hast thou been beaten and banded to
Promote the ends of turbulent-spirited men !
My lords, while they are striving for the mastery,
What if we fell upon them ?

 Mis.   Very requisite !

 Eva. Let us be private in't, and do it suddenly.
But first we'll have a baiting at your house.

 Arch. Your Highness will enrich me with the
  favour.   [*Exeunt.*

   Drums, trumpets, etc.

[*Enter the party of* HERMOCRATES, *driving* ANTAN-
 TER'S *party before them ; then* ANTANTER *enters
 and rescues his party, beats the others off;* HER-
 MOCRATES *enters with fresh supplies, and beats*

them in ; then enter at one door HERMOCRATES,
at the other ANTANTER.

Her. Have I singled thee ?

Ant.   Sir, know y'are saucy !
We use to keep at distance with such fellows !

Her. 'Tis likely : to come near us may prove
      dangerous !

Ant. Fellow, th'ast greater honour done thee
      now
Than e'er the wars bestowed on thee : thou
      grapplest
With no less than a King !

Her.   Of kitchen stuff !

Ant. I'll make thee do thy duty!   [*Fights.*

Her.   That's to beat you.   [*Wounds him.*
What will you take, sir, for your Kingdom now ?

Ant. Your head and quarters, sir, to fix on th'
      gates !

Her. And this next touch to boot?
                              [*Wounds him again.*

Ant.   'S death ! I think
I've fooled away my courage !
How do you now, sir ?   [HERMOCRATES *wounded.*

Her. As well as e'er I did, sir ! Have I reached
      you ?   [ANTANTER *wounded.*

Ant. Your arm 's too short, and your aim worse !
By Heaven !
Hadst thou indented with the Fates to live
But for a minute longer, thus I'd cancel it !
                                [*Wounds him.*

Her. And thus I meet thy resolution !

      [*Fall both on one another ; being down, they
      strive with one another. A great shout
      within.*

Enter EVANDER, MISSELLUS, ARCHBISHOP,
PLANETIUS, EPECIDES, *and* SOLDIERS.

Eva. Give order for the magistrates' enlarge-
  ment !
Her. Ah, how my fate afflicts me with fresh
  torments !
Evander living?
 Ant.   Whose injuries lie heavy
Upon our souls. Most gracious sir, howe'er
Our lives have been disturbance to your Kingdom,
In death, with you and it we sue for peace.
Forgiveness, royal sir !
 Eva.   We come not to
Possess our own with thoughts to be revenged ;
Or if we did, you have escaped it. Heaven
Forgive you as we do !
 Her.   May never foreign
Or home-bred jars wither your peaceful laurel !
 Ant. And thus our enmity does end. Thy
  hand !   [*Kisses it.*
 Her. Thy cheek ! Farewell ! [*Dies.*
 Ant. Plenty and peace perpetually dwell among
  you !   [*Dies.*
 Pla. Two as brave spirits
As e'er Sicily bred !

  Enter ICETIS, HIPPARINUS, MAGISTRATES.

Epe. The magistrates are here, sir !
Ice. Hip. At your feet, royal sir, we fall !
Eva. Rise in our favour.
Ice. Your mercy has no precedent !
Eva. Heaven make you stronger in your faith
  and duties
Hereafter to us ! What is past we pardon.
 Hip. All th' louring aspects of malignant stars,

That lately threatened ruin to this Kingdom,
Are at your glorious presence sunk beneath
Their primitive conceptions.

Eva.   Take up those bodies !—
My lords, with your assistance, we must do
A cure upon the Kingdom, in the seating
Its dislocated joints.   We shall not take
Notice hereafter who amongst you have
Had hands in her impairing, but receive you
With no less favour than the rest, not doubting
But that the smart you have felt by these changes
Will draw you home to constancy.—And the wool
That has so violently been taken from
Your sheep, for want of an indulgent shepherd,

                              [*To the* ARCHBISHOP.
Make you prize one the better.

Arch. Epe. Hip. Ice. May Heaven transform our
      shapes when our hearts change !

Eva. Then are we strong enough to combat fate,
And cure the wounds thus made upon the State !

                              [*Exeunt.*

THE SCOTCH FIGGARIES.

H

The Scots Figgaries: or, A Knot of Knaves. A Comedy. London, printed by W. H., for John Tey, at the White Lion in the Strand, near the New Exchange. 1652. 4to.

The Scotch Figgaries: or, A Knot of Knaves. A Comedy. London, printed 1652. Reprinted and sold by W. Mears, at the Lamb, and T. Boreman, at the Cock, on Ludgate Hill. 1735. 12mo.

THE editors of the *Biographia Dramatica* remark : "Great part of this play is written in the Scotch dialect ; and the author, who was a strong Cavalier, and had the highest detestation for the Scots, has drawn the characters of them and of the Puritans in this piece in very contemptuous as well as hateful colours."

The "Scotch dialect" introduced in this piece is similar to that put into the mouth of the Scotch mountebank in the preceding play, *The Distracted State*, by the same author, and to that subsequently used by Lacy in his comedy, *Sawney the Scot.* Its affinity to Scotch is most remote, as no such dialect or idiom ever obtained in any district in Scotland ; and any one thoroughly versant with the Scotch language, ancient or modern, would have great difficulty in translating it.

The same sort of gibberish is set down as that spoken at Newcastle during the time of Cromwell, in a song called "The Scotch War," which appears in the first volume of *A Collection of Loyal Songs written against the Rump Parliament, between the years* 1639 *and* 1661, 2 vols. 12mo, Lond. 1731 :—

> "Our sweets and silks made such a smother,
> Next day we knew not one another;
> For Jockey did never so shine,
> And Jenny was never so fine.
> 'A geud faith a gat a ged beaver then,
> But it's beat into a blew-cap agon
> By a redcoat, that still did cry, Rag,
> And a red snowt,—a the deel aw the crag!'"

As there is no record of *The Scotch Figgaries* having

been acted in the reign of George II., it becomes a matter of
surprise why the piece should have been reprinted in 1735.
This reprint has a curious frontispiece, in which the two
Scotch beggars figure prominently. They are both clad in
short tartan jackets, and tartan breeches, with hose gartered
at the knee. Over the right shoulder is a belt buckled
in front sustaining a claymore, while round the waist is
another belt with three pistols in centre, distributed like
the Prince of Wales' feathers. They have small bonnets in
their right hand, while in the left of each a paper is presented, which they are in the act of offering to Wornout, the
courtier. The scene is a chamber, and it is evidently intended to represent the first scene in Act first, which, we
gather from the action and dialogue, is made during the progress of the piece to do service both as an exterior and an
interior. The papers which the beggars exhibit are no
doubt the "certifice" of Jockey's alleged maltreatment by
the Sheriff of Cumberland, bearing the forged signatures of
the several justices, made by an idle "turnie's lod" whom
he met in the north.

Robert Dormer, to whom the first edition of this piece is
dedicated, was the third son of Robert, the first Lord Dormer,
who had been made a Baronet by James VI. on the 10th
June 1615, and elevated to the Barony of Dormer of Wenge
on the 30th of the same month. His mother was Elizabeth,
daughter of Anthony, Viscount Montague. From him the
present Lord Dormer is directly descended by the male line.
His eldest brother, William, died during their father's lifetime, leaving one son, Robert, who became, upon his grandfather's death, second Lord Dormer. He was a valiant
Royalist, took up arms in defence of Charles I., and subscribed
the King's declaration in 1642, for which he was prosecuted
by the Parliament. He had been elevated to the Viscounty
of Ascot and Earldom of Carnarvon by Charles, and was
slain at the first battle of Newbury, on 20th Sept. 1643,
after he had charged and routed a body of the rebel force.

Having returned carelessly back through the scattered troopers, one of them ran him through the body with his sword, of which wound he died in the course of an hour. Clarendon gives a character of him in which he appears to great advantage : " If he had lived, he would have proved a great ornament to his profession. He was an excellent soldier, and, by his death, the King found a sensible weakness in his army." He married a daughter of that unprincipled nobleman, Philip, Earl of Pembroke and Montgomery, and had one son, Charles, who succeeded him in his Barony and Earldom, but died without issue male at Wenge, on Nov. 29, 1709, whereby the Earldom became extinct ; but the Barony of Dormer devolved on the male issue of Anthony, second son of the first Lord Dormer, in the person of Rowland, his grandson. This, however, he, the fourth Lord Dormer, enjoyed only a short time, having died upon the 27th Sept. 1712, aged 61. The Barony then came to Charles Dormer, the fifth Lord, the grandson of Robert Dormer, Tatham's patron in this play, who was proprietor of the estate of Peterly, in the county of Buckingham, and who married Mary, daughter of Edward Bannister of Ilsworth in the county of Southampton, by whom he had eight sons and six daughters. It is very probable that Tatham had served under the Earl of Carnarvon in the civil wars, and had, from his personal intercourse during the conflicts with the Scots, formed a very poor estimate of that nation.

THE PERSONS.

SMALLFAITH, ... _A declining Magistrate._

DOMUCH, ... } _Magistrates continued._
SUREHOLD, ... }

FOLLY, ... _The Court Fool._

JOCKY, ... } _Two Scots Beggars._
BILLY, ... }

SCAREFOOL, ... _A Scots Soldier._

RESOLUTION, ... _An English Soldier._

WORNOUT, ... _A Courtier._

DOWNFALL, ... _A Lawyer._

SOONGULL'D, ... _A Citizen._

LAYMEDOWN, ... _His Wife._

MRS. SMALLFAITH.

ANYTHING, ... _A Parson._

A SEMINARY.

TRAPHEIR, ... ⎫
PINCKCARCASE, ... ⎬ _Blades of the Times._
TOWNSHIFT, ... ⎪
DRAWFORTH, ... ⎭

WITWUD, ... } _Two Bubbles._
WANTWIT, ... }

A CREW OF COUNTRY PEOPLE.
VINTNER, DRAWER, SOLDIERS, SERVITORS.
A PUBLIQUE NOTARY.

THE SCOTCH FIGGARIES.

Enter JOCKY, *with his Wallet.*

Jocky. A Sirs! thes eyr has a mickle geod savour.
I ha creept thus firr intolth' kingdom, like an
crivigg intoll a mon's lug, and sall as herdly be
gat oout. Ise sa seff here as a sperrow under a
penthoowse. Let the Sheriff o Cumberlond gee
hang himsell in's own gartropts, Ise ferr enough
off him, an's fellow officer th' hangman noow. I, a
Scot theff, may pass for a trow mon here ; aw the
empty weomb and thin hide I full oft bore in
Scotlond, an the geod fare I get here ! Be me saw
Ise twa yards gron about sin I cam fro Scotlond,
the deele split me gif I cam at thee mere Scotlond.
Ise eene noow ny the bonny court, wur meny a
Scot lad is gron fro a maggot ta a bran goose.
Marry! Ise in geod pleight. Weel, Scotlond, weel,
tow gaffst me a mouth, Anglond mon find me met;
'tis a geod soil geod feith, an gif aw my contremon
wod plant here, th'od thrive better thon in thair non.

Enter BILLY.

In the foul deel's name wha's yon? a sud be me
contremon by's scratin an scrubbin. A leokes
like Scotlond itsell, bar an naked. A carries

noought bet tha walth o Can aboot him, filth an virmin.

Billy. Aw Scotlond, Scotlond, wa worth the tim I cam oout o thee ! Ise like tha wandering Jew, ha worn my hoofes sa thin as pauper, and can get ne shod for um. Anglond has geod sooft grond, bet tha peple ha mickle hard hearts. Aw Billy, Billy, th'adst better ha tane tha stripe for stelling in Scotlond (bet thot 'tis sin ta rob the spettle) an ha thriv'd by't, than ta come ta be hangd here, or stervd. Tis keen justace a mon sud dee sick a deeth for macking use o' his hands. I ha ne oder mamber woorth ought.

Joc. On's mon what gar thee in these pickle ? how cam'st hither ?

Bil. E'en on me ten toes, sir, and thay err worn oout now, thay'l ser me ne longer.

Joc. Wha tha deel sall mend 'um ? Sham faw thee, a Scot an cannot shift !

Bil. Alack, sir ! amon mo not stell here for's neck ; and Ise mickle sham ta beg.

Joc. How mon, not bag ! Ons th'art nen a me contremon than.

Bil. Ey marry, that am I ; geod feith Ise a Scot, an boorn at Andrakeddin.

Joc. I thoought sa be thy iddle leife ; what gar thee cam hither ?

Bil. Alack, mon ! I sud a bein whopt aboot tha toown o Barwick for theiffing in Scotlond, bet brock gale and scapt it.

Joc. Hadst tow tha conscienc ta stell fro thy own contre, an hast noot tha fece ta bag in an oder ? Fy, mon, fy ! Ons hoow thinkst leive ? Leok her, mon, leok her, sa tha vertu o bagging. [*Opens his wallet and shows him meat.*] A, sir ! d'yee drop, d'yee drop at mooth, sir ?

Bil. Ey, sir; sike a seight may mack a mon sown.

Joc. Sow up your chops in tha deel's nam; gif you cannot bag, ye sall not eat, sir.   .

Bil. Geod feith an I ha noot eat un morsell thes twa daies; cam awey, mon, cam awey.

Joc. Nee, nee, sir; stey your fercnes, keep your fangs off, sir; yee ma ha the mang.

Bil. Ne, geod feith, Ise a clere skind lad.

Joc. Bet monstrous lozy.

Bil. Dooubt not that, sir; thay'l pin ta death, sir, for I ha noought to fed 'um bet sken, an that's twa toough for thair teth,—cam awey, mon; sum cherete, good contremon.

Joc. Weel, set doown; leok thee here, mon. [*They sit down to eat.*] Thes gis tha leg o a Anglish prest.

Bil. Sey yee sa, mon !

Joc. Reight weel thay bein mad up o' cappon and whit broth; thay mack their carcase fat, bet their solls len. D'yee thenk Sent Andra wad a fested sa mickle gif a cud a gat sike met as thes ? Ne, ne, by me saw Ise hang than; he was sterv'd, thay fare deliciously; he wos loowzy, and hod no sheft, they bien buried aleife in fin lenin an lown fleesses; he stunk abo grond, they bien swetten'd leiving an deed, abo an under gron. A me saw, Sent Andra had ner don sa meny marvailes gif a had stuft his carcase so full as thay.

Bil. Geod feith, I main pass for a sent ten, for me carcase is bar an thin enough.

Joc. Ey for sent theff, for he ner did mirackle. Thes torky leg cam fro a merchant's table, thes widgin's wing fro a citizen's, and thes goose's leg fro a lawyer's.

Bil. Bred, thay mack mere preambl 'boot thair

boody then aw tha peple in Cristendum de aboot thair saws. How hadst tow tha fece ta speek at sa meny dores, mon?

Joc. A, sir! I sall tach yee ta bag bravely; mind ye me noow, sir. I stoll twa coows fro me contremon, and gar tham agat ta Comberlond ta seele, bet tha plaggy shrief gar tham tack fro me, an sent me toll tha gale, bet I gat loose, an sa cam froward; an in tha Noorth I met a iddle turnie's lod, wha mad me thes certifice, an sat aw those Jestece nams tol't, that tha shreif o Comberlond had den me mickle wrong, an sa Ise cam up toll th' King for jestece.

Bil. Geod feith, wad I had sike an oder!

Joc. Cam awey, mon, hest thee, fill thy weomb, and get thee on yon sid, mon; an Ise kep of thes, and sa nen sall scap us. Hark ye me, mon, you mon tell 'um you cam o geod parentage, an ha lost aw your siller as ye cam for Anglond; you mon speeke a hy, mon, an noot lick a mole under gron pest herring.

Bil. Weel, weel, Ise be avis'd be you; gif you far weel, I sall noot far amiss.

Enter a COURTIER.

Joc. Gang awey, mon; gang awey, mon; seest tow yon braw mon tofore thy eyne.

[*Billy runs towards him.*

Bil. Bless your honor, Ise speek a word or twa ta your honor!

Cour. My honour! Pox on your fawning hide! what would you have with me, and be hang'd?

Bil. Ne, ne, sir, I pray your honour wax noot wrothfull; Ise a mon o geod ranck in my own contre, an ha kept geod beasts.

Cour. Ay, for some bodies else. Thou dost not look as though thou e'er wert worth one.

Bil. Ne, ne, sir, me non proper geods, geod feith. I cam we mickle siller in me purss ta Englond, weel clad.

Cour. With some old curtains that bore Sent Andrew's story, or children's blanquets stoll, and turn'd to trowsies.

Bil. Ne, geod feith, I ha een bien rob'd o aw.

Cour. Rob thee! Of what? Had he a mind to be lousy? But this is an engine laid to draw a piece of silver to you; is't not so?

Bil. Your honor speeks mickle weel.

Cour. There!——There's some of your country-men at Court live better by this trade than you.

[*He gives him.*

Joc. Un word ta your honor.

[*As he goes Jocky meets him.*

Cour. Hy day, another! I'm waylaid; hast thou been robb'd too?

Joc. Ne, ne, sir, ne; tha shreiff o Comberlond has dun me mickle wrong, sir.

Cour. Whipt you about the pigmarket?

Joc. A has tacken awey me cows, sir, an aw me geods. See here, sir, I ha aw thos worthy Jestece nams ta testifie!

Cour. There is no beggar like the Scotch beggar for tricks and impudence. Come, what must dis-charge me from you, sir, and your bellowing?

Joc. Geod feith, sir, I wont siller ta gat jestece.

Cour. Hadst thou had justice done thee, thou hadst been hang'd long before this.

Bil. Bred, he's a fortuneteller.

Cour. There,—that will serve to buy you oat-meal. Sir, there is no more of your catterwalling companions hereabouts, is there?

Joc. Ne, ne, sir, ant lick your honor.

Cour. Ne, ne, pox on your nees and your nose too; I'm glad I'm rid on you.   [*Exit.*

Joc. Noow, sir, ye had noot tha fece ta bag! Hoow lick ye it noow, sir? what ga he toll ye?

Bil. Thes smaw peece o siller.

Joc. A geod begining, mon. Tolld a ye noot sum o our contremen liev'd at Court by baggin.

Bil. I sea noow a Scot may ly by atorete, an beg wi permission. Weel, to Curt ta, an ly as fest as tha beest o 'um.

Joc. Be me saw an that's herd ta dee.

Enter MR. FOLLY.

Joc. Seest tow, seest tow, mon, yon braw fellow, wi' his gold rop aboot's neck, an's long cot lick a sark? Geod feith, he's ta herd for twanty o 'um.

Bil. He's tha feul, gis a noot?

Joc. Ey, ey, mon; a has feuld himsell intoll mickle fevor, gif a feul himsell noot oout agen,—sey, a cams aneust us, mon! wees speeke toll him.— Bless your honor, sir! bless your honor! Ise gled ta sea your honour in heelth.

Fol. Be me saw, th'art a bold fellow.

Joc. I'm your own contremon, sir; I ken your honor mickle weel; bless your worship.

Fol. Kenst tow me, mon?

Joc. Mickle weel, an't lick your honour. I ken your honor weel enough; your honour is the King's feul.

Fol. A, mon, he kepes mere feules than I; bred, he's kepe tow ta gif tow canst feul him. How far Scot art tow?

Joc. Marry, Ise a mickle wey oofe noow.

Fol. Bet I wad kne whar tow wert boorn?

Joc. Gin me moder's weomb, sir, forty years agast.

Fol. Ons, mon, speeke toll me i what plece o Scotlond wert tow boorn?

Joc. Geod feith, gin meny, sir; I ha bien boorn fro plece to plece a me moder's back, sir; and ha seffered mickle sorrow.

Fol. The fow deel tack thy large lug; wha was thy fader?

Joc. A mon, sir, surely.

Fol. The black deel a was, sir; whar liev'd a?

Joc. A, sir! at a plece your honor kens mickle weel.

Fol. Whar, mon, whar?

Joc. A, sir! A, sir! what pleice caw ye that, sir, whar your honor nurst tha tyny babe wi wull on's back, sir?

Fol. Oout, tha faw deel; oout, rog!—Bet wha art tow, mon?

Bil. I'm een yar contremon twa, sir; cam ta bien a curtier ta, sir.

Fol. Ons, a curtier!—a carter,—tha hangmon,— tha deel!

Bil. Ye ha geod friends thar, sir; ye may dee mickle for us.

Fol. Dee, mon! bred, he that sall deo for thee sall ha enough ta dee. Art geod for oought? wha canst dee for thy sell?

Bil. E'en what ye sea, sir.

Fol. Oout, this is base; it shams your contre, mind ye me. Wha o ye swain ha mest wot?

Joc. He that can sheft beest.

Fol. Reight weel.

Joc. And that's e'en I; this feule had noot a fece ta bag toll I boldened hum.

Fol. Oout, oout, mon; sham-feect!

Bil. Ne, ne, I sall grew bold enough gif I sall get oought by't.

Fol. Gif ye had clad,* sirs, what curs wad ye tacke to liew ?

Bil. Ise cud mack tha King, bliss his Worship, an't lick your honour, mickle geod puttins an potsloose.†

Joc. I'd bien oth' Mint, sir ; I loove to finger siller.

Fol. Weel, sirs, cam away wy me ; for contre's sack Ise gat ye sum purveyance, an sum lodging ; and tan we sall find oout sum woork for ye emong 'um here.

Joc. Bless your honor for your benefaites.

[Exeunt.

Enter TOWNSHIFT *and* TRAPHEIR.

Town. Pray recollect yourself ; I cannot do't
Without a loss to my repute and fame,
If you have but a foot of ground unsold.
Therefore consult your thoughts, my willingness
Shall not be wanting to procure your freedom ;
But I'd not have a dirty piece of land
Bring an obstruction to't.

Tra. Why ?   As I live
I have not an inch left ; whate'er I mortgag'd
Is either sold outright or forfeited ;
I lie not, on my credit.

Town. How's that, man ?
Have you credit, then ?   Why, that's as bad.

---

* Good clothing. In *Sir Tristrem,* "clad" is "covered with armour."

† Markham says black puddings are called "pots" in Devon.

It is not held convenient by the Huff,*
Lords of the sword, that any youngster should
Be one of us 'till he 'as not only lost
His 'state, but's credit too.

 Tra. Upon my life,
Dear Townshift, I've not credit for a thrips ;†
Thou know'st it well enough, my roaging laundress
Will not do't for the washing of a shirt.

 Town. Why, have you shirts, then ?

 Tra. One, as I live, no more ; and that so thin,
You may draw't through a needle.

 Town. What boots have you ?

 Tra. I cannot call these any, yet th'are all ;
And as for stockings, I have long ago
Held them unnecessary.

 Town. Why this cloak,
And th' weather warm and friendly ?

 Tra. 'Tis too much ;
The weight on't, I confess, 's not to be borne ;
I'll ease me of the burthen : it shall sink
In sack when I'm made free, prethee about it.

 Town. I would not for a world you should have
  any
Remnant of your estate left ; 'twould undo you.

Enter DRAWFORTH *and* PINCKCARCASE.

See, here's my brothers, Drawforth and Pinckcarcase !
May I presume to recommend you to 'em ?

 Tra. You may, you may, dear Townshift.

 Drawf. How now, Trapheir ?
What ! is all gone yet ?

---

* A sect of Swaggerers, similar to the Alsatians of White-
friars.
† Qy., a threepenny?

     I

Town. All, he swears by's twibell,*
His cloak excepted, and its time expires
Within this half-hour; shall we make him free ?
　　Pinck. Trapheir, you now are to begin the
　　　　world,
Which you cannot do handsomely, unless
Your land and you be separated, and if
Aught lye conceal'd, 'twill rise in judgment 'gainst
　　　　you ;
Therefore, pray, have a care; 'tis Christian counsel.
　　Drawf. It is not fit the least piece of your old
Adulterate fortunes should corrupt the new
Your wit must purchase.
　　Town. Right ; beside, he'll ne'er
Have a refin'd wit 'till he has nothing left.
　　Tra. The greatest enemy I have, gentlemen, is
　　　　my cloak,
And I promise you I'll see 't no more.
　　Pinck. Say you so ! then to the next tavern.
Boy ! boy ! a room.

Enter DRAWER.

　　Draw. Please you to walk into a room, gentle-
men ?
　　Town. What call we thee for else ?
　　　　　　　　　　[They pass in and enter again.
　　Draw. How like you this room, gentlemen ?
　　Town. Indifferent ! bring us wine and tobacco
　　　　of the best, sirrah.
　　Draw. You shall indeed, sir.
　　Tra. Dear Townshift, thou must show this
　　　　gentleman
The way to th' brokers.　　*[Pointing at his cloak.*
　　Town. Is he for sale, or mortgage ?
　　　　　　　* A halbert.

Tra. For sale, by all means. I'd not charge my
    memory
I've aught left worth redeeming.

Enter BOY *with wine.*

Drawf. Bravely resolv'd !—Is't racey ?
Draw. Right racey, sir, believe me.
Pinck. Trapheir, to thee !
Tra. Drink apace, dear Townshift !

[*To his cloak.*

The sight of that same gentleman's my tortour,
I prethee, rid me of him !
Drawf. Townshift, swear him !
Tra. I can't with a safe conscience swear as long
As that appears before me.
    Town. How shall I get it out o' th' house ?
    Tra. Leave thine here, and wear mine thither.
Oh, how I hate to call it mine !—away with't !

[*Exit Townshift.*

    Pinck. Trapheir, you now must exercise your wit
To live on others, as w'ave liv'd on you.
Wit's never good till purchas'd, what though't be
With th' loss of fortune's trumpery and trash.
Content ne'er dwells 'mong dirty land ; who sells it
Parts with a deal of care, and scurvy toil ;
Men never are ingenious that are clogg'd with't.
The generous spirit will not be coop'd up
In that same country cage, a mansion-house,
And confines of the buttery. Be free!
Thou art not worth a groat when this is spent.

Enter TOWNSHIFT.

    Tra. How much, how much, dear Townshift ?
    Town. But thirty, by my valour.
    Tra. Down with't, down with't !

[*The money laid on the table.*

I'll not put up a dodkin* on't.   Dear Townshift,
Drink, drink away ; I thirst until it's melted :
Your molten silver swallows best.
    Drawf. His oath, his oath !
    Town. Your sword.
                    [*Lays his hand on the hilt of his sword.*

            By this hilt, and this blade,
            Which at Hounslow was made,
            You swear to be true
            To what shall ensue.

First, you swear not to make it any scruple of
conscience to cheat your father : That you will hunt
after young heirs, and when you have courst them
out of wind, you'll refresh 'em with some scrivener,
broker, or draper : That you'll keep always three
strings to your bow, to make it bend till it break :
That having gotten a Bubble or Byshop, a lad of
the last adoption, that you make him sensible of a
wench, though to the charge of a surgeon, it being
reason all trades should live, and, if occasion be,
wink at small faults.   Next, be sure to keep them
continually at game, or drinking ; urge 'em to
quarrel, and then take up the business, but not
without profit to the Brotherhood : That what
quarrels soever arise among ourselves, must not
cause us to fight with one another, but the coins
of the Bubble or Byshop must make us friends :
That you must not pay your coachman but with
kicks, unless your Bubble or Byshop do, and then
he owes you a fare : That your Bubble, or Byshop,
and you keep but one purse, though two drabs :

---

* An exceedingly small coin, the eighth part of a stiver,
which is in itself a small coin (Dutch), in value about a
farthing. A doit was half-a-farthing, and the stiver was its
superior.

That when you have drained him dry, you make him free, if he sue for it ; if not, let him keep company with the titteretues, and live upon the sin of Sodom : That you'll take your chance of the day, where there is need of dipping, without grumbling.

> That while you can stand,
> With sword in your hand,
> You'll not be in awe
> Of the Halberteer Law ;
> Kiss this, —— Now y'are free
> > [*Kisses the hilt.*
> Of the Huffs' company.

Tra. Hey for the Brotherhood ! No wine stirring, boy ?
You rascal, where's your duty ? Absent ? Hah ! More wine.

Enter DRAWER.

Draw. You shall, sir, by and by.
Tra. Bring a glass will hold
A pint at least ! [*Exit Drawer.*] I hate a thimblefull.
We shall ne'er have consum'd this mighty mass
> > [*Pointing to the money.*
If we sip thus like sparrows.

Enter DRAWER.

Ay, marry, this looks like some brother to you all.
Drawf. Gramercy !
Tra. Sirrah, cover the boord with bottles ;
This is our coronation day ; the room
Shall swim in wine. Be frolique, Huffs, and drain
Me dry, yet I shall live when y'are all hang'd.
> > [*He begins to be drunk.*
Town. How now, how now, Trapheir ?

Tra. Drink, and be damn'd !
Must I wait on your drivelling ?

Town. Drawforth, to you !—charge him home.

Drawf. Trapheir, a whole bottle to thee ! I'm
    up to th' chin.

Tra. So, so, sir——y'are a fine fellow. Is all
    paid ?

Town. No, all's not come in yet.

Tra. I'll stay no longer.
                    [*He takes Townshift's cloak up.*

Town. Pray leave my cloak behind you.

Tra. Your cloak, sir ! How came it to be yours,
sir ? I have one somewhere.

Town. Yours is at the brokers, sir.

Tra. Is it so, sir ? I thank you for the informa-
tion.

Drawf. There lies the virtue on't.

Tra. So, sir, I thank you twice ; for once I care
not if I put my cloak into my pocket.
                    [*He snatcheth up the money.*

Town. But, Trapheir, Trapheir !

Pinck. Who pays the house ?

Tra. Let the house pay itself. Dip, dip and
be hang'd, you that have cloaks ; am I bound to fill
your insatiate gorge eternally ?

Pinck. What asses were we to let the money
lie so long, knowing his rascally humour ; he'll not
pay a penny when he's in drink. See what thou
canst work him to !

Town. Boy !

Enter DRAWER.

Draw. Sir——I shall, sir.   [*They whisper.*

Town. Trapheir ! a prize, Trapheir !

Tra. Of what ? Sprats ?

Town. A gudgeon, man ; a gudgeon's come to net !

The master of the house desires admittance
To play a game at tick-tack* for a piece ;
And thou knowst, Trapheir——hah——

                          [He shakes his arms.

   Tra. I know it, rogue ;
And thou shalt play with him for all he's worth.
I'll venture on thy hand my whole estate,
This my trusty blade.   Provided always, sir——

      Enter MASTER OF THE HOUSE.

   Town. That you have half. 'Tis granted—he's
    here !
Thou knowst I have no money.
   Tra. Thou shalt not want, dear bully; I'll not leave
Myself a George.†   *[He gives him his money.*
   Town. Spoke like thy self ! come, be so.
There, sir, pay yourself.
   Mr. Y'are kindly welcome, gentlemen ; fetch
    my quart.
   Tra. Death ! what's this ?
   Omnes. Ha, ha, ha ! Only the reckoning paid, sir.
   Tra. Y'are rogues, shirks, and cheats ! I'll indict
    you !
   Pinck. Buoy, good sir ; employ your tongue at
    Billingsgate.
Adieu, adieu !   *[Exeunt Town., Pinck., Drawforth.*
   Tra. Farewell, and be hang'd. For your part,
    sirrah,
I'll have you up for keeping of a bawdy-house.
                         [Exit.
   Mr. Do your worst, sir ; do your worst ! *[Exit.*

---

  * Trick - track, or tick - tack. A species of backgammon,
played both with men and pegs, and more complicated. Sometimes the phrase has been used in an indelicate sense.
  † A George-Noble, a gold coin worth 6s. 8d.

ACT II.

Enter FOLLY, JOCKY, *and* BILLY, *very gallant.*

Fol. Y'ar mickle braw, sirs; y'ar mickle braw. Bred, ye leoke mere lick Burgemasters noow thou hedg creepers. Ken ye your sells, sirs? ken ye your sells, sirs?

Joc. Geod feith, sir, gif aw that sud ken themsells wad ken themsells, nen wad ken us. A me saw, sir! I'd rader ha 'um trast me thon ken me; sur, gif thay sud ken me reight, thay'd sea me deed tofore thay' trast me.

Fol. Y'ar mickle wise, sir; ye ha rob'd a feul, sur.

Joc. We wish you weel, sir; we wish you weel.

Fol. Sey ye sa, sir? y'ar vary cheretable. Ken ye me, sirs? On's, ye are gron see loofty, you'l knee ne body. Wha set you up, in tha deel's nam? wha, wha put thes gay fethers on your back? E'en I! an noow yol flee awey ta tha deel. Harke ye me, sirs; gif ye bien sa high, Ise tack ye down wy a plague ta ye. Wha had y'ar intail'd virmine tane off ye wy a murren? Wha, wha gat ye a——

Bil. Oour faders and moders, sir.

Fol. Did thay sa, sir? Bred, gif thay gat ye, thay ner cud gat feod enough for yar side weombs. Are you provander prickt noow, sirs? Ha, wha am I? ha, sirs, ha, wha am I?

Bil. Oour geod friend, sir; bliss you.

Fol. The deel wound ye, sleight ye me? On's, Ise sa geod a mon gas aw in Scotlond, an ha mere siller in me purse.

Joc. Anglish stamp, sir; I beleev't.

Fol. Ye beleeft? Wha tha deel cares for your beleeff?

Joc. Geod sir, geod sir, be sober.

Fol. Bred, Ise not drunken; ha ye bien at cost wy me, sirs? Hah! Ise sall uncass ye, sirs, an ge your arse tha ayr agen; are ye sa hot, sirs? Want ye a cooler? Bred, Ise ge ye sick a rattle wy a rom ore tha riggins sall mack your ribs reore, sirs.

Joc. Geod, your honour, put up your wroth, an wees buckle oour wots; wees yar on contremons, ye knee weel enough.

Bil. An sud leove won oder. Y'ave a geod mester, sir, an oour contremon, wha macks mickle o you.

Fol. Bred, an Ise mack sa mickle o hum as I can.

Joc. He's a geod mon, sir; and you ha wot enough.

Fol. Ken you that, mon; ken you that? Ons, an ye bien not wud, ye ma ha wot ta chep enough; bet Ise ne body, my benefaits are noought woorth.

Joc. Y'ar aw body, sir; wees at your commandement.

Fol. Sey ye sa, sir? Why, noow ye speeke; be vis'd by me, an ye sall ooutwot 'um aw. Mind ye me, sirs; will ye be avis'd?

Joc. Sed ye, sir; wy aw our harts.

Fol. Ise ha ye turn dooctors.

Joc. Ise a dooctor! a dooctor! Geod feith, wees mack bra dooctors.

Fol. Mind me, mon; mind me. Thes Kingdom's mickle sick, tha Curt o tha cety, tha cety o tha Curt, an tha contre o beoth, an aw o 'um o tha Kirk an tha Law. Tha Kingdom's livergron wy iddlnes an raches, an noow noought can cur it bet a Scots dooctor, ne matter for your skill.

Joc. Geod feith, sir, wees ha skill enoough ta bleed its siller vains, Ise warrant ye.

Fol. Ha bet confidence, lie and dissemble hand-
somly.

Bil. Wees y'ar on contremons, sir; doobt it noot.

Fol. Tha nam o a Scot gis enough ta cur aw
their maladies. Ge 'um peson an thay'l tack it for
a cordall. Perswad 'um thay ar sick, thay'l beleeff
ye, and gif ye mack 'um sick, thay'l beleeff th'are
in beest helth; bet ye mon carry sem show
o holliness wy ye, an profess aw for thayr
geods.

Joc. Sa we sall, sir; an tack 'um whan we ha
deon.

Fol. Billy sall gaing toll th' contre, and tow salt
kep behind, an bien dooctor here, and gif tow
hest wot enoough tow canst noot wont werk.

Joc. Ne, geod feith, I sall mack mesell werk
enoough; for gif I can hel ne distampers, Ise mack
enoough emong 'um.

Fol. Cam awey than, cam awey !   [*Exeunt.*

Enter TRAPHEIR *and* BOY.

Boy. 'Twas morning ere he went to bed, sir.

Tra. All's one; tell who 'tis, and 'twill be
    warrant
Enough for your awaking him; 'tis business
I come about, and of concernment too,
That cannot admit delay. ·

Boy. I'll venture then to call him, sir.   [*Exit.*

Tra. Do so. If this design
Of mine proves prosperous, Townshift, it will be
Some comfort to me that I am even with thee.

Enter BOY.

Boy. He'll wait upon you presently;
He's rising.   [*Exit.*

Tra. A good lad.—Townshift, arm thyself,
For I am prepar'd to give thee an assault,
And dare thy action at law, if wit
And sword should fail, dear Townshift.

Enter TOWNSHIFT.

Town. By this light I have not slept
A minute. What's the news? You serv'd us
    bravely
The other night at tavern.
    Tra. Oh, this drinking!
This perilous drinking will destroy us all.
Thy pardon, my dear heart; the business now
I come about will try thy friendship.
    Town. How?
I hope no quarrel.
    Tra. Yes, with my base stars.
    Town. But what's the matter, tell me?
    Tra. That's my meaning;
A sort of rascally bailiffs dogg'd me hither,
And thou know'st if I be once ta'en I am
A slave perpetually.
    Town. What wouldst thou have me to do?
We'll send to Drawforth and the rest.
    Tra. 'Twon't do;
They'll make but a disturbance in the street,
Yet I may be surpris'd for all their valour,
And then I am undone. The hopes I have
In one I am to dine with lost, which might
Be worth to thee and me some hundreds, bully.
    Town. Send for him! now let him take up the
    business.
    Tra. What! ere I'm throughly known to him?
    Besides,
Should he take this up, twenty more would follow 't;

Who, knowing me so low now, do forbear
To execute their rigour.

Town. What wouldst thou have me do ?

Tra. Hark thee, I've thought upon a fine deceit.
Hast any patches in thy chamber ?

Town. Rare ones,
Of all sorts.

Tra. One to disguise my face, with a cloak, would
Do't to the life.

Town. Sure they are gone ; I'll send to see.

Tra. Oh, hang 'em, rogues ! th'are skulking at
    th' Lane's end,
Or some blind alehouse.   Dearest Townshift, do't.

Town. Do what ?

Tra. Lend me thy cloak, and I'll contrive a patch
Shall cover my left eye, they may not know me.

Town. I know not what to do.   I should go forth
Myself.

Tra. Nay, prethee Townshift——

Town. Will you leave
Your sword, then ? you'll have no——

Tra. Prethee wouldst have me
Pass by 'em unprovided ; put the worst,
They should descry me ?

Town. There's no trick in't, Trapheir ?

Tra. No more trick than you see.   I prethee
meet me in Fish Street at the Feathers, where
we'll dine ; there thou shalt see my friend, and I'll
restore thy cloak, dear Townshift.

Enter BOY.

Town. Well, thou shall't ha't.   Boy, fetch
My cloak and patches !
           [Boy exit and re-enters with cloak.
'Tis thine, there, take it !   *[Gives it him.*

Tra. Gramercy ! is't handsome ?

Town. Very well.   I must lie down and take a
nap.

At twelve I will not fail to meet thee.   [*Exit.*

Tra. Sirrah, boy, be sure you wake him.

Boy. I warrant you, sir.   [*Exit.*

Tra. Ha, ha, ha !

I'm sworn to cheat my father, and 'tis fit

He that first made the gin should hansell it.

                                               [*Exit.*

Enter SMALLFAITH, FOLLY, *and* JOCKY.

Smal. Sir, you are kindly welcome; and the oft'ner
You visit me, the welcomer you shall be.
I honour men of knowledge.   Master Folly,
I am oblig'd to you for his acquaintance.

Fol. Geod feith, sir, an he's worth yours.   I sall
Play him wy any Anglish dooctor in the warld.

Joc. Ne, sir, Ise can dee mere than Ise speeke,
    sir.

Smal. I believe you, sir,
By what I find of truth within myself.
I must confess, I am not altogether
So right as I would ; my body tells me
I may admit of physick.

Joc. Mickle weel, sir.

Smal. I'm troubled with the spleen, a strong
    disease
Amongst us magistrates, which makes me fear
'Tis not for cure.

Joc. Ise cure it in twa minutes, gif ye ha
Bien trobl'd wy it twanty years ; an aw
Your tribe, gif tha'll cam toll me.

Fol. Ne, ne, he's reight.

Smal. You'll do a wondrous cure, then.

Joc. I sall dee't, o me honor. Bet that's noot aw.
Your malade ; ye are noot soound at heart, sirs.

Smal. I know not that, sir.

Joc. Planty an iddleness ha bred gross humours
in you, whilk mon be pourged awey, or elke ye
dee for't ; bet Ise sall ge ye that, sir, sall mack ye
bare an leight enough.

Smal. I thank you, sir ; accept this, pray, and I
                              [*He gives him gold.*
Shall further gratify; but be speedy,
Good sir, with your preparatives.

Joc. Ise gang aboot it stret; Ise gang aboot it, sir.

Smal. Your servant, gentlemen ; I shall hear
    from you, sir?

Joc. Soon, mickle soon, sir.   [*Exit.*
Leok, mon, leok ! aw thay bien sick o gis sike fin
things as thes. Fiev golden lads, mon ! Fiev mere
are woorth a leard's land, sir ! Geod feith, gif their
veins wul ran sike drops as thes, wees drain um
dry.   A simple feuls ! that ken noot whan th'are
weel, bet wull bien wasting thair means toll set
thair boodies oot o frame.   A feuls ! feuls !

Fol. Ne matter, mon, gif oought can be gut wy
putting um oout o fram ; tha deel try his skill to
put um in agen for Jocky.   [*Exeunt.*

Enter BILLY, *and a* CREW OF COUNTRY PEOPLE.

Bil. Keep off, sirs, keep off; ga me wund toll
speek toll ye. Ise cam for aw your geods, mind
ye me ?

Omnes. Very well, very well.

Bil. Ise cur aw diseases, aw manner o malades,
an sall tack noought o ye for me peyn bet your
siller. Gif there bien or a kirk prest emong ye
choak'd up wy pluraltes o benefaits, tha poowder

in thes pauper macks the impostom breck, an tacks
aw awey clere.   Gif any prest bien vext wy tha
Babylonish mang, thes purgation, med in me non
contre, curs hum were he ner sa fer spent.

1 *Coun.* For our doctor, sir ! for our doctor !

2 *Coun.* For our vicar !   [*He disperseth*

3 *Coun.* For our parson !   *his papers.*

4 *Coun.* For our curate !

5 *Coun.* For our bishop, prebends, and curates !

Bil. Gif any emong ye bien troubl'd wy tha
neyce o organs in your lugs, thes poowder curs you
for ever.

1 *Coun.* For our town, sir !

2 *Coun.* For ours too, sir !   [*He disperseth, etc.*

3 *Coun.* And ours, and ours, sir !

4 *Coun.* And our whole county, sir !

Bil. Gif eny emong ye bien blind wy tha seight
o lawn sleeves, thes curs and restores ye.

1 *Coun.* For my landlord, sir !

2 *Coun.* For mine too, sir !   [*He disperseth.*

3 *Coun.* And mine !

4 *Coun.* And mine !

5 *Coun.* And mine !

Bil. Gif eny emong ye ha tha beon o a tith'd
soow's babey stick in your wund pip, thes saw cur
you stret, and tack aw awey.

1 *Coun.* For me, sir !

2 *Coun.* For me too, sir !   [*He disperseth.*

3 *Coun.* And me, sir !

4 *Coun.* And me, sir !

5 *Coun.* And me, sir, pray !

Bil. Gif eny emong ye bien troubl'd wy heart-
burnings, tha poowder in thes pauper curs ye stret.

1 *Coun.* For my neighbour, sir !

2 *Coun.* And mine, sir !

3 *Coun.* And mine too, sir, I pray !

4 *Coun.* And som of our whole town, good sir !

Bil. Gif eny o ye bien sore wy ore mickle burdens an weary o your riders, thes poowder macks ye strong ta orethraw um, or ta bar greater.

Omnes. For us all, sir !

Bil. Gif eny o your stomacks bien opprest wy law, thes pell sall remoove tha cause, and tack it awey. Gif eny bien hard boound, thes sall mack mickle free.

1 *Coun.* For my landlord, sir !

2 *Coun.* For mine too, sir !

3 *Coun.* And mine, sir !

4 *Coun.* And mine, sir !

5 *Coun.* And mine, sir !

Bil. Gif eny emong ye bien trobl'd wy a scurvy mooth, thes tacks aw felth awey.

1 *Coun.* For my wife, sir !

2 *Coun.* For mine, sir !

3 *Coun.* And mine, sir !

4 *Coun.* And mine, sir !

5 *Coun.* And my mistress, sir !

Bil. Gif eny bien trobl'd wy a loosnes, thes ties 'um fest as a rope or hawter.

1 *Coun.* For my wife, sir !

2 *Coun.* And mine, sir !

3 *Coun.* And mine, sir !

Bil. Geod peple, noow I ha gau ye aw remedies ta your malades. Twa dees hence Ise sall bien her or noot ta sey whot operation tha ha had upon ye. Ise sur ye sall ha remedy or non. An sa far ye wall. [*Exit Billy.*

Omnes. Farewell, sir, farewell ! [*Exeunt.*

Enter TRAPHEIR *and* WITWUD.

Wit. A pretty place this.

Tra. But the company !
The company, dear coz, hither resorts
Gives life and sweetness to't.   The rarest wits !
So rare, a man may lose himself ere he
Discover 'em,—for they are not to be   [*Aside.*
Discovered.   Besides, the women, ladies
Of such excelling beauty,—you would swear
They painted, and not be forsworn,—as merry
As Cupid when he wantons.
　　Wit. And you spent
Your means amongst 'um ?
　　Tra. And spent rarely well !
I've no remorse for't.   Can you sing ?
　　Wit. Not I, coz.
　　Tra. How, coz ! not sing ?   Why, then, you are
　　　　no company.
We have a merry life so long as't lasts.
I'll lay my life you fence not neither.
　　Wit. Yes,
My grounds I do.
　　Tra. Have you the grounds of fencing ?   that is,
To make the passado, to retreive, comply,
Defend, make up, close, and disarm ?
You know not this, I warrant ?
　　Wit. Not I, truly.
　　Tra. I cannot think what will become of you
When you meet men of valour.
　　Wit. I pray, keep me
Out of their company ; I love no quarrels.
I came to study th' law.
　　Tra. At a fine time.
Y'ave bought no books, I hope ?
　　Wit. Ay, but I have.
　　Tra. Return them to the bookseller; for shame !
A sword will prove more useful.   Hark ye, coz,
I am resolv'd to have you learn to fence.
　　　　　　　　K

Wit. I'd rather learn to sing.
Tra. That ye shall, too :
Your money will do all things.

Enter TOWNSHIFT.

Yonder's Townshift ;
How like a rogue he looks ! I will not shun him.
                                        [*Aside.*
And cousin, as I was telling you——
                    [*Townshift pulls him by the sleeve.*
  Town. With your leave, sir.
  Tra. 'Twas well askt, sir.
What's your will with me ?
  Town. My cloak, sir ; where's my cloak, sir ?
  Tra. Even at the brokers, sir——
  Town. How ? you are a rogue !
  Tra. That's nothing, sir : your railing will not
    fetch it out again.
Townshift, I love thee ; thou knowst I do.
  Town. A pox upon you !
  Tra. Thou knowst the oath : I'm not to spare
    my father ;
And though we quarrel, yet we must not fight.
I'm punctual to my oath ; but if thou hast
The conscience, I am ready.   [*Offers to draw.*
  Town. Is he sunk for ever ?
  Tra. No, it may rise again, if you be civil.
  Town. Is that your friend ?
  Tra. And kinsman.
  Town. Wilt thou cheat him too ?
  Tra. My oath is past, I will not be forsworn
For a king's ransom.
  Town. Nay, then, I'm satisfied.
  Tra. Come, be known to him. Coz, this is my
    friend.

Town. Sir, I kiss your hand.

Wit. I thank you heartily, sir.

Tra. Fie, coz, fie; there's a compliment!

Wit. He does not look as though he needed aught,
Save what thou want'st,—a cloak.

Tra. Good wit, coz; good wit!

Town. Oh, rogue! how he claws him!

Tra. Where shall's dine?

Wit. I'll to the ordinary.

Tra. Where?

Wit. In Fetter Lane.

Tra. To feed on bruis, and be serv'd with linen
As sable as the chimney? No; we'll take
A coach, and hence to Fish Street.

Wit. What shall we do there?

Tra. Eat fish; the world does not afford the like.

Wit. But th' coach is costly.

Tra. Pough! I'll be at that;
'Tis said the milk of asses makes men fat.

[*Exeunt.*

ACT III.

Enter JOCKY *and* Mistress SMALLFAITH.

Jock. Fy, mastres, fy! geod feith, y'ar mickle
oout; I ga hum nooought bet convenable stooff.

Mrs. Small. Y'are a rascall, a Scotch horseleech!
A doctor? a dolthead! Oh, the madness of the
men of these times; if any of them be but a little
out of temper, none can set them right but a
Scotch doctor, forsooth, as though all the English
ones were fools. But, sirrah! sirrah! it is well
known my husband [*she runs at him*] was never
distempered till he came acquainted with such a
decoy as you. Curse on the time—— [*Weeps.*

Joc. Geod mistras, hark ye toll me.

Mrs. Small. Hang you, rascal! my husband was never troubled with whimsies in his head, nor never rail'd against his superiors; he was ever a quiet man, and an honest man, and had the love of the whole Court; and so had I too. Many a good turn have the good gentlemen done me, which I must never expect now again, so violently my husband rails against the Government. But if he suffer for't, thou shalt not wear a nose to thy face. A nose on thy face, said I? nay, if there be a sign-post in all this town I'll hang thee on't. Ah, poor heart!

Enter Mr. SMALLFAITH.

Here he comes. See what a pickle you have put him in! My fingers itch to come at thy face, that ugly face of thine.   [*She runs at him.*

Joc. A me saw, she's a deil, and wull spell aw my market gif I ser her noot lick him. Thes gis o tha sem powder, whilk gif sha smell ta, wull mack her sa lick him as may be.

Mrs. Small. Sweet heart!

Mr. Small. Oh, art thou there? 'tis well. There
   has bin ne'er
A pursevant here yet to fetch me, has there?

Mrs. Small. A pursevant for you! for what
   cause, husband?

Mr. Small. I am too honest, that is cause enough.
There is a council table, yes, forsooth,
And at it is contriv'd men's ruins. Hah!

                                        [*Starts.*

Who's that? who's that? Is't not for me they ask?
I shall be lost quite, if I look not well
About me.

Mrs. Small. True, y'are in the way to undo

Yourself and me and all your family.
But this is thy gin, rascal.   Oh, I could tear thee !
[Runs at him.

Joc. Mistras, ga me whil toll speeke toll ye.
Thes wudnes* o his cam fro tha corruption o his
hart.   Aw that I ga hum was sike as thes, be me
saw,—smeel, laddy ; smeel, laddy.

Mrs. Small. I have not patience.

Joc. Ne, ne, be noot wud, smell toll it.
[She smells.

Mrs. Small. Methinks 'tis very comfortable.
[She starts.

Joc. Hoow doll ye, geod sir ?

Mr. Small. Oh, Mr. Doctor, is't thee ! art safe ?
'Tis wonderful there's nothing charg'd against thee !
There is an office call'd the Green-cloth, too ;
Has no man had thee there yet ? *[She starts again.*

Joc. They ken me sa weel, sir.—It warks brawly.
[Aside.

Mrs. Small. Hark you, husband, what is that
you said but now ?   I believ't; what was't ?   The
King is pestilent, wilful,—hah !   Was't so ?   Why,
then, for aught I know, he must be beaten into
better manners.

Joc. Reight weel said, geod faith.

Mrs. Small. Honest Mr. Doctor, pray come in, sir ;
You are the welcom'st man come to my house
This fortnight.   Husband, love him ! has he not
A taking countenance ?

Mr. Small. No body at the gate ?   *[Starts.*
I am possest with fears and jealousies.

Mrs. Small. And well you may be, husband ; I
   am sure
You have had cause enough.   Good man, I grieve,
I grieve to think on't.

* Insanity.

Mr. Small. Mr. Doctor, be advis'd ;
Pray go not unprepar'd. To-night you shall
Take my house for your shelter ; things work
 strangely.
Mrs. Small. Sweet Mr. Doctor, you shall be so
 welcome.
It passes ! truly, y'are a man upright
In every thing, I warrant ; pray come in, sir.
Joc. Geod feith, tha cass is awter'd.   [*Exeunt.*

Enter a CREW OF COUNTRY PEOPLE.

1 *Coun.* Bring forth your prongs, neighbours.
All men stand up for the truth ; and he that will
lie on the Sunday is not to be trusted the week
after.   What say you, neighbours ?
  2 *Coun.* I say a Sunday's lie may go as far as a work-
day's ; my reason is, it has more leisure to travel.
  3 *Coun.* For my part, neighbours, let them lie
that will ; I have no more to do with a lie than a
lie has to do with me.   If any lyes with my wife,
it shall go hard but I'll do as much with his.
  1 *Coun.* Ay, if he have one, neighbour.
  3 *Coun.* Why, if he have none, neighbour, I must
go without.   No man will be a slave, I think.
  2 *Coun.* A slave !   Who has such a mind let
him have it still.   For my part, neighbours, I'll
work hard—earn my bread with the sweat of my
brows,—none shall eat away the fruit of my labour ;
but I will sit down when it is done, and laugh in
despight of all the Kasars in the world.
  4 *Coun.* Hold a pluck there, neighbour ; 'tis ill
playing with edge-tools. That word 'despight' comes
not in handsomely, and may bring us all to the pot.
  3 *Coun.* What ! have we a scab'd sheep amongst
us ?   Let's clear our flock of him !
  4 *Coun.* Hold, neighbour, hold !   I am for you

with all my heart, but give me leave to speak to you. I am but a fool, 'tis confest, but children and fools tell truth sometimes, you know.

Omnes. And what of that? and what of that?

4 *Coun.* I say again, 'tis dangerous meddling with edge-tools. There's store of trees hereabouts, and there may be gibbets made of them, and you know well enough what fruit gibbets bring forth. I say no more, but be careful what you do.

Omnes. Away with him, away with him!

4 *Coun.* One word more, neighbours, one word more. It is not well to mock our superiors, much worse to threaten them; for, as I have heard, there was a suit at law commenced about a fart.

Omnes. Ha, ha, ha! how, man, how?

4 *Coun.* Why, I will tell you, neighbours; be but patient. There was a fellow, I'll not tell his name, was pissing against the wall; the Mayor came by,—now you know the proverb, Tell a tale to a mare and 'twill let a fart; but here the case alters, for the fellow let the fart, and the Mayor took it in the nose, and caused the fellow to be carried to the town hall as prisoner.

3 *Coun.* The Mayor was a horse, or a whorson knave; what's this to us?

4 *Coun.* Now to th' suit.

2 *Coun.* 'Tis worn out, we'll have none on't.

4 *Coun.* Neighbours, lay down your prongs, take my devise; 'tis an old proverb, Be merry and wise.

Omnes. Away with him, away with him; we will break the cords of our slavery!   [*Exeunt.*

Enter JOCKY, *and* FOLLY, *and* ANYTHING.

Fol. Thes gis tha doctor I toll'd ye o, sir; mickle
   wise an holy:
My non contrymon ta, sir.

Any. Sir, the character
The town receives of you makes me ambitious
Of your acquaintance.

    Joc. I complamen noot, sir; Ise doownreight
      Scot ;—
Aw verety an honesty.

    Any. The better, sir ;
That language is the freest from deceit
That carries most simplicity.

    Joc. Ne, ne, Ise noot sa sample neder.

    Any. Pardon me ;
I speak not in that sense, but have regard
Unto the metaphor.   I don't conclude,
'Cause th' organ of the soul may be infected,
The soul must be imperfect ; for I've known
Men rarely endu'd, that Nature has deny'd
The benefit of expression to.

    Joc. Y'ar a scollard, sir.

    Any. And I presume you one.   I have read
      something
Of th' metaphysicks, though I took not on me
The function or the practice.   But no more
Of that, sir ; 'tis not wisdom in a man
Unskill'd, to hold a weapon 'gainst a fencer.

    Joc. Mickle weel sed, geod feith.

    Any. All my discourse
Draws to this period ; that is, you'd be pleased
T' afford me your opinion.   Something I ail,
But know not what, save this, a deprivation
Of breath, and find it prejudicial to
My calling.

    Joc. You ha bad lungs, sir, whilk macks ye
short wound.

    Any. I could have told you that, sir.   My defect
Proceeds from thence ; but for the remedy—
I know my failings.

Joc. You'll faw, sir, intoll a consumption very soon, sir, gif ye tack noought ta keep ye fro it. Aw the dregs o Rome mon be tane fro ye.

Fol. Gead feith, gif he tack yee in hand, sir, y'ar aw hole.

Joc. Y'ar ta fat at hart, sir ! pluraletes bred bet iddlenes, an iddlenes, bad humors ; yee mon keep a spar diet, sir, an be brought low we purgations, sir ; an whan tim sers ha sim comfortives, sir.

Any. Sir, I shall trust my body to your care.

Joc. Bet Ise net trust me saw to yours. [*Aside.*

Enter a SERVANT.

Ser. Sir, Mr. Soongull'd desires you would come with the doctor to him presently.

Fol. I sal, swett hart, my Jo. Doctor, you mon ta Mr. Soongull'd wi me.

Any. You are sent for, sir, I see.

Joc. Bet I sal ha ye in mind, sir.

Any. As soon as may be. Farewell, sir !

[*Exit.*

Joc. Fer noot, sir ; fer noot ! [*Exeunt.*

Enter TRAPHEIR, WITWUD, *and* TOWNSHIFT— DRAWER, *with wine.*

Draw. This is the best room, gentlemen.

Wit. It stinks of tobacco, don't it, coz ?

Town. How ! tobacco ? Tobacco is companion for a prince !

Wit. I take none, though.

Tra. Then you want education. Fill, boy, fill ! Townshift, to thee. [*Exit Drawer.*

Town. Let it come.

[*Enter Drawer with pipes and tobacco.*

Draw. Sir, ther's some gentlemen in the next
room desires your company.

Town. What are they?

Draw. I think their names be Drawforth and
Pinckcarcase.

  Tra. Plain Drawforth and Pinckcarcase; well,
     admit 'em!
Shall it be so, coz?

Wit. I hope there'll be no quarrelling.

Tra. What if there be?
Have you not here your men of iron by you?

    Enter DRAWFORTH, PINCKCARCASE, *and*
             WANTWIT.

Can you be better back'd and breasted, sir?
Townshift, the rogues have got a bubble.

Town. The more the merrier.   Your servant,
Gentlemen.

Drawf. This is our friend, and desires your
acquaintance.

Pinck. Gentlemen, a man of worth, I'll assure
you.

Wit. What countryman, I pray, sir?

Want. An Essex man, sir; your servant.

Drawf. The better flesh, I'll warrant.

Want. I know not that, sir; I have ne'er bin
tried.

Wit. Nor ne'er shall be for me.

Pinck. Drink, drink about!

Town. To thee, Drawforth!

Drawf. A health to thy friends, Mistress!

Tra. Well done, about with't!

Wit. I thank you, gentlemen.

Tra. What! not begin another?

Wit. I've drank too hard already ; this same
glass and no more.
Gentlemen, your ladies' health, sir.

Pinck. Why, Trapheir, whence this gallantry ?

Tra. What an idle question
Is that of thee ! Why, who should do't, but this ?
He sent his tailor to take measure of
The buildings of our bodies.

Town. And th' appurtenances
Came to us by like Providence.

Drawf. Drink, drink about !

Tra. Coz, let me give thee o'er our wine some
counsel.
You are a landed man, be careful what
Strange company you keep ; for there are cheats,
And desperate cheats, abroad, will make no
conscience
To bring you into bonds, and make you sell
Or mortgage all you have. Take heed, good coz,
What company you keep.

Wit. He that cheats me shall have good luck,
coz.

Pinck. When does your tailor fit your body with
A fashionable suit ? This bears an antique
And worn-out date. A gentleman of your fortunes,
And walk so like a cow-driver !

Want. I will have one 'gainst Sunday.

Pinck. Some six yards makes me one, too; let it
be so. Hah !

Drawf. The like proportion fits me ; twelve ! us
both.

Want. Well, it shall be done, gentlemen.

　　　　　　　　　　　　[Begins to be drunk.

Town. Drink, drink about, your friend is gone !

Drawf. I'll send yours after him.

Wit. I—must—be—gone ; 'tis—late !

Tra. No, sure ! What by thy watch ?

Wit. The hand is up—on—on—twel—ve.

Drawf. He's drunk !

Tra. A pretty watch ! I prethee lend it me,
To have another made by.

Wit. 'Tis—a—watch—of price, coz.

Tra. I would not borrow it else.

Pinck. What store of chink have you ?

Want. Money—enough, money—enough !

Pinck. Lend me a piece or two.

Want. There—there, boy.

Drawf. The like to me, sir; come, I shall, I shall.

Want. There, sir. I'll—be—gone.

Pinck. The house, the house to pay.

Enter DRAWER.

Draw. Twenty-two shillings, and y'are welcome,
gentlemen.

Drawf. Make it up five and twenty, and you two
shall cast dice which pays it. Are all parties agreed?
I know our noble friend will not be backward.

[*Exit Drawer.*

Town. Nor ours. Heroic spirit, wilt thou ?

Enter DRAWER, *with wine.*

Draw. Here's more wine, gentlemen.

Town. About with it, about with it !

[*Exit Drawer.*

Drawf. The dice, the dice !   [*They throw.*

Tra. Come, 'tis a good throw, coz.

Drawf. But that's better, sir. Your friend pays.

Wit. Hang him, he cheated ; he's a cheat !

Want. Ne'er go not I, gentlemen.

Wit. You lie, you lie !

Pinck. How ! the lie ? Will you take that ?

Want. How shall I help it, pray ?

Tra. Well done, coz.

Wit. Hang him, he's but a country puppy calf.

Pinck. Throw a pot at's head.

Want. I—shall—not—hit—him.   If—I—do,
I—am—no—more—puppy—than—yourself.

[*Throws a pot.*

Drawf. Why, that was well done.

Wit. I'll kick you, sirrah ! I learn'd that of you,
coz.

Pinck. Gallants, expect to hear from us, and
suddenly.

Drawf. A coach there !

Wit. I hope, they—wait—not for us.   Hah !

Tra. What if they do? we fear 'em not. Pay, pay !
Boy, there's your reckoning.   Call a coach, boy.

[*Exeunt.*

Enter SCAREFOOL.

Scaref. Ha ye wark for a Scot sawger, wha ha
bien aw tha wirld ore ons ten toes ; ser'd aw
religions, an can tha better be o eny. I ha kil'd
tha whar a Babilon, body an saw, brent aw her
rawlecks wi tha feer o zeal.   I can carry twa feces
under won hood. I can be a sent, an I can be a
deil, gif ye ha wirk for me. I ha seen a powre
a riches in me dees, but ha broought noought heom
wi me bet St. Andra's Cross, want an poverty.

Enter BILLY *and* JOCKY.

Bil. A sir ! the bonny siller came a pece, gif I
tol'd um a tale, they'd ga mickle heeds. Geod
feith, won pell ser'd a malades.

Joc. An whot pell wos thot, mon ?

Bil. The pell o sedition.

Joc. A ! ken you thot, mon ? Tha sam set tha magistrat an's wife intoll fears an jealousies, turn'd tha insid o tha kirk, mon, ooutwards, and noow's aw gall ; tha ceteson gis as bitter. Tha leyer cannot stond, he's brought sa weeke wy me purgations; and tha curtier noot worth tha grond a goes on. I ha let aw his geod as weel as he's bad bleod oout.

Scar. Saw ye, gentlemen, gif ye ha a mind ta bien saw'd ; ken ye me, sirs ?

Joc. How sud we ken thee, mon ?

Scar. Wha, noot Scarefool, your contremon ?

Bil. Whar hast bien, mon ?

Scar. Aw tha wirld ore, sirs ; an noow aw pleces are wary o me. Ise cam ta Anglond toll seeke wirke.

Joc. Here's wirke enoough gif ye bien wise ta deele wy tha Anglish, mon.

Scar. Geod feith, Ise chet 'um thay wern ner sa cheted. Show me toll 'um. Whar liew thay ?

Joc. In th' cety, and contre ta. Marry, bet cam awey wy us, mon ; wees tack a drinck first, an tawke mere on't.

Bil. Cam awey, *Jo* ; cam awey.   [*Exeunt.*

ACT IV.

Enter SOONGULL'D *and his Wife* LAYMEDOWN.

Soon. Down with this Babell-builder, this Court
        pride !
Dagon and his idolaters shall down.

Lay. Ay, down with 'em, husband ; down with

'em : they have stood long enough. I am sure their long standing have made you come short many a time and often ; but I hope now, husband, you'll take 'em down a button-hole lower.

Soon. Am not I a man ?

Lay. You think so, husband, I warrant.

Soon. Why, a king's no more.

Lay. Nay, is he that, husband ? Troth, I dare say our man William is as good a man as the best of you. For, as they say, a man is a man and he has but a hose on's head.

Soon. Well, I am resolv'd ; William shall forth.

Lay. Forth ! How do you mean—forth ? I hope you will not leave me unprovided at home. You know your own business abroad, and I am certain he can do your business at home better than your self. Oh, husband, husband, here's the Scotch doctor !

Enter JOCKY, FOLLY, BILLY, *and* SCAREFOOL.

Soon. Mr. Doctor ! what news, Mr. Doctor ?

Joc. Nen good, sir ; nen good, sir : bet me frond ha had hes cass pul'd ore his lugs.

Soon. By whom ? by whom ?

Fol. Wha ! wha bet tha prod prelates, sir. Ise tolld 'um o thair knavery, an thay gar tack awey me brawery. Bet thoough thay ha tacken awey me cot, thay sall ner tack awey me conscience ; that's holl an sound, an ned nen o thair pachings o thair preachments.

Lay. O wicked, wicked children of darkness !

Joc. Her's a frond o min, sir ; a mon o meight an mettell, wha ha endured meny a brunt and storme, he sall stond betwixt ye in aw harme.

Soon. I shall be glad of your acquaintance, sir.

Lay. True truly sir, you have a face like man. You'll do the business, I warrant, let you alone. But gently to the women, sir, for we are twigs, and may be bow'd which way you list—mere tender twigs, sir.

Scar. Bred, bet sam o ye bien toough enoough.

Lay. We are a long time indeed a bringing up, but then we are soon cast down. Women have tender hearts, and tender flesh, and tender consciences, though naughty men report that we have none. Husband, shall they walk into th' parlour? I do love to enter into dialogue with these gentlemen, they talk so prettily.

Soon. Ay, with all my heart.

Lay. You will meet with, sir, fine plunder 'mong the ladies. You shall dine with us too; you may make me amends with a Court smock. I look to wear one in truth, they are so fine and so perfum'd, it passes.

Soon. Come, sir, we'll discourse of our affairs after w'ave din'd. You'll dine with us too, gentlemen?

Joc. Wees tack ye ot yar word.   [*Exeunt.*

Enter ANYTHING, *and Boys following him.*

Any. Nay, you may do't, sirs, you may do't; you have warrant for't. 'Tis well enough known, the pomp of the prelates, the whore of Babylon herself in her feathers, the kings of the earth commit fornication with her pluralities of benefices, makes men but idle, saies Mr. Doctor, and idleness makes you fat, and fat makes you pursy, and so by consequence short-winded. It is a trick of Rome to starve our religion. Let Jezabell be brought before the elders, and the whore of Babylon to the whipping post; let her have lash upon lash; let her smock be given to the rag-men, it may come to be paper, and her condemnation writ in't; let the whelps and the cubs be brought to the stake,— bait 'um, bait 'um, bait 'um! I am your warrant, saith Mr. Doctor.

Boys. Master Doctor's an ass.

Any. Children, you talk not like men, you are but middling Christians,—'tis well known to the parish—

Boys. That Bedlam's fit for you.

Any. Those that will follow me, let 'um follow me,—

I am for the truth,
And the Covenant in sooth.   [*Exit.*

Boys. Hi, hi, hi! Stow the Friar, stow the Friar!
[*They sing.*
[*Exeunt after him.*

Enter DOWNFALL *and* WORNOUT.

Down. You see what he has brought me to—my
   crutches!
I was e'er held an able man, you know,—
Had my tongue at command, and my head too,
But now they both are so enfeebled, I
Have scarce the use of either; if I had,
It were all one. The country people are
Bewitcht into belief they have as much
Reason and law as I, and will become
Their own solicitors, and counsel too.
I cannot last long, but expect still when
My crutches will deceive me, and I fall
To th' ground for ever.
   Worn. I am brought to nothing
As well as you. I little thought a Scotchman

L

Could e'er have drain'd my veins and purse so dry.
I am not worth the ground I go on; so
Dejected are my thoughts, my spirit lost,
And all the hopes of my recovery
Extinct and buried.

Down. I should not have known you,
Had you not told me who you were; you are
So changed from yourself.   Oh! those were times
Worthy to call to mind—though to our grief—
When you and I, like twins, deriv'd a being
From one another's sustenance; the monopolies
That you projected, and I perfected!
Like two expert limners,—the one employ'd
To fashion th' face, the other to finish it.

Worn. Ay, those were times indeed; but all I got
Then has been since consumed, and I guess
You are not much the better.   I am weary,
I protest, of my life, and would thank him
Would do me so much good as take it from me.

Down. Patience is the best remedy where no
Better can be obtain'd.   'Tis vain to crave
The thing we want when 'tis not to be had.
Your dancing days are done, and all the breath
The Scot has left me scarce will heat my fingers.

Worn. And my affliction does the more increase
To see my friends disabl'd, as I am,
From helping one another.   'Tis a grief
That's inexpressible, and not for cure.

Down. What Fortune sours, content must
      sweeten.
He is the best man o'ercomes his misery.

                                   [*Exeunt.*

Enter SMALLFAITH *and his* WIFE.

Small. For my part, I am but a man, and I owe

but a death; let them take it, as they say they will;
give 'um good on't. Let them come, let them come!
Where are they? Stand, stand, stand!

Wife. Husband, now you talk of standing, pray
let me lye down, and then let 'em do their worst.
I defy 'em.

Small. And so do I. We'll to the terret,* woman,
and there we are secur'd 'gainst devil and pursevant.

Wife. I'm weary'd off my legs with doing
nothing but running up and down in e'ry nook
and corner like a rat for fear of catching.

Small. They are coming, they are coming. Let
me come in, woman, let me come in!

Wife. I would you would come in, husband,
once. You have been out long enough to small
purpose, I'm sure. [*Exeunt.*

Enter SUREHOLD *and* RESOLUTION.

Res. Believe it, their design aims at our ruin;
And though the cord they make be somewhat finer
Than ordinary, 'twill choak us at the last.
I hold a naked freedom better far
Than an adorned prison. Golden fetters
And iron ones produce a like effect ;
What differs them's but curiosity.†

Sure. Into what a lethargy have these rabble
Scots
Betray'd the people's senses. Tell them on't
And they'll abuse you for't. Nay, though they see
Distraction brought unto their very doors,

---

* Terre tenant—*terra tenens*—is he who has the actual possession of the land, which we otherwise call *the occupation.*
39 Eliz. 7.—COWEL Ed. 1708.
† "Qualities are so weigh'd, that curiosity in neither can
make choice of either's moiety."—SHAKESPEARE'S *King Lear.*

They'll look on't, and not know it till they feel it,
And then will tamely kiss the rod that whipt 'em.
A nation proud and arrogant as the beggar,
That when h'as got a bonnet 'bove his wearing,
Will scarce bow to the giver.   All the service
They ever did this nation was to help
The people eat their victuals, and share their
    fortunes.
    Res. Th'are good for nought, but to eat, louze,
    and sleep,
And stink a street up ; tell you stories of
Don John of Austria, the Mogul, great Cham,
Their valour at Madrid, Levant, or where
You will ; and this in some blind chimney corner,
In fume and smoke, rouz'd up with lanted ale,
'Till that their faces do resemble th' towns
They set on fire ; and yet dare not encounter
A rat or weasel.
    Sure. Yet the world reports
Them men for siege the best, and can endure
The greatest hardship.
    Res. Very true ; if they
May but lie still, they'll feed on one another
Rather than venture on their enemy
To get the least provision ; and, indeed,
The worst will serve their turn, for they are men
Loves anything but beating, yet they'll take
That too, if need be ; take 'em down a little,
And you may fillip dead a score of them.
It is a shame the English should become
Such mules to such base burdens.   I'm resolv'd
To turn the chance o' th' die that favours them,
Though to the hazard of my being.
    · *Sure.* 'Twill
Be ta'en a piece of service fit for chronicle,
And you shall want no furtherance.

Res. If I bring not
The soldier, doctors, and their crew of cheaters
As tamely to be hang'd as puppy dogs,
Let me receive no credit from you after.

[Exeunt.

Enter SOONGULL'D *and a* SEMINARY PRIEST *going to
weigh the Covenant with the Pope's Bull.*

Soon. Sir, though I hate your bulls and your
    decoys,
And know you have two ends to all your ways,
I fear you not, for Truth will show herself
In spite of all the clouds you cast upon her.
   Sem. You are in th' right. Truth will appear,
    and that
To th' shame of your trim'd Covenant ; for though
She be but plain, she is more glorious
Than all the gloss and colours that set forth
That new devise, created to deceive
Poor simple people, and at last yourselves.
   Soon. These are but bandying. I'll pursue my
    wager.
   Sem. I'll venture ten pound more y'are lost in
    weight.
   Soon. You'll lose yourself, sir, with your con-
    fidence.
   Sem. Bar treachery and I care not.   *[Exeunt.*

Enter TRAPHEIR, WITWUD, *and* TOWNSHIFT.

Wit. I cannot endure this fighting, coz, a dad !
Tra. Pox take your dad ! is that an oath for a
    gentleman ?

A lad at ten swears more profoundly.   You'll
Be quarrelling, and then you dare not fight,
As though I were a wall of steel or brass
To stand betwixt you, and receive the darts
Cast at you.   Sir, why did your cowship send
An answer to your challenge, if you found
Your blood so cool and phlegmatic ?
    Wit. 'Twas your doing, — I had not had the
      heart else.   [*Aside.*
    Town. For preservation of your honour, sir,
Could you do else than answer him ?
    Wit. What was he
That brought the challenge ?
    Town. Pinckcarcase by name.
    Wit. A devilish name, and full of devilish ends.
This fighting is not lawful.   Prethee, coz,
Take up the matter ; I have little maw to't.
    Town. What ! now the hostage reputation
Is past, will you recant, reneage, revoke,
Recoil, revert ?   Stand to your principles.
    Wit. I shall not stand an inch of ground, believe
      me.
    Tra. 'Tis pity th'art worth any.   Let me see, —
How shall we do't with honour ?
    Wit. 'Tis no matter
For that thing honour ; let her walk alone,
I don't desire her company on such terms,
Sweet coz, sweet coz !
    Tra. Let me see, — I'm resolv'd
That you shall fight him.
    Wit. Coz, I had forgot,
I swear, a strange infirmity, — that is,
I zound when as I hear a gun shot off,
And tremble at a pistol's ; all my senses
Become as useless.
    Town. Why, 'twas your own motion.

Wit. No matter, 'tis but so much charges lost.
I will not fight with bullets; I've more conscience.

Tra. Why, then, you must prepare a case of
rapiers
For Townshift and myself; ours are grown dull
With often usage.

Wit. Oh, the better, coz !
They'll do less mischief.

Tra. Then your fencing master
Must make you at your chamber fit for th' field.

Wit. That's past his skill, I'm sure. More
charges, coz.

Tra. It cannot be avoided, if you mean
To fight on foot, and put off your horse combat.

Wit. In my mind 'tis horse-play to fight on foot.
But hark you, coz, don't you make winking at
That weapon ye call sharp ; I'm not so set.

Tra. Fye, winking ! no, how will you see to hit
him ?

Wit. No matter, so he hit not me. But mayn't I
Bar points, being the challenged ?

Tra. That's base, and player-like.

Wit. I'd rather play so than work otherwise.

Town. Come, come, resolve ! you know the time
draws near.

Wit. I would it did not ; I love not to think on't.
Can we throw nothing in Time's way to make
Him stumble and stop a little ?

Tra. Resolve upon your weapon ere he be
Furnish'd with horse and pistols.

Town. I'll lay my life he's that already, then
'Twill be unworthy in you to——

Wit. Good sir, talk not to me of worthies ! my
father was none of the nine. He ne'er kept company with your Huffs, nor puffs; he could drink
in a tavern and ne'er quarrel about the reckoning.

He lived without knocks, and died in the love of
his parish.

Tra. But he has left a quarrelsome son behind
Must pay for all.

Wit. I shan't stand much upon
That point, so I may be discharg'd from beatings.
Methinks a skin set out with eyelet holes
Appears not handsome, nor a face to be
Painted with black and blue ; I hate those colours.

Town. What will you give him shall take up the
business without loss to your honour ?

Wit. A man cannot lose
That which he never had.   My father was
A man of bags, and might have been a knight
When knighthoods went a begging.

Town. But to the matter,
What say you to my proposition ?

Wit. Troth,
It sounds well.   Let me see now what in conscience
You will demand ?

Town. But twenty pieces.

Wit. So l
To save a man from beating, very good !
How many such d'ye meet with in the year ?

Town. Hundreds, hundreds, sir !

Tra. Men must live, coz; men must live !

Wit. Anywhere but on me, good coz ; but, sir,
Before my coz here, I'll give you ten.

Tra. Ten is too little in all conscience, coz.

Town. Consider, sir, the danger.

Wit. And the charge
Already I've been for horse and pistols.
But those I hope you will return me when
The peace is made.

Tra. Not one ; expect not one !
Th'are forfeit goods to us lords of the soil.

Town. 'Tis true y'ave been at charges, and for
    that
Reason I'll undertake it at your rate ;
Forbid but I should bear a conscience too.
Meet us at th' Mermaid !
    Tra. At the hour of twelve.
    Town. The precise time.
    Tra. Cozen, he will deserve it.
    Wit. Would I had his art
To live by when I and my fortunes part.
                      [*Exeunt.*

    Enter WANTWIT, DRAWFORTH, *and*
            PINCKCARCASE.

    Pinck. He is the challenged, and justly may
Design the way of fighting, and the place.
But though you have provided us with horses,
Swords, pistols, and so forth, yet there's a thing
Call'd money we do want ; put case he should
Fall by your hand, in what a case were we !
    Drawf. Suppose that you should fall !
Ay, there's the danger.
    Pinck. We must fly for't, and that we cannot do
Conveniently without a sum ; the oratory
Of silver makes our passage free and safe,
The want of it detains us.   Open, open
Your close-mouth'd bags, and let them speak to us.
    Want. Troth, gentlemen, I'll tell you, and I lie
    not,
Th'ave got a hoarseness since they came to town,
And speak so low, a man can hardly hear 'em.
    Pinck. One mortgage, sir, will raise their voice
    again.
    Want. Well, well, he might have ta'en another
    way

To work. Had I been he, and he been me,
I would have askt him mercy.
 Drawf. But, you see,
He is a man of spirit—spirit, sir !
 Want. I would he had no more than I : a gnat
Is better furnisht. I have heard my mother
Protest, and solemnly, I had a heart
No bigger than a hazel nut.
 Pinck. Why, saw she't ?
 Want. No, but she felt it. 'Tis an imperfection
In nature I can't help, and 'tis as cold,
I warrant, as a cucumber.
 Drawf. And riseth
So little in your stomach !
 Want. Troth, as little
As may be, sir. How shall I heat it, gentlemen ?
 Drawf. Drink wine and drab.
 Want. Why, so I do, you know.
Yet, when the flame of drinking's o'er, I fall
Into the noose of taverns, like a pigeon.
 Pinck. Only then y'ad best fight when y'are
  drunk.
 Want. And so
Be hang'd when I am sober. No, I bear
Too great a conscience.
 Drawf. If it be a burthen
Too hard to bear, we'll teach you how to throw
It off, and live as we do without any.
 Want. Take up this quarrel, gentlemen, and
  have
My heart for ever.
 Pinck. What to do ? to throw
The hounds ye starve ? Yet that's so little, 'twill
Not be a mouthful. 'Tis your money we
Value the most, let your heart go as't came.
 Want. Why, I shall mortgage next week.

Pinck. Are you serious ?
May we give credit to you ?
Want. I've occasion.
Drawf. Thou shalt have more rather than want.
   My bully,
We are thy guardians ! Who assaults our ward
Suffers, unless he be on a sure guard.   [*Exeunt.*

ACT V.

Enter JOCKY *and* BILLY.

Bil. Bred, thos Anglish ar deeles ; w'are aw lost
men. Aw oour knavery is oout, nen wull tack
oour parts. Tha cetesons hong thare heds doown
lick bullrushes, an won noot bien sen for us.
   Joc. Hoow cam thay, in tha deele's nam, sa aw o
won mind ? Ise sur Ise ded whot Ise cud toll
mack 'um het on oder ta deeth. Tha deele feere
'um ; thar lick serpans, that gif ye smit 'um asunder,
wull join agen.

Enter SCAREFOOL, *with his sword drawn.*

Scar. W'are aw lost ! sheft, sheft, tha deel's a
comming toll tare tha Covnant. Sha yeer heeles,
sha yeer heeles ; spang awey, sirs, spang awey !
         [*Exit running.*
   Joc. On's, gif tha men o war flee, whar sall we
hid our sells ? Aw sir, sir !

Enter RESOLUTION, *with two or three.*

Res. Take them into your custody ! they are
Your lawful prize.   [*Exit.*

Bil. A sirs! a sirs! geod feith wees ment ne bad.

1 Soul. What, Mr. Doctors! have we found ye? Who can cure the citizen of his headache but the Scotch doctors? who their wives of the toothache but the Scotch doctors? The Scotch doctor is all in all. The kirk will take no physic but of the Scotch doctor; the country will be cheated by none but by the Scotch doctor; the Court and gentry will be beggar'd by none but the beggarly Scotch doctors. Come away and be hang'd!

[Exeunt.

Joc. Bil. Mercy, sirs! mercy, mercy, mercy!

Enter SCAREFOOL *running, with his sword drawn.*

Scar. Hawd—hawd—hawd, sir! *[He trembles.*

Res. Nay, I don't intend
To take th' advantage of you as I may;
I owe a greater honour to true valour.
I have heard nobly of your countrymen,
And therefore to assure myself report
Lies not, I have expos'd my person to
This single hazard. *[He trembles.*

Scar. A, sir! I dee leov you.

Res. And I shall love you too, if that I find
You prove as gallant as y'ave spoke yourself.
Consider what dependances are on you,
Whom y'ave involv'd by your large promises
To this engagement. Let them see you dare
Do something for their money.

Scar. Be me saw, sir,
Y'are a mickle gallant mon; Ise thra me swerd an hert at your non feet, sir.

Res. That's base, not soldierlike. Submissiveness

In this case speaks you coward, and if so,
My breath has been ill spent.   What ! will you
    fight ?
Scar. Noot a neust ye, sir; geod feith I leove a
Anglishmon wy aw my hert.   A sir ! a sir ! send
aw reight, send aw reight.   Her, tack me weppon !
Ise your non prisoner, sir, geod feith.
                            [*He offers his sword.*
Res. Since thou art so base,
And not fit for a noble treaty, take
This, this, and this.   [*Kicks him.*
Scar. A, geod sir, use me like a gentleman !
Res. A gentleman ! a swineherd, hang ye,—go !
                            [*Kicks him.*
The bubble's broke the wind gave being to.
                            [*Exeunt.*
                Within.
Y'are welcome, gentlemen; show a room there,
    boy !

Enter TRAPHEIR, WITWUD, TOWNSHIFT, *and*
        DRAWER.

Tra. Sirrah, there will some gentlemen ask
    for us,
Direct 'em hither !
Draw. I shall, sir.   What's your wine ?
Town. Sack, boy, the quickening sack; and such
    tobacco
As may inspire a spirit into clay ;
Quick, and as sharp as lightning !
Wit. Oh ! good sir,
I can't endure to think upon a storm.
Talk not of lightning, it does bode some quarrel-
    ing ;

The calmest language is the best when there's
A peace intended.

Enter DRAWFORTH, PINCKCARCASE, WANTWIT,
and DRAWER *with wine.*

Tra. Here they come !   Now, coz,
For your honour seem somewhat averse
To an agreement ; carry yourself stoutly,
With an unalter'd countenance.
Wit. 'Tis not in
The power of human frailty.
Tra. Gallants, welcome !
Y'are men, I see, for credit.
Want. What must I say ?
Drawf. Carry yourself manly.
Want. What would I give now for an inch of
    manhood !
How he does eye me ! would I had a look
            [*Drawf., Tra., Town., and Pinck. whisper.*
But half so piercing, I'd encounter then
With basilisks.   It carries daggers in't
Will penetrate a coat of mail.   There is
            [*Witwud and Wantwit stare at one another.*
No safety but in distance.
Wit. How he looks at me !
With such a hungry countenance, as though
He meant to satisfy himself upon me.
But if he knew but what a piece of flesh
He had to deal with, he'd not be so greedy.
I was not cut out for a royster ; sure
Nature ne'er meant me for the field, unless
To call my cattle home, or try my hounds.
I am so great an enemy to a sword,
I wear none when I ride.   Oh ! how yon fellow

Would spurn me, like a mushrome, could he get
Me but alone! But he shall be hang'd first.

    Tra. What! all this while and speak not to each
        other?

Why, you have hearts of oak! Not bow, dear
    coz?

    Wit. I cannot help it.

    Town. Come, we must have you friends.

    Want. With all my heart, sir.

    Wit. How's this? The man's bewitcht.

See what the gold can do!

    Want. If you please, sir, I am your humble
        servant.

    Tra. And what say you, coz?

    Wit. Hum, I smelt, 'tis so;

The fellow is a coward, on my life.
Are they not all so? 'Tis a blessing, then.

    Drawf. Come, sir, our friend is willing to pass
        by

All the affronts you gave him, if you'll waive
His challenge.

    Wit. I'll wave nothing but my sword

Against my enemy.

    Town. Shall we be friends?

    Wit. A friendly blood runs not yet current
    in me.

Be challenged by a dunghill cock? I scorn it.

    Tra. Why, this is rare! Coz, I'll spit in thy
    mouth.

    Pinck. Sir, 'tis your friend's desire, as well as
    ours,

To prevent bloodshed.

    Wit. Let such things as you,

That dare not waste their blood, be sparing on't.
For my part, I'll not value if he tap
From me a pailful.

Tra. Who the devil conjur'd
Up such a spirit in him ?
   Pinck. Your friend's grown !
Take him down, or by this light
I'll kick him.
   Tra. Pough ! let me alone for that.
   Want. The gentleman grows angry. I'll be gone !
                                    [*To Drawforth.*
   Drawf. Hang him, a coward ! a mere coward,
      friend.
   Want. How, a coward ! he speaks not like one.
I would his hands were tied behind him, I
Would make a trial on't.   But he has teeth
Strong as the tusks of boars, and legs more stiff
And big than any bedpost.   I should do
No good upon him.
   Tra. Come, coz, throw
Your ranting habit off ; the scene of war
Is past, and now put on your robe of amity,
The bride-garment of peace.
   Wit. Peace ! who shall peace ?
'Tis sauciness to tell me so.
   Tra. How's this,
You worm ?   'Slight, if I lay my hands
Upon you once, I'll tear you into nothing,
You cowardly simple puppy.   Sirra, I'll——
                            [*He takes him by the shoulder.*
   Wit. Not so loud, good coz ;
You know I have but follow'd your directions.
   Tra. Be hang'd ! and overdone it, han't you,
      sirrah ?
The gentlemen shall know you have not spirit
To look a cat in th' face, if that you ben't
More sociable.
   Wit. Good cozen, I'll do anything.

Tra. Well, I have brought him to't with much
   ado :
  [*Takes Want. by the hand and brings him to Wit.*
Here, shake hands, sir, you must be friends.

Wit. Well, if I must, I must ; patience is a
   virtue,
And I'll embrace it : I am your friend, sir.

Want. I shall never be your foe, sir.

Wit. So said, and so done, sir, will do well.

Tra. The rascal acts it handsomely.

Pinck. To your credit.
Ours is the silliest rogue.

Drawf. Boy, more wine !

Enter DRAWER.

Would we had music here to celebrate
This nuptial !

Draw. I will send for some.

Tra. Do so. Come, here's to the married couple !

Wit. I do believe we both can get a boy
Will prove a soldier.

Enter FIDDLERS.

Pinck. Ah, sirrah ! are you there ?

Fid. I am your own man, sir.

Pinck. Let's have a good air ; but drink first.

Town. Drink about, gallants,—what ! the music
   dulls you ?
Hast e'er a new song, fellow ?

Fid. Yes, of the Scots coming into England.

Tra. That, that by all means.

Fid. Please you to hear me ; 'tis but a ballad
   put to
One of their own tunes.

M

Pinck. The better, the better; let's hear't.

Song.

Cam lend, lend y'ar lugs, Joes, an Ise speek a song;
   Sing heom agen, Jocky; sing heom agen, Jocky.
O hes bonny deeds, an hes prowes emong;
   Sing heom agen, heom agen, O valent Jocky!

Sirs, Jocky's a mon held o mickle note;
   Sing heom agen, Jocky, *etc.*
Tha breech o tha Covnant stuck in hes throte;
   Sing heom agen, heom agen, *etc.*

For Jocky wes riteous, whilk ye wad admire;
   Sing heom agen, *etc.*
He fooght for the Kirke, bet a plunder'd tha quire;
   Sing heom agen, heom agen, *etc.*

An Jocky waxt roth, an toll Anglond a cam;
   Sing heom agen, *etc.*
Fro whance he'd return, bet alack a is lam;
   Sing heom agen, *etc.*

An Jocky wes armed fro top toll toe;
   Sing heom agen, *etc.*
Wi a poowre o men, an thare geod Deuke, I tro;
   Sing heom agen, *etc.*

Sa valent I wis thay wer, an sa prat;
   Sing heom agen, *etc.*
Ne cock nor hen durst stond in their gat;
   Sing heom agen, *etc.*

In every streete thay ded so flutter;
   Sing heom agen, *etc.*
Ne child dorst shaw hes bred an butter;
   Sing heom agen, *etc.*

Noow, whan oour ferces thay herd on o'er night;
  Sing heom agen, *etc.*
Next morne they harnest themsels for a fight;
  Sing heom agen, *etc.*

Thare Deuke was tha mon that wad be sen stoote;
  Sing heom agen, *etc.*
He feect us a while, stret twurn'd arss aboot;
  Sing heom agen, *etc.*

Our men that ater these valent Scot went;
  Sing heom agen, *etc.*
Had ner fond him oout bet by a strong scent;
  Sing heom agen, heom agen, O valent Jocky!

Tra. Ha, ha, ha! it's good enough for the subject.

Enter DRAWER.

Pinck. Drink about, drink about! More wine,
  boy!
Here, Witwud, to thee.
  Town. Let's discharge the music.
  Wit. With all my heart.
  Town. There, ye rascals.
  Fid. Thank you, gentlemen.   [*Exeunt Fiddlers.*
  Drawf. Trapheir, to thee.
  Tra. Let it come; a pint and thou dar'st.
  Pinck. Art mad? Trapheir is drunk enough;
  he'll be
Not company for a dog immediately.
  Tra. To your Mightiness, sir.
  Pinck. I shall pledge your Highness, sir — to
  you, sir.
  Wit. Excuse me, pray, sir; I am almost spent.
  Pinck. Not pledge me!

Tra. No, he shall not pledge you, sir.
What then ? he is my friend.
   Pinck. But why should he
Be more excus'd than ours ?   Will you drink for
   him ?
   Tra. Not neither, sir.
   Pinck. Then he shall pledge me, sir.
   Tra. He shall not, sir.
   Town. Nay, Trapheir ; what dost mean ?
                        [*Pinck. throws the pot at him.*
   Tra. Hang him, turd— Are you good at that,
   sir ?
I shall return you answer by this messenger.
                                    [*Draws.*
   Wit. Good coz, no fighting; I will drink a gallon
Rather than lose one drop of blood.   It is
Too precious for the floor to drink.

Enter DRAWER.

   Draw. Gentlemen, your noise has drawn soldiers
into the house ; th'are coming up. As many as can,
get into that little closet !
   Pinck. I would not be in custody for a million.
The rode, the rode——
            [*Tra., Pinck., Town., and Drawf. get in.*
   Drawf. That's all our faults : in, in !
   Wit. Where shall we be ?

Enter SOLDIERS.

   Sol. Where's all these Huffs ?   What ! you two
make this noise ! hurl pots, break glasses ? You
are youths indeed ! Is this a time of night for you
to rant in ?   Come, you must with us.
   Want. Nay, good gentlemen.   [*Exeunt.*

Enter DRAWER.

Draw. Gentlemen, you may come forth ; the coast is clear.

Tra. Where's the two gentlemen ?

Draw. They have ta'en 'em with 'em.

Pinck. Did they pay the reckoning ?

Draw. No, sir.

Tra. A pox upon you ! why did you not ask 'em for't ?

Draw. I durst not, sir, for fear they should say the rest of their company was above.

Pinck. 'Tis right,—the devil's on't ! This was your doing, Trapheir ; ·
Will you pay the reckoning now ?

Tra. Not a penny ; I'll keep unto my oath. Throw who shall dip, or pay if you will.

[*Townshift throws.*

Pinck. Here's dice—throw. Twelve, hang ye, rascal ! [*Pinck. throws.*
Now, my chance—'tis passable. Throw.

[*Drawf. throws.*

Drawf. Mine is the worst.

Tra. But mine's the worst of all. Sirrah, boy, will you take this cloak for your reckoning ?

Draw. I know not, sir, whether I shall or not.

Tra. You shall not, sir, now, you know, as long as such spankers last. What's to pay ?

[*Shows his money.*

Draw. But thirty shillings, sir.

Tra. Death ! but thirty, sayest thou ? Well, there 'tis !
I shall be even with somebody.

Town. Why, this was handsome, Trapheir.

[*Exeunt.*

Enter two or three SERVITORS.

Ser. Make room for the magistrates !
The prisoners

Enter DOMUCH, SUREHOLD, RESOLUTION, SCARE-
FOOL, JOCKY, BILLY, SMALLFAITH *and his*
WIFE, SOONGULL'D *and his* WIFE, ANYTHING,
DOWNFALL, WORNOUT, SEMINARY, PUBLIQUE
NOTARY.

There——
Do. Which are the prisoners ?
Res. These, sir.
Joc., Bil. Mercy, mercy, Master Judge !
Sure. What are those ?
Res. The subjects on the which these villains
practis'd their subtleties and deceits. First, I shall
tender my charge against 'em, then produce my
evidence.
Do. Very well, very well ! Proceed.
Res. In brief, sir, then, they have infected most
Part of this nation.   Here's a thing,
A man of reputation once, and bore
                                  [*Pointing to Small.*
A place amongst you.
Sure. I do pity him.
Res. And now is fit for no place except Bedlam.
Here is another; a man, you would think,
                                  [*To Anything.*
The devil could not work upon, and yet
These Scotch ones have.   The lawyer—father of
Contrivances—is noos'd in one himself :
He cannot stand without his crutches, and

His head's so light, his nose is every minute
Ready to touch the ground.

Sure. What is that gentleman ?   [*To Wornout.*

Res. Do you conceive him one ? have they left
    aught
Upon him like a creature ? may we swear
He is a perfect man, no ghost ? 'tis hard.
The hurryings he has had with sleepless eyes,
Continual purgations, bleedings, what not,
That they could but invent to bring him low.
He's all left of a courtier, and deserves
Your pity. There's no double doors betwixt
His heart now and your eyes ; he's so transparent
You may see through him. 'Tis not these alone
Th'ave brought to this, but all the country people,
Both common sort and gentry.

Do. What say you for yourselves ?

Joc., Bil. Mercy, mercy, mercy ! wees leove tha
Anglish mickle weel.

Sure. Yes, it appears so. We'll requite your loves,
But cannot say with your own coin, because
You never were worth any ; but we'll find
A way to pay you home.

Res. When they had thus
Spread their infection, they began to think
Their safety would not last without the soldier ;
And to that end and purpose do persuade
The giddy people, which they had before
Distemper'd with their poisons, to receive
This man of feather as their grand Protector ;
They take him, and to Covenant they go.
Two hundred thousand pounds—a sum would
    buy
Their Kingdom !—must be raised and paid to them.

Do. Very fine!

Res. But mark, sir, the event !

I am resolv'd to open what they did
For all this money.

Do. 'Twill do well, indeed.

Res. They gave a piece of paper, in the which
Were strange things promis'd then, as if that all
The courage of the world contracted were
In their, and but their, nation.

Sure. And what found you?

Res. I now proceed to that. I found them, sir,
Like bullrushes, that tremble if the wind
But blow on them; they run and tumbl'd o'er
The necks of one another, like to tiles
A storm forces from houses' tops. This anything
But man, who own'd the name of their Protector,
In the most abject'st manner, and beneath
The spirit of a man, threw at my feet
His sword, and himself too, on simple terms,
Without a stroke. Scarefool they call him, and
They must be citizens or none that fear him.
A rat shall make him run to his own country!

Scare. Ise a gentleman, sir, mind ye me; Ise
gang toll me non contre wy aw me hert, gif you
wull.

Sure. Not in such haste, sir; we'll reserve you
for
Another purpose. Take him hence to prison.

Scare. The faw deel fier thot tong.

[*He is carried off.*

Res. What think you, sir, that paper costs so much
Is worth in weight? Here's one will tell you, sir.

Pub. No. I am a publique notary by profession,
And dare speak nothing but the truth; the wager
Past on this gentleman's side, the Pope's Bull
weighed
It down by much, the other was not worth
In weight a penny loaf.

Omnes. Ha, ha, ha !

Sure. But what make you here, sir ?

Sem. Not to harm, sir.

Do. Stay not here upon

Your peril, sir ; your Bulls have too long tails.

Sem. I stay but for a wind, sir.

[*Exit Seminary.*

Soon. I must confess we have been much deluded,
Cheated, and cozen'd by these perjur'd Scots,
Under the show of zeal and honesty.

Lay. Hang 'em, rogues ! they complain they are
pillaged. You made them not bare enough, sirs ;
you should have taken their skins off too, they
would have made monsters of us. But truly my
husband is a natural man, and I am his own wife.
I hope you do not think we are otherwise than we
should be.

Mrs. Small. I have a husband here too. Help
his head, he was a man once, and I was a woman,
as this gentleman the courtier knew well enough ;
but now I am nobody, thank you, pick-purses !
Pray spare 'em not ! I'm sure they would not
spare me when time was, do what I could.

Sure. Take them hence ! There will be order
   shortly
To pack them to some foreign parts ; they are
But caterpillars, and what place soe'er
They come at will be the worse for't. Take them
   hence !

Joc., Bil. A mercy, mercy, mercy !

[*Exeunt Scots.*

Omnes. You have done justice !

Sure. Y'ave seen these Scots dissected, gentlemen,
And what d'you find them now to be but
   rascals ?

Mere mountebanks, that have, instead of cure,
Bred strange diseases and distempers 'mongst
    you !
Jugglers, that looked you in the face, and told
You a fine tale, to keep your senses busy,
While they did pick your pockets !
    Lay. Our pockets,
Say you, sir ? Ay, and something else too, could
They have come at it ; but soft, soft, two words to
    a bargain.
    Sure. Master Smallfaith, we shall do what lies
    in us,
Upon your recantation, to bring
You into favour with the Commonwealth,
And seat you as before, as capable
Of her preferment.
    Small. I thank you.
    His Wife. Blessing on your hearts !
    Sure. We make the same profession, sir, to you,
On the like terms. You may do much
Upon the giddy people by th' example
Of your own reformation.
    Any. Sir, I shall
Do what befits an honest man, abus'd,
And servant to the Commonwealth.
    Do. And you, sir,
Are not exempted here the benefit
Of favour, if you will take hold of it.
    Soon. I thank you.
    Lay. Ay, and hold it fast, husband ! Had I a
good thing to handle, I'd make much on't a long
time, I warrant you !
    Sure. As for these gentlemen here, Master
    Downfall
And Master Wornout, we shall do our best
To set the one upon his legs again,

And restore the other, though not to his full
Ability, yet to a health contentable.

    Down., Worn. We are your servants.

    Sure. When all our minds and hearts are fairly
        knit,

Let the Scot do his worst, by sword or wit!

                          [*Exeunt.*

THE RUMP;

OR,

THE MIRROUR OF THE LATE TIMES.

The Rump: or, The Mirrour of the Late Times. A new Comedy, written by J. Tatham, Gent. Acted many times with great applause at the Private House in Dorset Court. London, printed by W. Godbid for R. Bloome. 1660.

Ibid. *The second impression, newly corrected, with additions. London, printed by W. Godbid for R. Bloome. 1661.*

INTRODUCTORY NOTICE.

In the First Edition of this curious drama the names of the principal performers differ from those assigned to them in the second one. Thus Bertlam stands for Lambert, Woodfleet for Fleetwood, Stoneware for Wareston, and Lockwhite for Whitelock. Why this original attempt at mystification was attempted is not very intelligible, unless it was that the author was doubtful how far he was safe in bringing the mighty lords of the Commonwealth *personally* before the citizens of London. Monk's arrival in London, and his extinguishing the Rump, speedily removed all difficulty on this head.

The following Dedication occurs after the Title-page of the Second Edition :—

To my deservedly Honoured Friend, WALTER JAMES, of Ramden House, in Smarden, in the County of Kent, Esquire.

SIR,

As you were pleased to honour me with your acquaintance and friendship,—a hard thing in those *iron days*,—so your merit and favours obliged me to this duty. You had the sight of the brat in its swaddling clouts—my loose papers —ere it was fully shaped for the stage. Yet through that obscurity you were pleased to discover something of hope, that it might live and prosper; and from thence I derived an encouragement to cherish the youngling till it was fit for service, and then turned her off to shift for herself. How she hath pleased is not for me to boast— only I may say this, that those to whom she hath relation wish they had her again, and would make more of her; for though her name may seem to blemish her, I will assure you she carries no obscene pot about her. Transferred to other hands she became a traveller—for which I am to beg your pardon, in that she went without your license, and indeed my privity. But being now upon a second adventure, and somewhat mended in her apparel, I present her to you for your letters of credence; which granted, trebly binds me.

Sir,

Your most affectionate Friend and faithful

Servant,

J. Tatham.

The absence of any Dedication to the First Edition shows that the author did not venture to compromise his patron unless his comedy succeeded.

THE ARGUMENT OF THE PLAY.

FLEETWOOD is fool'd by LAMBERT to consent
  To th' pulling out of the RUMP PARLIAMENT;
Which done, another GOVERNMENT they frame
In EMBRYO, that wants MATTER for a name.
  In brief, by force, FOOLS supplant crafty men,
  The bauble exits, enter KNAVES agen.

J. T.

N

DRAMATIS PERSONÆ.

LAMBERT, ...	} *Competitors for the Protectorship.*
FLEETWOOD, ...	
WARESTON, ...	{ *A Scotch Laird, President of the Committee.*
DESBROUGH,* . . .	)
HUSON,†	} *Colonels, and of the same Committee.*
COBBET,‡	
DUCKINFIELD,§ . . .	)
LADY LAMBERT, . .	*Wife to Lord Lambert.*
MRS. CROMWELL, . .	*Oliver's Widow.*
LADY FLEETWOOD.	
PRISSILLA, ...	*Woman to Lady Lambert.*
TROTTER,‖	*Secretary to Lord Lambert.*
1 TROTTER.	2 A FRENCHMAN.
4 PRENTICES.	4 SOLDIERS.
2 CLERKS *and* 2 DOORKEEPERS *to the Committee.*	

* John Desborough, or Desborogh, was the brother-in-law of Cromwell, whose sister he married, and who wished him to sit as one of the judges at the King's trial. This, however, he declined to do. His first wife predeceased him, whereupon he took a second one in the beginning of April 1658. Granger says "he was clownish in his manners, and boisterous in his behaviour." He is supposed by Noble to have survived the Revolution. See *Lives of the English Regicides*, vol. i. p. 178. London, 1798. 8vo.

† Hewson, originally a shoemaker, rose to high rank as a commander under Cromwell, who placed him as a peer in his Upper House. He had the good fortune to escape to the Continent at the Restoration, where he died.

‡ Miles Corbet, or Cobbet, was a lawyer and clerk of the Court of Wards in 1644. He was a regicide, and was beheaded at Tyburn in 1662, his head placed on London Bridge, and his quarters over the city gates. The latter part of the sentence is conjectured not to have been carried out in consequence of the loyalty of his relations.

§ Robert Duckenfield was proprietor of a good estate in Cheshire, where he was a great supporter of what was called the popular party. He was deputed to sit on the trial of the King, but had the good sense to decline the appointment. His son Robert, who succeeded him, was made a Baronet by Charles II., June 16, 1665.

‖ Probably intended for Secretary Thurlow.

In both editions of the play the following Prologue comes after the names of the performers :—

The author, not distrusting of his play,
Leaves custom's road, and walks another way.
Expect not here, language three stories high:
Star-tearing strains fit not a comedy.
Here's no elaborate scenes, for he confesses
He took no pains in't. Truth doth need no dresses,
No amorous puling passions ; here the lord
And lady rather differ than accord.
What can be in't, you'll say, if none of these ?
It is all one; he's sure the thing will please
The truly Loyal Party ; but what then ?*
Why, truly he thinks them the better† men.
    But if in's progress he does chance to hit
Hab-nab on something that may sound like wit,
Pray take no notice on't; for if you do,
·You'll spoil the poet, and the players too ;
They will grow proud upon't ; and in the street,
Instead of cringing, nod to those they meet.
Yet, now I think on't, 'twill not be amiss,
We'd rather have your Plaudit than your Hiss;
And promise faithfully we will endeavour,
If you do favour this, to please you ever.

* The Loyal-hearted Party ; and what then?   Second edition.
† Wiser.

Geneste, in his account of the English stage, has stated inaccurately that the *Rump* was first acted *after* the Restoration. Such was certainly not the case, as it must have been placed before the public when Monk dethroned the Rump. It had been hastily put together by the author to try the effect it would have upon the metropolitans in regard to the Puritanical autocrats, whose rule was becoming more and more unpopular every day. The failure of the Rumpers to attach Monk to their party, his refusal to coerce the Londoners and take away the city charter, and his compliance with the demand of the country for a new and free Parliament, at once disclosed the unpopularity of the usurping faction. The rejoicings which followed its downfall spread like wildfire through England, and evinced the delight entertained, with few exceptions, by all classes of society. At such a period the comedy of the *Rump* must have had fully as much effect on the public mind as at a later period Lilli-bu-lero had in the expulsion of the Stewarts. Lord Wharton, it is said, "whistled" James II. out of the Three Kingdoms, to which his brother Charles had been called back by the voices of the multitude twenty-eight years before.

That the present comedy had a powerful influence in preparing the people of London for a restoration of monarchy can hardly be doubted, when the preparatory rejoicings, as given by Pepys and Aubrey, cotemporary witnesses, are remembered; and whatever may be said against the drama as a comedy, we apprehend that as an *historical* play descriptive of the times, the living actors, the intrigues of the competitors for power, their instruments, the wives of the would-be rulers, it is admirable,—in a word, that as calculated to further the object in view nothing better could have been constructed.

The text is taken from the first edition, with such corrections and additions from the second one as were necessary. Pepys says he bought a copy in November 1660. This seems to have been the first edition, as the second one did not issue from the press until 1661, so that the previous one must have been a print of the drama immediately after the overturn of the Rump by Monk, an event which occurred in the beginning of February 1659-60.

Previous to this time the friends of the Commonwealth had, with a singular want of sagacity, done all they could to destroy the prestige which had attached to the government of the Protector, by their miserable contentions as to the individual having best right to be his successor. In place of uniting to sustain Richard Cromwell, whose right was originally allowed, they, after permitting him to accept the high office, made his position so uncomfortable that he was without difficulty induced to resign.

Having done so, they set about intriguing which of them should obtain the government of England. Fleetwood and Lambert each had their followers. The former was son-in-law of Oliver, having married his daughter, the widow of Ireton, Lord-Deputy of Ireland, who died on 26th November 1651. The latter, one of Oliver's peers, was, as Lord Lambert, placed in the Upper House. He was a major-general, popular with the army, and greatly liked by the public for his agreeable manners. He had fought gallantly for the late ruler, especially at Dunbar. It was said that his lady had found favour in the eyes of the Protector Oliver; * and Noble, in the third edition of the *Memoirs of the Cromwell Family*, 8vo, London 1787, vol. ii. p. 369, states that Mrs. Lambert "was an elegant and accomplished woman," adding, she was "supposed to have been partial to Oliver the Protector." A very rare poem, entitled "Iter Australe," London 1660, small 4to, after showing how Oliver became Protector by the Black Rod whipping "the Rump out of doors," remarks, some

"Would have him a *David*, 'cause he went
''To *Lambert's* wife, when he was in his tent;'
Other people styled him *Moses* from ' his shining nose.' "

The reference to David is obvious, but where the writer ascertained that Moses had a "shining" nose is not disclosed by him.

On the other hand, General Desborough, the brother-in-law of Cromwell, was an advanced Republican, to whom the appellation of King or Protector was equally distasteful. He was before the Rebellion a private gentleman, subsequently

* See "Newes from the New Exchange; or the Commonwealth of Ladies, Drawn to the Life in their severall Characters and Concevements. London: Printed in the year of women without grace, 1650." Small 4to, p. 10.

a lord of Parliament, and one of Cromwell's major-generals. "His conduct," says Noble, "was as impolitic as his behaviour was rude and uncourtly."[*] Notwithstanding the honours bestowed and trusts conferred upon him, he had sense enough to refuse sitting as one of the judges at the trial of Charles I., and in consequence was not included in the bill of pains and penalties. He was, however, considered a very dangerous person, and, during a long life, was "always watched with peculiar jealousy."

It appears that before the year 1658 Desborough lost his first wife, as Noble quotes an extract from a letter from Swyft, secretary of Lockart the ambassador, then in France, dated London, 17th April 1658, in which he states he had delivered all the letters, "except that to General Desborough, to whose present lodging his servants in the Spring Gardens could not direct me. His lordship was married on Monday last, and has ever since continued at his lady's house." These second espousals must have occurred previous to the Protector's death, which happened at Whitehall on Friday the 3d of September 1658. His son was proclaimed Protector next day. On the 4th of December following he called a Parliament in the ancient form, and summoned his House of Peers to meet upon the 17th January following, and on that day addressed both Houses, as is usual at the opening of Parliament.

Upon the 12th of April 1659 Parliament was dissolved by commission under the Great Seal, whereupon it was understood that the Protectorate of Richard expired. In consequence of this, Fleetwood and some of the general officers of the army published a declaration, inviting the members of the Long Parliament to return to their seats in Parliament, whereupon some forty-one of these worthies attended upon the 7th day of May, who took upon themselves the power to act without a Protector or House of Peers, and commanded that all writs and patents, etc., should run in future in the name of the Keepers of the Liberties of England. A council of state was constituted possessing exclusively the executive power. To this extraordinary usurpation of power the unlucky but well-disposed Richard was compelled to succumb by his sister's husband and his own relations, including his brother Henry, then Lieutenant of Ireland. Thus by their own suicidal act the

* Noble's *Lives of the English Regicides.* London, 1798. Vol. i. p. 178.

Cromwell family extinguished every chance of recovering power in the State. See Pepys, vol. i. p. 12.

From all that we have been able to gather of the life of Fleetwood, we are inclined to believe him to have been a canting hypocrite, who, from possessing a more than ordinary fluency of expression, was enabled to gratify his followers by doses of that unintelligible mystification which gives so much delight to the initiated, but is not particularly delightful to ordinary people. It was for this peculiar gift that the Protector no doubt gave him his daughter. When he did so, he little imagined that his preaching son-in-law would be the first person to assist in the downfall of his own issue.[*]

In overturning the previous government, the originators overlooked the fact that England had not become a kingdom of Puritans; that the army was not composed entirely of saints; that the citizens of London, by a great majority, were not addicted to praying; and that Lambert was not a man to surrender his fair claims to the Protectorship to a set of fanatics. Accordingly, he did not long retain his allegiance to the Rump, for, having given great offence to their high mightinesses, he was, with other dissentients, turned out of Parliament, 12th October 1659. He left London for the north on the 5th November, and reached Newcastle, where he and his troops remained, until the latter, in consequence of General Fairfax having declared for a free Parliament, deserted, and joining him, took possession of York,[†] where they kept up a correspondence with Monk, who, upon Sunday the 1st of January, crossed the Tweed and entered England, from whence he advanced to York, where he was entertained by Fairfax, who, with the gentry of York, entreated him to procure a free Parliament. Lambert was

---

[*] Noble, in his *Memoirs of the Cromwell Family*, 3d edition, London 1787, vol. i., remarks " that the Protector gave his daughter Bridget, upon the death of Ireton, to Lieutenant-General Fleetwood, as he bore, from his property of praying, no small influence in an army composed of Puritanic bigots." Oliver generally made his domestic concerns subservient to his ambitious purposes. Fleetwood had not the abilities of her first husband, which gave his wife much concern, as she saw with much regret the ruin his conduct would bring on herself and children—p. 134. She died at Stoke Newington, and was buried there September 5th, 1681.

[†] 24th December 1659.

considered, during the Protectorate, " as second to Cromwell in courage, prudence, and capacity, but was equal to him only in ambition.   The Protector regarded him with a jealous eye ; and, upon his refusal to take the oath to be faithful to his Government, deprived him of his commissions, but granted him a pension of £2000.   This was an act of prudence rather than of generosity, as he well knew that such a genius as Lambert's, rendered desperate by poverty, was capable of attempting anything."*   Pepys, in his *Diary*, who was a cotemporary, also refers to the poverty of Lambert.

After his dismissal by the Protector, he retired to Wimbledon House.   He became, according to Roger Coke, a successful florist, and had the finest collection of tulips and gilliflowers that could be procured for love or money; "yet, in these outward pleasures, he nourished the ambition he entertained before he was cashiered."†

In August 1659, Lambert defeated Sir George Booth,‡ who commanded a large body of the Royalist forces in Cheshire.   For this important service the Rump Parliament rewarded him with a thousand pounds sterling to buy a jewel.   Whether dissatisfied with the reward, or displeased with his Parliamentary companions, who were more occupied with attending to their own interests than endeavouring to raise him to the Protectorate, he left them in the month of November, and marched northwards with his army, which deserted him, as mentioned previously, and went over to General Fairfax.

Lambert, deprived of his forces, was compelled to return to London, where the Rumpers, as they were designated by the Loyalists, arrested him, Sir Henry Vane, and other members of the Committee of Safety (9th January), and placed them in confinement.   Upon the 6th of March Lambert was committed to the Tower, from which he contrived to escape upon the 9th of April following.   He was captured by Ingoldsby on the 22d, with Cobbet or Corbet, Creed, Okey, and Axtel, near Dauntry, without any attempt at resistance, which was remarkable, for he was a gallant soldier, and had distinguished himself on every occasion.

* Granger, vol. iv. p. 2.   London, 1824.   8vo.
† Coke's *Detection*, vol. ii. p. 76.
‡ Created Lord Delamere after the Restoration

THE RUMP;

OR,

THE MIRROUR OF THE LATE TIMES.

—◆—

ACTUS PRIMUS.—SCÆNA PRIMA.

Enter 3 or 4 SOULDIERS *severally.*

1 *Soul.* Ah, rogues ! the business is done.

2 *Soul.* In a dish, I warrant you.

1 *Soul.* And thrown out o' th' windows :
The town's our own, boys !

3 *Soul.* And all the wealth in't !

1 *Soul.* And wenches to boot, boys !

2 *Soul.* Boot me no boots, 'tis bootless till we
have 'um.

4 *Soul.* Those are commodities, I confess, I fain
would truck for.

1 *Soul.* Thou shalt have them by the belly, lad !

4 *Soul.* Rare recruits after a long march !

1 *Soul.* Gramercy, Bertlam !

2 *Soul.* Heroick Bertlam !

3 *Soul.* The man of men and might !

1 *Soul.* We were oppos'd, and even at push a
pike for't.   Though a wet morning, 'twould have
been dry service had we gone to't.

o

2 *Soul.* Dry blows would ne'er have done't,—some must have swet blood for't ; but 'tis prevented.

1 *Soul.* The nail of Providence was in't.

2 *Soul.* Or the parings rather; but no matter which, 'tis done.

1 *Soul.* Leymor was a stubborn lad, yet Bertlam fitted him, and in his kind too. His rhetoric silenc'd the mouth of his pistol ; it had sent a bad report else, and a home one. But Bertlam, brave Bertlam, that carries charms on the tip of his tongue, acted the part both of a souldier and a courtier, an enemy and a friend, exposing his breast to danger, under the canopy of security ; and all this for us, you knaves ! He told 'um a fair tale, but means to trust them no farther than he can fling 'um.

2 *Soul.* That's some out of commission.

4 *Soul.* Or into prison, or both.

1 *Soul.* We may, lads, in time grow up to something.

2 *Soul.* Ill weeds grow apace, brother, and thou art one of them, and in time mayst reach the gallows.

1 *Soul.* Speak for yourself, brother, I need not your oratory. Well, Bertlam has wit at will; Woodfleet's an asse to him.

2 *Soul.* A meer milk-sop !

3 *Soul.* A whey-brain'd fellow !

1 *Soul.* And of courage as cold as a cucumber !

4 *Soul.* A fool in folio !

1 *Soul.* Ambitious puppet !

2 *Soul.* A general in the hangings, and no better !

3 *Soul.* What think you of Vane ?

1 *Soul.* As of a vain fellow.

3 *Soul.* And what of Haslerigge ?

1 *Soul.* A hangman for Haslerigge, I cry !

2, 3, 4 *Soul.* One and all, one and all !

1 *Soul.* 'Tis Bertlam for my money, boys. He is our general, our protector, our king, our emperor, our Cæsar, our Keasar, our—— even what he pleaseth himself.

2 *Soul.* If he pleaseth himself, he shall please me.

1 *Soul.* He is our rising sun, and we'll adore him.

3 *Soul.* For the speaker's glory 's set.

1 *Soul.* At nought, boy. How the slave look'd when his coach was stop'd ?

4 *Soul.* Like a dog outlaw'd. The pallat of his breech fell down with fear.

1 *Soul.* He told us he was our general.

2 *Soul.* Of what ? bills, bonds, and obligations, or green-sleeves and pudding-pies ?

1 *Soul.* And we told him he was an old, doating fool; and bade him get him home and take a cawdle of calves' eggs to comfort his learned coxcomb, for he look'd but faintly on't.

3 *Soul.* And what said he ?

1 *Soul.* Said he ! I prethee what could he say that we would admit for a reasonable answer ? We were better principl'd then so. Reason and our business were two things ; what we did we did, that was our will; and the word of command lodg'd in our hilts. Alas, poor worm ! Cobbet and Duckinfield show'd him cockpit law, and o'errul'd his rolls. He understood not the souldier's dialect ; the searching language of the sword puzzl'd his intellect—the keenness whereof would have prov'd too sharp for his wit had he been obstinate or persisted in the interpretation ; and therefore very mannerly he kist his hand and wheel'd about.

2 *Soul.* To the place from whence he came.

3 *Soul.* And ere long to the place of execution.

1 *Soul.* No, hang him, he will have his clergy.

2 *Soul.* Is he such an infidel to love them ?

1 *Soul.* Yes, as we do barbers, that is, while they are trimming us.   He'd fain go *à la mode* to heaven.

2 *Soul.* If his foot slip not ; but if it do, his finery is spoil'd, he will be so sootifi'd.

1 *Soul.* He that deals with pitch must expect no better.   Black will to black, quoth the devil to the collier ; but, dost thou think there is a heaven or hell ?

2 *Soul.* Why dost thou ask me that question ? I am a souldier, and so art thou ; let's ne'er trouble our heads about it.   A short life and a merry life, I cry.   Happy man be his dole.

3 *Soul.* And so say I.   While we are here, we are here ; when we are gone, we are gone,—for better or for worse, for rich or for poor.   Amongst the good or the bad we shall find room, I warrant thee, lad, and our General can expect no more.

2 *Soul.* And now you have put us in mind of our General, I mean Bertlam (not Woodfleet, that son of a custard-maker, always quaking), let us as bravely spend his this day's benevolence as he nobly intended it.

3 *Soul.* A good resolution.

1 *Soul.* Rather a proposition, brother.   But where, how, and in what ?

2 *Soul.* Not in rot-gut beer, I will assure you, or muddy ale,—wine for my money !

1 *Soul.* Wine is the life of action ; 'tis decreed
    and I obey.
Blood requires blood ; then from the purple grape
I'll suck my fill, spite of you, Jackanape.
There's poetry for you, gentlemen !

2 *Soul.* A pin for your poetry !   March upon't.
                                        [*Exeunt.*

They go out, and come in again at the other end of
the stage.

1 *Soul.* Bring us wine, there !   Come, who sings ?

A SONG FOR THE SOULDIERS.

2 *Soul.* Though the morning was wet,
          We are merrily met
     In a house more dry then our skin, boys ;
          We'll drink down the day,
          Ne'er question our pay ;
     Let them heartily laugh out that win, boys.
Chor. Then drink a full brimmer to him
               that intends
          For the good of the souldier to labour
          his ends.

     Let him flatter and lie,
     What is't to thee or I,
And ape Noll in ev'ry condition ;
     If we thrive upon't,
     Let all the world want,
And the city kneel down and petition.
Chor. Then drink a full brimmer to him
               that intends
          For the good of the souldier to labour
          his ends.

Souldiers. Hey, boys, come away !   [*Exeunt.*

Enter BERTLAM *and* WALKER *his Secretary.*

Bert. Trotter !
Sec. My lord ?

Bert. Has Lockwhite been here yet ?

Sec. Not yet, my lord. Sir——

Bert. What wouldst thou have ?

Sec. Nothing, my lord, not I.

Bert. Thou hast not thy name for nothing. I see thy tongue will keep pace with thy wit, and still be trotting. I prethee leave off thy impertinences, I have told thee enough on't.

Sec. Why, my lord, and it shall please you——

Bert. I tell thee it does not please me ; 'tis my fear thou'lt be my shame. I sent thee into France to learn some breeding, and thou renderest me the poorest and the pitifull'st accompt that ever porter gave on a sleight errant. Dost thou keep company ?

Sec. Yes, my lord.

Bert. What are they ? of what sort ?

Sec. Of the better, sir.

Bert. 'Tis strange ! thy knowledge being so bad. Are they men of intelligence ?

Sec. I think so, my lord.

Bert. You think so ! sad, I professe 'tis very sad. Were it my case as it is yours, and it behoves you as you assume the title of a secretary, I'de draw men's souls out by inspeculation, and in the inquest of their faculties cull out such matter as would yield advantage to him I had relation to ; and without this, thou neither dost deserve the place thou hast nor art thou fit for company.

Sec. My lord, I have done my endevour.

Bert. A weak one; let Thurloe be your president.

Sec. When your lordship is translated to your highness, and that you have command of the publick purse, I shall be as ready to waste it as he or the proudest of 'um, but I am but a fool to explain myself.

Bert. That time is drawing near.

[*He turns about in wrath with his dapper dagger at his breech.*

Sec. In the meantime I have not been idle; I have done something.

Bert. What hast thou done that may deserve recording?

Sec. Why, I have endevoured to find how the common cry of the town goes as to this day's business.

Bert. That's something, indeed; and how do the people rellish it?

Sec. Rellish it! why, truly, sir, it is thought——

Bert. Thou wilt return to thy vomit.

Sec. Why, truly, sir, it is thought, and if I may speak my thoughts freely, the Rump was but a stinking Rump, and scented so ill in the nostrils of the people that they fear'd a sudden plague attended the concavity, and with much joy blest the rue and wormwood you brought to their conservation.

Bert. Dost thou know what thou sayst?

Sec. I could say more, sir.

Bert. To as little purpose—begone! I would be private; yet if Lockwhite come, admit him.

Sec. Nay, my lord, I warrant here will be the whole fry presently.

Bert. Thou a secretary, and talk so like a fisherman. What fry, you fool?

Sec. Woodfleet and the rest, sir.

Bert. My mind is not at rest while thou are here. Begone——   [*Exit Secretary.*

I wonder Lockwhite comes not; he's a man
Has run all hazards, with as good success,
Except old Noll, as any man I know.
He was his creature, and he now is mine,
And hitherto he has perform'd his part

In my revenge upon that family;
So home, even to their doors, that my disgrace
Lies buried in their infamy.   How now ?

Enter SECRETARY *and* LOCKWHITE.

   Sec. My lord, he's come.
   Bert. 'Tis well ; leave us.
My lord, how goes causes ?
   Lock. They cannot go amiss, sir,
Whilst you are advocate.
   Bert. The sword, thou meanest,
That must decide all controversies.
   Lock. It will do much, sir, but pollicy puts the
best edge to't.
   Bert. And that you have.   Come, my lord, be
      free,—
Where shall we set up our rest ?
We have had tossing times.
   Lock. Indeed, my lord, time hath been tost in a
blanquet; but I hope now we shall use time better
than so.
   Bert. As how ?
   Lock. You may trim him, sir.
You have him by the foretop.
   Bert. If I thought so, I'de hold him fast.
   Lock. Now or never.   If you let slip your hold
you are undone—*aut Cæsar aut Nullus.*
   Bert. But the Remora to that is Woodfleet.
   Lock. Alas ! you know him, sir.
   Bert. True, he's but of a softly nature.
   Lock. A fine commendation for a general, that
should be rough as warre itself.   But he has a soft
place in his head too, and that's worse ; however,
he's a fit subject for your purpose, and therefore,
sir, use him as Cataline did Lentulus,—drill him

along with hope that all this tends to his onely advancement; fools are soon persuaded. And believe me, my lord, that was the very engine made him consent to th' blowing up of his brother, a gentleman in some sense better qualified.

Bert. Ay, but a small nutshell, I am confident, may with ease contain both their courages, yet I know Woodfleet will fleer (he dare not grin) after honour, and is as greedy on't as a cat is of a dish of milk.

Lock. 'Twill be ill bestow'd, sir, if it light on him.

Bert. What, a dish of milk?

Lock. You misinterpret me; honour I meant, sir. If you make him groom of your close-stool, 'Twill draw more from your goodness then his merit, And keep his wife in smocks too, during pleasure. That will be, sir, your highness' pleasure.

Bert. It is not come to that yet.

Lock. Oliver had it; his time is past, and your time's coming on. Princes have power o'er the persons of both sexes.

Bert. Name him no more; I hate his memory.

Lock. I confess I do not much care for't, yet I hate nothing brought or brings me profit. I lov'd the father of the heroicks, while he had a power to do me good; that failing, my reason did direct me to that party then prevailing,—the fagg end of the Parliament. What though I took the oath of allegiance to Oliver; your lordship and others did (without the which I could not have sat there); yet, it conducing not to our advantage, it was an ill oath, better broke than kept; and so are all oaths in the stricter sense. The laws of nature and of nations do dispense with matters of divinity in such a case; for no man willingly would be an enemy to himself. The very beasts do by instinct of nature seek for self-preservation ; why not man, who is the lord of reason ? Oaths ! what are they but bubbles that break with their own emptiness ?

Bert. You say very right, my lord, I am of your opinion.

Lock. Yet the pulpiteirs belch forth fire and brimstone against it. But, my lord, how could I have serv'd my countrey by setting the Dane and Swede by the ears, while the thread for a protectorian interest was spinning here ? How could I have carried on, or rather promoted, the design for Jamaica (though it were in Revilo's name) ? How could I have lopt off those ill branches to the Commonwealth, the Cavaliers and Essex, his discontented reformadoes ? How could I have show'd myself loyal to your interest, by foolling Fleetwood in the disseating of Dick, by his dissolving the Honest Parliament, as they call it, and bringing in the odious Rump ? How could I, in my speech at the Councel of State, have raked up Revilo's ashes, by bespattering him and his family, and told Ireton how Providence had brought things about, and that the hand of the Lord was in't, when I meant nothing lesse ? How could I, under favour, have advised you to this day's enterprise, if I should have startled or scrupl'd at oaths, preferred honesty or divinity before temporal interest or humane reason ? I desire, my lord, in this case you will be my judge.

Bert. Nay, my lord, you are your own judge in this case ; but, in my opinion, you have done yourself but justice.

Lock. And he that will not do justice to himself, will never do it to another.

Bert. You advise well.

Lock. My lord, take it from me, he that will live in this world must be endowed with these three rare qualities, — dissimulation, equivocation, and mental reservation.

Enter WALKER.

Bert. How now? the news with you?

Sec. The Lord Woodfleet, sir.

Bert. What of him?

Sec. My lord, he is come, sir.

Bert. Prethee——thy wit and his may walk together; admit him——I knew I should be troubled with him.   [*Exit Walker.*

Lock. I doubt not but you have prepar'd yourself for the encounter.

Enter WOODFLEET.

Bert. I am pretty well antidoted 'gainst the poyson, — he's here. My lord, your most submissive servant.

Lock. My lord, I cannot complement, but I am in heart your creature, that is, at your disposal.

Wood. Seriously, I profess, I cannot reach your meaning, gentlemen.

Bert. Our meaning's not amiss, sir ;
We know, sir, what we say.

Wood. Indeed, I profess I believe so, gentlemen. I hope things are now in the Lord's handling, and will go on well, and become the doings of Christians.

Lock. The Government has been all this while in the horrid hands of infidels, Jews, Pagans, and Turks. [*Aside to Bert.*]—I must make him up a medly.

Wood. Yea, abomination hath been in the hands
of iniquity.

Bert. But, my lord, those hands are now cut off,
and all our ambition is, that your lordship would
take the Government into the white hands of your
goodness.

Wood. Who? I! Gentlemen — seriously — I
profess—indeed—and by yea and nay law—you
shame me—so you do! I can say no more, alas!
I!

Lock. You! Why, my lord, if you knew yourself as well as I do, you would say more.

Wood. Truely, I think, I have been something
in my time.

Bert. Something! you have been more than
something.

Lock. That's stark nought, my lord, but it shall
pass.							[*Aside.*

[*Within*—Where's my Lord Bertlam? where's
my Lord Bertlam?

Enter WALKER.

Bert. What's the meaning of this?

Sec. The Lord Stoneware, the Lord Huson,
Colonel Cobbet, Colonel Duckinfield, and others
desire your favourable and courteous admittance,
sir.

Bert. By all means, let them enter. But, my
lord, be sparing of your speech, for these are catching fellows, and will interpret strangely. Our aim
is onely to advance your interest.

Wood. You know, my lord, I can keep my
tongue within my teeth sometimes.

Lock. 'Tis a high point of wisdom in you, sir.

Wood. Odd, so they are here. I cry mum.

Enter STONEWARE, DESBOROUGH, HUSON, COBBET,
and DUCKINFIELD.

Lock. The less you speak the better 'twill be,
sir.

Bert. My Lord Stoneware!

Stone. Many benisons lite on you for this day's
wark, my geod loord.

Des. How do you do, my Lord Woodfleet? how
do you, my Lord Bertlam? how do you, my Lord
Lockwhite? and how do you all? Hah!

Wood. The better for your asking, sir.

Des. Say you so? then I'll ask again; and how?
and how?

Hus. And what? and what?

Cob. Your language cannot be translated, brother.

Hus. Let them take me by the meaning, then.

Stone. By th' members, hawd there, my loord, 'tis
sere and faw pley, sirs.

Duck. My lords, I have not been backward in
this day's business, nor any here, I think.

Bert. 'Tis confest, sir; what would you infer
farther upon't?

Duck. And therefore requisite we should know
how things will go.

Lock. As they may, sir. Soft fire makes sweet
malt. You know that, Colonel?

Des. And that I know very well too; and you
have said very well, as much as a man can say, and
no more.

Hus. And that's enough.

Duck. But we are in a chaos, a confusion!

Hus. A meer chaos, a confusion!

Cob. And the people expect suddenly something
from us.

Lock. Why, gentlemen, Rome was not built in a day.

Stone. Mickle wisdome, geod feath, in that, sirs; there's mickle wisdome in that, Ise sure yee.

Bert. At three a clock we'll meet at Wallingford House, and discuss the business further. What say you, my lord?

Wood. I profess I say so too; at three a clock be't, gentlemen. What say you?

Duck., Hus., Cob. We'll wait upon you, my lords. Your servants.

          [Exeunt Duckinfield, Huson, and Cobbet.

Des. I protest I am glad of this with all my heart, for I have business in Smithfield, where my horse stands. Now it comes in my mind, on my conscience the roguish ostler has not given him oats to-day, and the knave's hay is musty, too. Well, my man is such another asse. Farewell, gentlemen, I'll see you anon. If I come not soon enough, pray keep me a place in the councel, or let my vote stand for one,—no matter how.   *[Exit.*

Stone. Au geod rason too, my loord; he's a braw mon this, my leords; yee kenn him weele enough.

Lock. And you too, sir.

Bert. Come, my Lord Stoneware, we presume you are a knowing man; to what kind of Government stand you affected?

Stone. E'en tol what ye plase, sir.

Lock. What think you of a single person? here's my Lord Woodfleet.

Stone. Marry, an he's a braw mon, sir; bet are ye in geod earnest, sirs?

Bert. What else, my lord?

Stone. Bred a God, Ise for him than.

Lock. You see, my lord, how Heaven does raise you friends.

Wood. Seriously I profess, my lord, you know, 'tis none of my seeking.

Lock. [*Aside.* Nor is like to be of your enjoying.] My lord, a word with you,—what if my Lord Bertlam were the man ?

Stone. Reight, sir ! Ou'z in on word ya ha spoken. Aw sir, he's a mon inded, mon, gif Stoneware ha any braines, sir.

Lock. You will live, I see, sir. My lord, he's your friend now.

Bert. No matter whose; he's a required property, and must be used by somebody. And why so melancholy, my lord ?

Wood. I profess not I,—I was thinking 'twas dinner-time.

Bert. Will your lordship please to take part of our small cheer ?

Wood. No indeed, my lord, I thank you, not I ; my wife, I profess, stays for me. Adieu, gentlemen all. [*Exit Woodfleet.*

Omnes. Your servants, my lord.

Bert. Nor you, my Lord Stoneware.

Stone. Ne, in geod feith, sir, pardon me, Ise invited by a gay mon, sirs, tol platters of bra capons, sir, and aw the foles in the eyre, sirs ; I an marry, sirs, tol one a my none countreymen ta, geod feath noow.

Bert. If you please to stay, my lord, y'are welcom.

Stone. God's benizon and mine lite on you, sir ; geod feath, y'are like a bra mon, 'twould berst a mon's hert to part fro yee. Ise e'en yar humble servant, my geod loord.

Bert. You'll stay, then ?

Stone. I marry, sir, wi yar none sell tol deeth, sir, gif ye ta plase, sir.

Lock. I knew a small hair would have drawn him to your table, without this adoe.

Bert. My lord, lead Lockwhite the way.

Stone. Ater yee is geod manners, sir.

                                [Speaking to the L. Lockwhite.

Lock. That's more than you know. My lord, I am your servant.

Bert. Well, I'll break off the complement, then.

                                           [Exeunt.

Act ii.—Scene i.

Enter the Lady Bertlam *and* Prissilla *her Woman.*

Lady Bert. Pris ! Pris !

Pris. Madam.

Lady Bert. Why, how now, Pris ? where hast thou left thy breeding ? in thy other pocket ? Art thou not read in times and seasons ?

Pris. I never was such a fool to put trust in almanack-makers yet, madam.

Lady Bert. What a wench art thou ! and why madam, prethee ? There's a word, indeed, as common as the cries about the town.

Pris. Your ladyship hath us'd me to't.

Lady Bert. I'll break that custome ; 'tis a rude one. Hast thou no wit, wench ? Canst thou pick out no better title for me ?

Pris. In sooth I cannot reach it yet, madam.

Lady Bert. Reach a fool's head of thy own; sure thou art mad, wench !

Pris. The secretary, indeed, sayes, I am a mad wench, but I thank my stars I can make a fool of twenty such as he is, madam.

Lady Bert. Agen ! Can flesh and blood endure this ! I must new mold thy manners. Madam ! There's a gammer's title ;—out upon't !

Pris. Seriously, I know not by what other names or titles to distinguish you, madam.

Lady Bert. I profess thou art dull, abominable dull. Dost thou not know upon what score my dear and second self is gone to Wallingford House ?

Pris. How should I, madam ? I cannot divine.

Lady Bert. Lord help thy head ! Why, he is gone to be made a man, wench !

Pris. Was he not so before ? if not, your lady-ship hath had but an ill time on't.

Lady Bert. The prince of men, you baggage ! Thou art such a dull one !

Pris. I cannot help it, madam, while I remain in ignorance.

Lady Bert. I see I must open thy eyes by way of explanation ! Then know that from henceforth I will be call'd her highness.

Pris. Nay, now you tell me what you would be call'd, I shall obey, your highness.

Lady Bert. It will do well, and 'twill be but your Duty. Prethee tell me how dost think I shall Behave myself in't ?   [*She struts it.*

Pris. Highly well ; you cannot choose, you begin so soon, if it shall please your highness.

Lady Bert. I think I am better shap'd for't than Joan, or what do you call her ?—Cromwell.

[*She surveys herself.*

Pris. Abundantly, for at her best she was but a bundle of f——, madam : Lord, I am so forgetful ! Highness, I should have said.

Lady Bert. That's the word ; con it and be per-fect in't, or I profess you and I shall part.

[*Pris. repeats to herself* — Highness, highness, highness, highness !

P

Enter WALKER.

Lady Bert. What's the news with you ?
Am I sent for to Wallingford House ?
   Sec. No, madam.
   Lady Bert. What a beetle-headed fellow's this !
   Pris. Highness, you changeling ; you must call
her highness.   [*Pris. pulls him by the skirt.*
   Sec. No, and it shall please your highness.
   Lady Bert. It pleases me very well.
                  [*She struts it and surveys herself.*
What's your business ?
   Sec. Gammer Cromwell would speak a word or
two with your highness.
   Lady Bert. Bid the poor woman waite without ;
I'le do her what good I can for her children's sake.
   Pris. Or, rather, for husband's sake, if it shall
please your highness. Good turns ought not to be
forgotten.
   Lady Bert. Thou say'st true, one good turn re-
quires another. He was, I confess, a man, every
inch of him.
   Pris. Ay, and though he was out with my lord
many times, he would be in with you, as the say-
ing is, and please your highness.
   Lady Bert. Well, I care not if I go to her.
   Pris. Your highness will decline much your state,
then.
   Lady Bert. Say'st thou so, Pris ?   Walker, admit
her, I'le hear what the poor creature can say for
herself.   [*Exit Walker.*

Enter WALKER *and* MISTRESS CROMWELL *the elder.*

   Mrs. Crom. I thought I should have staid at the

door till midnight. Marry, come up, Mrs. Minks! Is there such a doe to speak with you? No marvel, indeed.

Lady Bert. Prethee, woman, what wouldst have?

Mrs. Crom. Thy husband by the throat, had I him here! and I could finde in my heart in the meantime to claw thy eyes out, and make thee wear black patches for something, thou proud imperious slut, thou!

Lady Bert. The woman, sure, is lately come from Billingsgate! Pris, ask her how goes oysters there?

Pris. She's very quick of hearing, and't please your highness.

Mrs. Crom. Highness! In the devil's name it is not come to that, sure, yet, is it? Hah! thy husband may be hang'd first, like a crafty knave as he is! Did my husband make him a lord for this,—to ruine our family, or as the word is, indeed, trapan 'um? Curse on the time thy husband was born. He fool'd my son-in-law to betray the innocent babe, my poor child Richard, that our fames are now brought to the slaughter-houses, and the very names of the Cromwells will become far more odious then ever Needham could make the Heroicks! Wo worth the time!

Lady Bert. Pris, I pitty the creature, ne'er trust me. Alas! it weeps.

Mrs. Crom. Thou ly'st, baggage! I scorn thy pitty; my spirit is above it! Let me come at her! As old as I am, I can spoil that fine face my dear deceased lord did so much dote on. Let me come at her! [*Pris holds her.*] Hands off! I'le do't, thou Jezebel!

Lady Bert. She begins to rave. Send her to Bedlam, among her consorts.

Walk. I promise you you shall have clean straw, Mrs. Cromwell.

Mrs. Crom. Out, rogue, rascal, vagabon! a fellow rais'd from the horse heels! dost thou upbraid me too? I'le be the death of thee, if thou com'st near me. O Dick, Dick! hadst thou had but thy father's spirit, thy mother ne'er had come unto this shame! *[She falls back into a chair.*

Lady Bert. Pris, a cordial presently! Odds so, she faints!

Pris. I run, and't please your highness; I have it here. *[Pris. goes in and enters immediately.*

Lady Bert. Prethee give it her. I would not for a hundred pounds she should die here; we should be put to th' charge of burying her.

[Then Pris. offers her the cordial; she starts up, and with her hand casts it on the ground.

Pris. 'Tis a pretious cordial-water of my own making, madam; I hope there's no offence in that.

Mrs. Crom. I need it not, proud woman! I divine this scorne will be reveng'd on thee and thine! *[Exit.*

Lady Bert. Farewel, nought; Th'art better lost then sought.

Pris. She has a notable spirit of her own.

Lady Bert. 'Twill get her nothing, she beats against the wind.

Pris. She's wind-fall'n, and't please your highness.

Lady Bert. 'Tis an ill wind, they say, bloughs nobody good; let her rave and raile, my dearest second self will fare the better for't.

Pris. The fox fares best when he is curst.

Walk. Pris! Pris! a word or two, sweet Pris.

[As they are going off, the Secretary pulls Pris. by the sleeve.

Pris. Why, how now, sawce ? plain Pris ! Am not I her highness' maid of honour ?

Walk. I know thou art a maid of honour, but the meaning of this, dear Pris ?

Pris. The meaning of what, thou novice ?

Walk. That madam is so suddenly turn'd to highness. Is my lord made Protector ?

Pris. No, you dunce ! Well, thou art the simpl'st secretary ! What, must I find thee brains and understanding? Know, then, and grow wise upon't, she will be Protectoress whether he be Protector or not. If he has any honour it must come from her, for aught I see ; she is beforehand with him, and hath install'd herself already. I'm sure my voyce was herald to't, thou piteous thing ! Question the pride and pleasure of a woman ! I will have thee, scribe, to know, the time will come I shall have honour too, and be courted by the better sort.

Walk. Have I been wanting in that duty, Pris ?

Pris. Wanting ! why, thou art always wanting, never provided, still behindhand, never beforehand to a woman ! This I profess, and to thy shame be it spoken. And therefore walk upon't, I have no more to say to thee.

Walk. But I have something to say to thee, O ungrateful Pris !

Pris. Ungrateful ! and why ungrateful, pray ?

Walk. Hast thou forgot the small token I sent thee ?

Pris. It was a small one, indeed, if it came from thee.

Walk. The tweezers out of France ?

Pris. Did travail hither, but were as dull as he that sent them ; they would not cut a feather. Is that your pretious present ? If thou hast no better, walk alone for Pris, she's not for thy company.

Walk. Nay, dear Pris, shall we be married ?

Pris. What, are you so hot, sir ? There's a jest, indeed ; marry before your prenticeship is out !

Walk. What dost thou mean, wench ? prethee kiss me.

Pris. I'le see better clothes on your back first.

Walk. Why, are not these good ?

Pris. Enough, had not a fool the wearing of 'um.

Walk. Thou may'st say anything, Pris ; I may have better.

Pris. When that time comes, and thy wit is more refin'd, I may say something to thee.

Walk. Oh, my dear Pris ! in the meantime let me but kiss thy hand.

Pris. That you may ; but, hear me, be not proud on't, nor take this as a punctual promise from me ; I love myself better then so.

Walk. Yet I may live in hope ?

Pris. If it were not for hope, the heart would break, they say. But odds so, I forget my duty to her highness.

Walk. And so do I, thou hast transported me.

Pris. Not to Jamaica yet !   [*Exeunt.*

Enter MRS. CROMWELL *and the* LADY WOODFLEET.

Lady Wood. Good lady mother, be patient !

Mrs. Crom. Good lady fool, hold your prating ! Was ever mother so unhappy, or children so senselessly ungratious ?

Lady Wood. I beseech you, think not so. Things will make for the best.

Mrs. Crom. Oh, fond girl ! what hope canst thou create unto thyself can save us now from sinking ? We must perish, undoubtedly we must. Though Bertlam carry a smooth tongue to thy husband, it speaks not the language of his heart, for that is rugged.   It will deceive him as it did thy brother, and the late idolized Parliament he set up, out of a malice to thy father's memory, to make it odious, because he pull'd the Babell down ; yet now he has usurp'd that privilege himself.   Let his pretence be what it will, it bears no other weight but that of his ambition, to which thy husband is a property.

Enter WOODFLEET.

Wood. Mother, I profess I'm glad to see you here, ne'er trust me, law.   How do you, forsooth ?

Mrs. Crom. The worse for thee.   I wish I ne'er had known the time occasion'd thee to call me mother.

Wood. Why, forsooth, mother, if it please your highness.

Mrs. Crom. Oh, monstruous, not to be endur'd ! I have been tame too long.   The fool hath found a way t' upbraid my misery.   She had a husband, dear Ireton, my best of sons,—had wit, and by his councel stilted up our honours, which thou pull'st down as fast by thy simplicity.

Wood. I profess, ne'er trust me, I speak ingeniously,—ne'er stur now, I am no such baby neither, as you take me to be, mother.

Mrs. Crom. A mere stalking-horse to Bertlam's pride.   His wife, that minion, doth assume that title I once, and my son Richard's wife, enjoyed. She will be called her highness with a horse pox, while I am call'd old Joan, old Bess, old Bedlam, old witch, old hagg, the Commonwealth's nightmare !   'Tis well if any have the modesty to call me Gammer, or old Mrs. Cromwell, and leave out

many other horrid nicknames.   This infamy and
more thou hast brought on us.   [*She weeps.*

Lady Wood. Good mother, do not weep.

Mrs. Crom. Would I were dead !   Nothing
torments me more than that thy father, who whilst
he liv'd was call'd the most serene, the most illus-
trious, and most puissant prince, whilst that the
fawning poets' panegyricks swell'd with ambitious
epithetes, is now call'd th' fire-brand of hell, monster of mankind, regicide, homicide, murtherer of
piety, a lump of flesh sok'd in a sea of blood, traytor
to God and goodness, an advancer of fiends and
darkness !   Such as these, and worse, could I but
think on 'um, are daily cast into my ears by every
idle fellow.

Wood. I pray, take their names; I profess, mother,
I'le order them, as I am here.

Mrs. Crom. Thou order 'um! alas they value not
so poor a thing as thou art.   Had Dick continued,
he had kept our fame up fair in the world, none
durst have blemisht it.   They tell me that the
time is coming I must make a stall my court, and
learn to thrive by footing stockings; and if that
won't do it, must be (what I ne'er was) a woman of
carriage, either for tubs of ale, as suiting best with
my original condition, or else for oysters.   I was
made for burthens, and am too old and ugly to cry
oringes.   If these trades fail me, then I must turn
bawd ; they think me tough enough t'endure that
tempest, and tell me there's a place call'd Sodom
will receive me and my retinue.   I know it not,
but thus I am made a publick scorn by all men.
And in that, thee nor thine, nor any other that
claim relation to us, are exempted.   And all this by
thy foolery !

Wood. I profess, mother, I will be even with

'um. I know what I know, and there's an end, as I am here.

Mrs. Crom. I would there were an end to our disgraces, which I do prophesie is but beginning. What will become of that fair monument thy careful father did erect unto thy memory before (lest none should do't after) thy death, next to thy husband Ireton's; nay, even of his, thy father's too, and all that living bore a love to him and us? The raging malice of proud Bertlam is so irrisistible, 'twill destroy all.

Wood. I profess, mother, my lord Bertlam is a very honest gentleman, and he loves me well, I profess now to you. Well, I know what I know; few words are best. I am, and must be, the man, when all is done, as I am here.

Mrs. Crom. 'Tis very likely, when all is done, thou'lt be the man will prove their scorn and laughing-stock!

Wood. I profess now, mother, in sober sadness, I scorn the words, so I do. You know what I told you, sweetheart, as I am here?

Lady Wood. Very well, and do believ't, though you, forsooth, are so doubtful.

Mrs. Crom. Doubtful of what? Of that I never heard?

Wood. No more words, but mum, I say, I charge you, sweetheart!

Enter a MESSENGER *from the Committee of Safety.*

Mes. My lord, the councel waites your coming.

Wood. Why, law ye now, as I am here, you thought, I warrant, I should not be sent for neither. I profess, forsooth, mother, you are very hard of belief—— Tell the lords I'm coming.

Mes. I shall, my lord. Most honoured lady, your most humble servant. Your humble servant, madam. [*Exit.*

Mrs. Crom. I have seen this fellow's face before. Methinks he does retain something o' th' duty he paid me formerly.

Lady Wood. Be thou patient, mother, I'le warrant things will go according to your wish.

Wood. Ay, if you'll have some patience ; if not, I profess, mother, I cannot tell how to help it, for I must to coach, that's the truth on't. Sweetheart, pray make much of my mother. [*Exit Woodfleet.*

Lady Wood. Will you please to walk in, forsooth ?

Mrs. Crom. My heart was very heavy when I came hither, 'tis somewhat now at ease, by the disburthening of my oppressing griefs.

Lady Wood. I hope, forsooth, you'll have no cause to create more of them. [*Exeunt.*

Enter Lady BERTLAM *and* PRISILLA.

Lady Bert. Hast thou summoned those inferiour things ?

Pris. What, the ladies of the last edition ?

Lady Bert. Thóse whose husbands have been stygmatiz'd by Noll and Dick with the title of baronets.

Pris. I gave order to Trotter to trot about it, an't shall please your highness.

Enter TROTTER.

Trot. The ladies are coming forth.

Lady Bert. They were not bound to their good

behaviour, but——'tis well, they understand their
duties. Set us our chair of state, and then admit
'um.

Enter LADIES.

Lady Bert. Gentlewomen, for ladies we cannot
call you, your obedience to our commands is well
resented ; if you persever in't you will oblige our
favour. Pris, proceed.

Pris. By what authority, and from whom do you
derive your titles of Madams, I pray ?

Ladies. From our husbands.

Pris. What are they ? of what standing ?

1 *Lady.* Of no long standing, we confess.

Pris. That's a common complaint, and a general
grievance.

Lady Bert. And shall be taken into consideration
for a thing we know. Pris, prick that down in your
notebook. Who made your husbands knights ?

Ladies. Oliver the First.

Lady Bert. Of horrid memory ; put that in your
notebook, Pris.

Ladies. And Richard.

Pris. Of sottish memory. Shall I put down that
too ? 'tis remarkable !

Lady Bert. By all means ; put it down in the
margin, as a hand directing to the rest.

Pris. Of their foolish families ; 'tis done, an't
please your highness.

Lady Bert. What coates of armes do your husbands bear ?

1 *Lady.* Who ? mine, madam ?

Lady Bert. Ay, thine, woman.

Pris. You a lady, and show so little manners !
Forget her highness !

Lady Bert. I pass by their dirty breeding. Woman, we say, what coat of arms does thy husband give ?

1 *Lady.* He bears argent upon a bend gules, three cuckolds' heads attyr'd or.

Pris. Three cuckolds' heads ! Why, one is sufficient in all conscience.

1 *Lady.* 'Tis a paternal coat belonging to the family of the Wittals.

Pris. It may be they were founders of Cuckolds-haven.

Lady Bert. No more of cuckolds, Pris, 'tis approbrious, and intrencheth much upon the honour of our sex. Put that down in your notebook as a publick grievance, and it concerns us to look after, and the Committee of Safety to remedy.

2 *Lady.* 'Tis a material and punctual point to a woman.

Lady Bert. And what does thy husband give, prithee ?

2 *Lady.* He bears three gantlets dexter or.

Pris. Or again ! Your highness may perceive they have had golden times on't.

Lady Bert. Dexter or ! Well, we know he has been an ambidexter all his lifetime, and he shall now give another coat,—a body without a head in a field sable. And what's thine, prithee ?

3 *Lady.* Ours is but *Parte per pale.*

Lady Bert. Parte per pale ! what's that ?

Pris. A motley coat of two colours.

Lady Bert. 'Tis a wonder with what impudence those fellows Noll and Dick could knightifie your husbands ! For 'tis a rule in heraldry, that none can make a knight but he that is a knight himself. 'Tis Zanca Panca's case in Donquixott.

1 *Lady.* If none can make a knight but he that

is a knight, how shall our husbands receive honor from your husband, who is no knight himself?

Lady Bert. Let me alone to dub him.

Pris. You have done that already, and 't please your highness.

1 Lady. If dubbing our husbands will carry it, we can do that ourselves.

Lady Bert. But ours is of greater honor and antiquity, and therefore ought to take place. Receive that as a maxime from us; dispute no further.

Ladies. We shall not.

Lady Bert. Since, being infranchis'd through our grace and favour, you are become members of our Commonwealth, declare your grievances, and we'll hear 'em, whether publick or private.

1 Lady. Begin with the private first, sweet Mrs. Pris.

Pris. This lady complains her husband prays too much, and it takes him off his other business.

Lady Bert. There can be no charity in that man is remiss in his benevolence. Receive that as another maxime. Pris, you mind us not!

Pris. I'm pricking of it down, and't please your highness.

Lady Bert. But it may be he prays when's zeal's on fire, as bells ring, backwards.

1 Lady. And then he rails against the whore of Babylon, and then the people think he calls me whore.

Lady Bert. That's gross, and shows small breeding; we'll have it rectifi'd, it concerns us.

2 Lady. And my husband says I talk in my sleep, and call on men to come to bed to me, and discover his infirmities.

Lady Bert. Oh! have a care of that.

1 *Lady.* Have a care of what ? Were he capable
of more care of me, I should have less care of myself.

Pris. I commend the ladies' resolution.

Lady Bert. And what say'st thou ?

3 *Lady.* Why, truly, I cannot say much. My
husband is a man of reason, and is willing I should
satisfie myself. He knows the failings of women,
and imputes it to the frailty of our sex.

Lady Bert. He's an honest man, I warrant him.

Pris. Such a husband for my money.

1 *Lady.* As you are a lover of women, let the
Act of the 24th of June against fornication be re-
peal'd. Methinks it frights as there were a furnace
in't.

Lady Bert. As there were conveniences in that
Act, which ty'd up men's tongues from babling, so
there were destructive inconveniencies in't, famili-
arity not so frequently used between man and
woman. When know, society is the life of Repub-
licks—Martins the First and Peters the Second.
Indeed, things were rather done in fear then free-
dome.

1 *Lady.* In a free State, who is not free ?

2 *Lady.* I beseech you, in the next place, that
the Cavaliers may not be lookt upon as monsters,
for they are men.

1 *Lady.* And that it may be imputed no crime
to keep 'em company, for they are honest.

3 *Lady.* And men that will stand to their tack-
ling.

Lady Bert. Well, we'll have these amended. What
have you more to say ?

1 *Lady.* Now, Mrs. Pris, to the publick, I prey.

Pris. Whereas several abuses have lately crept
in amongst us.

Lady Bert. That's a small abuse; love must creep till it can go.

Pris. Her highness hath the feeling sense of it, and gropes out the meaning already, you see.

1 *Lady.* We could not go to Hide Park nor Spring Garden so much as with our own busbands.

Lady Bert. Why, what had you to do to go with them ? Could you find no better company ?

1 *Lady.* Good men were scarce ; and then to avoyd suspicion.

Pris. In my foolish opinion that rather bred it. What ! walkt with your own husbands ? How contrary to conscience and high breeding is that !

Lady Bert. When things are settl'd, we'll have an Act that no lady or gentlewoman shall be put to that slavery, but shall have liberty to walk, or —— talk, with whom they please. Now, may a multitude of men's blessings light on you ! Pris, proceed.

Pris. Here's a lady desires a patten for painting.

Lady Bert. 'Tis too great for a subject, we intend it for ourselves, and to that end have employed several persons as our agents in forraign parts, to find out the readiest and securest way for making it, that it may not eat into the cheeks, beget wrinckles, impare the eyesight, or rot the teeth.

3 *Lady.* I have found the woful experience of that.

Lady Bert. We have intelligence of a water that will in two hours' time take the wither'd skin off the face, and a new one shall supply the place. That no lady or gentlewoman, though she have outworn sixty, shall appear above five-and-twenty years of age.

Pris. That makes your highness look so smooth upon't.

Lady Bert. There's no invention for sleeking, glazing, or annointing but we have notice of; and for powders and perfumes, we may be scented a street off.

Ladies. Oh, sweet woman !

Lady Bert. Then, for attyring, and to find out the mazes of fashions,—there's no lady but must follow us.

Ladies. You are at a great charge, sure !

Lady Bert. We are so, but 'tis princely.

[*She rises.*

1 *Lady.* We hope your highnesse will remember the foregoing premisses ?

Lady Bert. Pris, be it your care to mind us. We must to Wallingford House and have 'um confirm'd.

And in the meantime, let our music play
To celebrate the glory of this day !

[*Exeunt.*

ACT III.—SCENE I.

Enter one of the DOORKEEPERS. *He trims up the table, lays the paper and standishes in their places; then enter two* CLERKS *to the Committee.*

1 *Clerk.* The lords are coming !

Door. Are you sure on't ?

Clerk. They are upon us already.

Door. That they are not, I'le assure you, gentleman. However, I will attend my charge. Keep back there ; keep back there ! I say, keep back there ! Make room for the lords there. God bless your honours !

Enter BERTLAM, WOODFLEET, LOCKWHITE, *and*
STONEWARE.

Enter DUCKINFIELD *and* COBBET; *they pass a complement to the rest,* COBBET *takes* STONEWARE
by the hand, DUCKINFIELD *and they walk
together whispering;* BERTLAM, WOODFLEET,
and LOCKWHITE *do the like. After a turn or two*
BERTLAM *speaks.*

Bert. It must be done, my lord; we have nothing
else to take him off.

Lock. Scots, we know, generally are greedy of
gain, and since we have made him President, and
sensible of our secrets, 'tis requisite we do something to stop his mouth.

Bert. Lest he——no matter, it must be done,
my lord.

Wood. Say you so? I profess seriously, if I
thought good would ensue of it, with all my heart.

Cob. My lord, believe us, all we can serve you in
you may command.

Duck. And you shall find it so when occasion
serves, and the Government's new molded.

Stone. Marry, sirs, an I'se sa mold itt; 'twas
neere so molded sen the dam bound the head on't!

Cob. I know there are some ambitious spirits
would have it settled in a single person, but we are
quite against it.

Stone. The faw deel splitt his pipe will be for't
than, for Archibald.

Duck. But my lord Bertlam is a stirring man,
you see.

Stone. Bertlam! Lett Bertlam gang tol bedlam,
in the deel's nam! What ha I to da with him?
I'se yeer humble servant, gentlemen.

Q

Enter DESBOROUGH *and* HUSON.

Des. How do you? how do you? and how do you, my lords and gentlemen all? how do you?

Hus. And how do you? how do you?

Stone. Ah, my geod loords, ken yee me, sirs?

Bert. We shall have up our number anon. Will you please to assume the chair, my lord?

Stone. Marry, and I'se your humble servant, my geod Loord Bertlam.

Des. Come, come, what Government must we have? what Government must we have?

Hus. I, I, I; what Government? Let's know quickly. Come, you talk of Conservetat,—Conservetat,—'tis a hard word, hang't; but there's *tors* in't, I'm sure of that.

Duck. Conservator, my lord! Conservator!

Hus. Conservators let it be, then! When shall we have 'um, when shall we have 'um?

Bert. My lord, we'll think on that hereafter.

Hus. Hereafter comes not yet, then, it seems?

Des. But while the grass grows, the horse may starve.

Cob. Howe'er, gramercy horse, though't has no tail to't.

Stone. Geod feath, sirs, and I'le tell you a blithe tale of a Scottish puddin will gar ye aw tell laugh, sirs.

Bert. That puddin will have no ent to't, good my lord.

Des. I love to hear of a puddin, so it be a bag puddin.

Hus. So do I, if it be a good one.

Stone. Bred agoad, as geod a puddin as e'er was cut up.

Wood. I profess my hair stands on end.

Duck. No more swearing, my lord, 'tis not season-able in this place.

Stone. Harke yee mee than, sirs, mind yee me now or neore. There was a poor woman, sirs, bog'd o'th' Karle the Speaker, sirs ; an heede gie her noought, whilke gard her to let a crack, sirs. I marry, quo the woman, quo now I see my rump has a speaker too. Haw lick yee my tayle noow, sirs ?

Omnes. Ha, ha, ha !

Bert. My lord, I know you have many of 'em, but pray let's mind our business.

Des. Business ! why, there's the thing. I think every man ought to mind his business. I should go and bespeak a pair of mittins and sheers for my sheerer, a pair of cards for my thrasher, a scythe for my mower, hob-nayl shooes for my carter, a skreen for my lady wife, and I know not what. My head is so full of business ; I cannot stay, gentlemen.

Lock. Fy, fy, gentlemen ! will you neglect the business of this day ? We meet to gratifie our friends.

Des. Nay, then, do what you will, so I may rise time enough to see my horse at night.

Lock. Is that it ? Clerk, read what we past the other day ; I mean the heads of 'em. What papers and petitions remain in your hands, referring to this day's business.

Cob. Forbid we should be backward in rewarding such as have done service to the Commonwealth.

Lock. There's money enough, gentlemen.

Duck. If we knew where to find it. However, Clerk, read. To Walter Walton, draper, £6929, 6s. 5d., for blacks for his highness.

Bert. For a halter ! Put it down for Oliver Cromwell's burial. We'll have no record rise up in judgment against us for such a villain.

Lock. But first, let's consider whether that were good service or not.

Bert. However, we'll give him a paper for't; let him get his money when he can. Paper is not so dear, gentlemen, and the Clerk's pains will be rewarded.

Stone. Geod consideration, my geod loord. Bred, sir, that Cromwell was the veryest limmer loone that e'er cam intoll our countrey; the faw deel has tane him bith' lugs by this time for robbing so rich a countrey! bred, sirs, I!

Wood. I profess, my lord Stoneware, you are to blame; I promise you, you are. Why do you swear so?

Stone. Geod feath, I gi you thanks for your chastisement. Ise fit ye, sir, au profess ta, an se gif you ha mee.

Cob. That may bring you profit indeed. Clerk, proceed.

Clerk. To Walter Frost, treasurer of the contingencies, £5000. To Mr. Edward Backwell, £4600. To Mr. Hutchinson, treasurer of the navy, £200,000.

Stone. Ounds, there's a sum! marry, it cam from a cannon sure!

Clerk. To Mr. Backwell more, £326, 16s. 5d. To Mr. Ice, £400. To Mr. Loethur, late secretary to his——

Lock. To Oliver Cromwell, say; leave out highness. You were ordered so before, where'er you find it.

Clerk. Secretary to Oliver Cromwell, £2999, 5s. 7d., for intelligence, and trapanning the King's liege people.

Stone. Marry, sirs, an ye gif so fast, yeel gi aw away fro poore Archibald Johnson.

Lock. Oyl the wheel, my lord, your engine will go the better. Move for him first.

Bert. Be it your business ; I'le do as much for you.

Lock. Content, gentlemen, since we have set this day apart for other business, purposely to gratifie our most concerned friends, let us consider the worth of the Lord Stoneware, a person of eminent fidelity and trust.

Stone. Geod feath, and I ha been a trusty Trojan, sirs.

Wood. We know it very well, sir, I profess, my lord.

Duck. And 'tis but reason you should be rewarded.

Des. I'de scorn to let a dog go unrewarded.

Hus. And so would I, he fawns so prettily.

Cob. My lord, you are witty ; I hope we shall have no more on't.

Hus. And performs his graces to a Scottish pipe so handsomely.

Duck. You may content yourself with that, my lord, he is our friend.

Stone. Geod feath, sirs, an sa I am ; wha denyes it ?

Hus. Nay, my lord, we are not foes ; I am for you.

Des. And so am I, as live.

Stone. Geod feath, weel sed ; ye ken well enough I'se sure I'se a man can serve ye aw, sirs ! Sin ye are so kind, sirs, Scribe, read my paper to.

Lock. You have a petition, then ?

Stone. Geod feath, I had been a very foole els.

Bert. Give us the substance of it.

Clerk. That your honours would be pleas'd, in consideration of his faithful service, and the constant charge he is at, both at home and abroad, to grant him some certain considerable summe of money for his present supply.

Duck. Order him two thousand pounds.

Bert. Seriously, let it be three thousand, gentlemen. You must understand he is much in debt.

Stone. God's benizon lite on your saw, my geod Loord Bertlam.

Hus. Three thousand pounds! Why, half such a sum will buy all Scotland.

Stone. Bred, sir, ye leoke but blindly on't than.

Bert. Gramercy, my lord!

Cob. Well, brother, the time was, a mite of it would have bought all the shooes in your shop (I will not say your stall, for your honour sake), though now you doe abound in Irish lands.

Stone. Y' are my good friend, sir; geod feath, y'ave eene hit him home. Clerk, gang a tyny bit farder.

Clerk. That your honors would be pleased to confer some annual pension upon him.

Bert. Gentlemen, I think it but reason. He has been faithful, and I hold him a good Commonwealth's man, and the rather because Hazlerigge hath so bespatter'd him. Since you have consented to his present supply, let him not suffer for want of a future one. What think you of £400 per annum. 'Tis but small; say, are you willing to it, gentlemen?

Omnes. I, I, I!

Bert. Are you pleas'd, my lord?

Stone. Bred, thare's a question indeed; ounz, sir, ye ha won my heart.

Bert. Then, gentlemen, since my lord Lockwhit's modesty is such he cannot speake for himself, give me leave to become a humble suitor in his behalf.

That you will be pleased to make him Constable of Windsor Castle, Warden of the Forrests, etc., Lieutenant of the Castles and Forrests, with the rents, perquisites, and profits thereof. Gentlemen, I need not instance his faithfulness to us and our designments hitherto. No man here, I presume, but hath been, and is satisfied in himself of his reality; and therefore I am confident you cannot confer a place of so great honour or trust upon a person more deserving. But I submit to your wisdom.

Omnes. 'Tis granted.

Stone. Bred, my good lord, what can ye ask that we sall not grant?

Bert. I have heard some say, that honour without maintenance is like a blew coat without a badge.

Des. Or a pudding without suet.

Bert. You have made him Keeper of the Great Seal! 'Tis honour, I confess, but no salary attends upon't; and bribes, you know, are not now so frequent as they were in Noll's time. Besides, my lord is a person of that honor.

Hus. Well, my lord, let us be brief and tedious; let us humour one another. I love my Lord Lockwhit well.

Bert. I move for a salary, gentlemen. Scobel and other petty clerks have had £500 a year apiece granted to them; I hope he merits more.

Hus. Let him have a thousand pound a year, then; you shall not want my voice, my lord.

Lock. 'Tis a liberal one, my lord.

Wood. I profess soberly, with all my heart.

Bert. Does that please your lordship?

Lock. Your faithful servant, my lord; but if I may be so bold to know from whence I shall receive it.

Cob. Out of the customes; the best place, I think.

Stone. Sure pay, my loord; bred a goad, I'se uphold you now, gang your wayes. On scribe, let us mind meere good warks, wee sall prosper then, aw my saw, sirs.

Bert. Clerk, proceed where you left off.

Clerk. Honyleybres, £3000 upon accompt; Backwell, for £9600; Worseley Aubrey, for £2500.

Stone. Bred, holt for tham. Where the deel sall they ha aw this siller, sirs?

Lock. Ne'er trouble yourself for that, my lord.

Bert. These things must be granted; we know the persons, they are our friends.

Wood. I profess, indeed, brotherly love ought to go along with us all; but when all is gone, when shall we have more?

Bert. Pough! my lord, the city's big with riches, and neer her time, I hope, to be delivered.

Hus. I'le be the midwife, or, what you will call me. I'le undertake to do my office as well as Dr. Chamberlyne can do his.

Des. Well said, brother. What's the matter there?

> [*The Lady Bertlam strives to enter; the Doorkeeper goes to the Lord Bertlam, and whispers him, he riseth and goes to her.*

Bert. I'le wait on you immediately, gentlemen.

Hus. Is the Lord Bertlam gone?

Wood. I profess I know not.

Bert. Why, how now, sweetheart; what make you here?

Lady Bert. Nay, what make you here, then?

Bert. This is not a place for women.

Lady Bert. How so, sir, pray? While thou art here I have as much right to the place as thou hast, if I am John Bertlam's lady; and for aught

I know, my advice may do as well here as thine, for all you perk it so.

Bert. Good sweetheart, return to thy coach.

Lady Bert. Good sweetheart, tell me, am I her highness or not her highness, or what do you intend to make of me ?

Bert. Thou makest thyself seem to be a mad woman !

Lady Bert. Do I so, sir ! I'le be madder yet. Then I'le to the board, and know what they intend to do with me.   [*She strives : Bertlam holds her.*

Bert. Thou wilt not, sure.

Lady Bert. But I will, and hear what they will say to me ! I will be put off no longer !

Bert. Be not so loud.

Lady Bert. I'le be louder, sir ! and they shall hear me ! If I am not her highness they shall not sit there.

Bert. Thou shalt be as high as can be, if thou wilt be patient.

Lady Bert. Patient ! Ay, thou knowst too well I am a patient fool ! Pray, when will the time come I shall be styl'd her highness ? for that I will be.

Bert. I'le tell thee that anon. Prethee, sweetheart, take thy coach.

Lady Bert. Ay, thou thinkst with thy fine words to work me to anything, but if you defer the time too long, you'll find the contrary. Call my man there ! D'ye hear me ? Pray, make haste home.

         [*Exit.*

Bert. Well.

Hus. My lord, we thought you had been gone.

Bert. No, my lord, I have been better bred then so to leave you in the heat and midst of business.

Lock. Nay, I think the heat of our business is

over for this day.   Clerk, see have you any more
papers ?

Clerk. Not any.

Hus. Let us rise, then ; I think we have sate a
pretty time by't.

Des. And my colon begins to cry out beans and
bacon.

Wood. I profess, my lord, it is not I think fit to
put you in mind ; I hope I need not, I profess.

[*They rise.*

Bert. Oh, to move concerning a single person ?

Lock. By all means, for his lordship.

Bert. Seriously, my lords, I hold it would have
been unseasonable ; but at the next sitting it will
fall in course, my lord, and then, my lord——

Lock. We are your creatures.

Wood. Say you so ; I profess, let it be so then.

Des. Come, let us go ; I'm mad to be gone. What
should we stay here for ?

Stone. Marry, an yee speke right, sir.   Scribe,
see aw theise orders be ready for my hond aneust
morne ; meere especially my none, and my geod
loord's heere, that they may gang to the pattent
scribe.   Here ye mee ?

Clerks. They shall, my lord.

1 *Clerk.* Come, sirrah ! here be thriving times ;
some men rise with their breech upwards.

2 *Clerk.* And 'tis very probable may be lasht
for't.   How they divide the kingdome's treasure !

1 *Clerk.* I commend them, they make use of their
time,—make hay whilst the sun shines.   I wonder
my Lord Desborough mist that proverb at the table.

2 *Clerk.* Was ever such language heard at a
council table before ?   They are all made up of
proverbs and old sayings, except *his tamen semper,*
Bertlam and Lockwhit.

1 Clerk. Oh ! those are two precious divels ; but for a fawning and colloguing divel, give me the Scotch divel.

2 Clerk. No more of this, the doorkeeper has ears.

1 Clerk. I would his ears were off, they are not worth the sense of hearing. But come, let's put up our trinckets. A pox on't, I did not think they would have sate so long !

2 Clerk. Thou hast some baggage or other to go to, I'le be hang'd else.

1 Clerk. Thou mayst be hang'd in time ; however, we'll goe.

Door. Well, go your wayes ; you are a precious couple.   [*Exeunt.*

> [*A noise within, crying* — Tom, Will, Harry, Dick, have you a mind to be murdered in your beds ?

Enter a CORPORAL, *and* SOULDIERS *after him in a confused manner, as from their several lodgings.*

1 Soul. What's the matter, corporal ?

Cor. The city's up in arms.

1 Soul. I am glad on't.

2 Soul. And so am I. There's plunder enough,— I am mad to be at it.

Cor. The Committee sate all this night about it. 'Tis said they are up everywhere.

1 Soul. I warrant that dog in a doublet, Haslerigg, is the ringleader.

Cor. 'Tis likely. The news came but within this houre, and the danger that lurks in't hath call'd the Committee together. To-morrow the Prentices intend to petition the Lord Mayor for a free Parliament.

1 Soul. Let 'em; 'tis good fishing in troubled waters.

2 Soul. Must the Rump come in agen?

Cor. I know not. Good lads, make haste, the captain stays for us.

1 Soul. Pox on't, let's ne'er stand buttoning ourselves; we'll leave our doublets behind us.

Cor. No, by no means.

1 Soul. And is't come to that? then, hey for Lumbard Street! There's a shop that I have markt out for mine already.

2 Soul. You must not think to have it all yourself, brother.

1 Soul. He that wins gold, let him wear gold, I cry.

Cor. Well, we shall have enough; 'tis a rich city. Never came better news to the souldiery.

1 Soul. We'll cancel the Prentices' indentures, and bind them to us in surer bonds.

2 Soul. And they shall ne'er be made free by my consent, till they have paid for their learnings.

1 Soul. Methinks I see the town on fire, and hear the shrieks and cries of women and children already; the rogues running to quench the fire, and we following the slaughter. Here lies one without an arm, and he cannot hold up a hand against us; another without a leg, and he shan't run for't; another without a nose, he'll ne'er smell us out; another without a head, and his plotting's spoyl'd; here lies a rich courmogeon burnt to ashes, who, rather then he would survive his treasure, perisheth with his chests, and leaves his better angels to wait on us, you knaves!

2 Soul. Oh, brave Tom!

Cor. I know you have all mettle enough, but our captain stays.

1 *Soul.* Not a minute longer. Hey for Lumbard Street, hey for Lumbard Street!

Omnes. Hey for Lumbard Street, hey for Lumbard Street!   [*Exeunt.*

ACT IV.—SCENE I.

Enter a Company of PRENTICES *with clubs.*

1 *Pren.* Come, boyes, come; as long as this club last, fear nothing, it shall beat out Huson's tother eye. I scorn to take him on the blind side, I'm more a man than so!

2 *Pren.* Thou a man! a meer pigmy!

1 *Pren.* Children are poor worms; I would have you to know that I am the city's champion.

2 *Pren.* Thou the city's champion!

1 *Pren.* Yes; and will spend life and limbe for Magna Charta and a free Parliament.

Omnes. So we will all, so we will all!

1 *Pren.* Why, then, you are my boys, and true sons to the city. Cry up a free Parliament!

Omnes. A free Parliament, a free Parliament!

1 *Pren.* Boys, this was done like men; but do you hear the news? My intelligence is good.

2 *Pren.* What is't, champion? what is't?

1 *Pren.* There's a proclamation come from the Committee of no Safety.

Omnes. For what, champion?

1 *Pren.* To hang us all up if we depart not to our homes. How like you that, gallants? how like you that?

2 *Pren.* This hanging is such a thing, I do not like it; well, I'le go home.

1 *Pren.* Why, now you show what a man you

are. I was a pigmy, as you said but erewhile, but now I say, and will maintain it, thou hast not so much spirit or spleen in thee as a wasp.

Omnes. Oh, brave champion !

1 *Pren.* Will you, like cowards, forsake your petition, and have no answer to't ? Rather let's die, one and all !

Omnes. One and all, one and all !

1 *Pren.* Why, this is bravely said. Now, I'le tell you what you shall do. When the Sheriff begins to read the proclamation, every man inlarge his voice, and cry, No proclamation, no proclamation !

Omnes. Agreed, agreed ! No proclamation ; no proclamation ; no proclamation ! [*Exeunt.*
[*Waving their clubs over their heads.*

Enter HUSON *and his Myrmidons, with their swords drawn.*

Hus. Was ever such a sort of rogues seen in a city ? Come, follow me, I'le so order um.

Soul. Oh, brave colonel ! [*Exeunt.*

Enter PRENTICES *at the other end of the stage, crying, Whoop, Cobler ; whoop, Cobler ! and he pursuing them.*

Hus. Shoot, shoot ! I charge you kill the rogues, leave not one of them alive !
[*A musket is let off within.*

Enter PRENTICES *again, crying, Whoop, Cobler.*

1 *Pren.* Cain has kill'd his brother, Coll. Cord-mayner. He has spun a fine thread to-day.

2 *Pren.* It may bring him to his end.

1 *Pren.* St. Hugh's bones must go to the rack,
and there let him take his last,—Whoop, Cobler !

Omnes. Whoop, Cobler ; whoop, Cobler !

[*Exeunt.*

Enter HUSON, *again pursuing the* PRENTICES ; *they
continuing their cry, Whoop, Cobler ! Turnip
tops are thrown at him as from house tops. Boys
run in.*

Hus. From whence come these ? Search that
house, and every house. I vow there's not a street
free from these rogues. [*Exeunt.*

Enter the PRENTICES *severally.*

2 *Pren.* Where hast thou been, champion ?

1 *Pren.* Where none but a champion durst be.

2 *Pren.* Where's that ? where's that !

1 *Pren.* Stand here and admire. You are be-
holding to me, I have past the pikes to meet you,
and swet for't. I tell you I have been at Guildhall, and what I have done there let histories
record. I'le not be my own trumpet.

Omnes. What didst thou do there ?

1 *Pren.* Do you see this small engine ? 'Tis a
good one, and has been trusty to his master. I say
no more.

Omnes. Nay, good champion ; what, what ?

1 *Pren.* How dull you are ! With this, I say,
heartily charg'd and ram'd, under my apron closely
hid, *Latit anguis in herba* (there's Latin for you,
rogues !), I got into the yard.

Omnes. What then, what then ?

1 *Pren.* By good fortune I espy'd a very fine
fellow, some officer, no doubt, he did ran dan so.

Omnes. But, prethee, be plain and short.

1 *Pren.* No, it was home; the sting of my serpent hath either kill'd him or lam'd him downright, I warrant he troubles us no more this day. [*A drum is heard within.*] Heark, the rogues are marching! Let them go and be hang'd, they shall not abide here; I have given them an earnest penny already, and if they come again, I'le double it. Well, boys, when they are past, we'll go and drink the King's health, say boys.

Omnes. Viva le roy, viva le roy!   [*Exeunt.*

Enter LORD BERTLAM *and* LORD LOCKWHIT.

Bert. My lord, you will still endear me.

Lock. A duty so oblig'd cannot be paid too often. My prayers go with you, my most honoured lord.

Bert. If I return, my lord, command my heart. In the meantime, let not your friendship cool.

Lock. My body shall be ice first.

Enter SECRETARY *and* LORD STONEWARE.

Bert. My Lord Stoneware, this is a high piece of kindness, indeed.

Stone. Marry, I'se come toll kiss your none hand, sir, ere ye gang anenst the limmer loowne.

Enter WALKER *and the* LADY BERTLAM.

Bert. Your servant, my lord. Walker, are you ready?

Sec. Yes, my lord.

Bert. Direct the Lord Stoneware to the blue chamber, where I'le attend your lordship.

Stone. Your very humble servant, my loords.
     [*Exit Secretary and Stoneware.*
Bert. I know she's clogg'd with passion, and 'tis not fit a Scot should understand it.

Lock. You have done wisely in that, my lord.

Lady Bert. Have I stay'd long enough ? May you be spoken with yet ?

Bert. Why not, sweetheart ?

Lady Bert. Am I a wife, or no wife ?
         [*She weeps.*
Bert. My only joy and comfort. Why dost weep ? There's not a tear but wounds me. Prithee, leave ; I'm sure th'ast no occasion for't.

Lady Bert. Did Noll do so by his wife Bess, that puss ? He had some care of her, and made her what her heart could wish ; but I have nought but empty promises.

Bert. Will you believe me ? This gentleman——

Lady Bert. He's a lawyer, and may lie.

Bert. He's my friend.

Lady Bert. 'Twas a by-compliment, I confess ; but I believe he knows more then you do. Pray, sir, say, shall I be what I will be, as he says ?

Lock. The power is now in his owne hands, and doubtless my lord's so wise he will not part with't.

Lady Bert. Say you so ? Then, prithee, kiss me, John ; ne'er stir, I shall so love thee.

Bert. But we forget the Lord Stoneware.

Lock. H'as got a Scottish fog in's mouth by this time.

Lady Bert. Hang him, 'tis such a boorish, stammering fellow, I can't endure him.

Bert. But he's a property, if I return victorious, I must make use of ; therefore, prithee, sweet, be moderately sparing in thy language ; let it not soar so high, lest it prevent my tow'ring thoughts of

R

their fruition, and clip those wings should hover thee to greatness.

Lady Bert. I'le not tye my tongue up for no man's pleasure living. I think I am a free woman, no bond-slave, sir!

Lock. But under favour, madam, when you weigh the advancement——

Lady Bert. I weigh it not a rush, nor shall I fee you for your counsel, sir!

Bert. He's a good man, sweetheart.

Lady Bert. Let him be ne'er so good, I'le have my will.

Bert. I prethee do.

Lock. I trust I have not angred you, madam?

Lady Bert. Again madam! Let his goodness be what it will, I'm sure he hath but ill breeding.

Enter WALKER.

Walk. My Lord Stoneware is going, sir.

Bert. Odds so, indeed, we have been too uncivil; come, sweetheart, my lord, will you please to walk in.   [*Exeunt.*

Enter two or three SOULDIERS.

1 *Soul.* How now, gentlemen? you are upon the merry march, I hear!

2 *Soul.* Ay, a pox on't; we shall have little cause, I fear, to call it a merry one.

1 *Soul.* Well, I thank my stars our regiment stays here at the well-head, you rogues, where there is plenty of all things.

2 *Soul.* What says Pluck?—The worser knave, the better luck!

3 *Soul.* But do you hear me, sirrah? for all that, your colonel may be hang'd, for killing his brother Cobler.

1 *Soul.* I hear no harm; I'm not to answer for him. But prethee tell me, d'ye think there will be bloody noses?

2 *Soul.* Those that have a mind to't, let 'em give or take 'em; hang him that fights a stroke, for my part.

3 *Soul.* Or mine either. Our company swear they'll all be hang'd first.

1 *Soul.* The General is like to be well hop'd up with such souldiers.

2 *Soul.* Why, what would you have us to do? If the General cannot agree them, let 'em fight it out themselves, and the devil part 'em, I cry!

3 *Soul.* If they will fight, we'll make a ring for 'em.

1 *Soul.* They say that General Philagathus is a gallant stout man, an excellent souldier, and a marvellous honest man.

2 *Soul.* Then we have the less reason to fight against him.

3 *Soul.* Nor will we fight against him.

1 *Soul.* But, brothers, let me advise you to have a care what you say, lest you make your words good, and be hang'd in earnest; there are rogues abroad.

2 *Soul.* Ay, too many; I thank you, brother, for your advice.

3 *Soul.* Alack! we talk away our time; let's go, let's go.

1 *Soul.* Nay, sure, brother souldiers, we will not part with dry lips.

2 *Soul.* What you intend to do, do quickly.

1 *Soul.* Come away, then.

Enter WALKER *and* PRISSILLA.

Walk. Now, Pris, what think you now ?

Pris. Why, truly, Secretary, I think thou wilt be a brave fellow when my lord returns.

Walk. You will let me kiss you now, I hope.

Pris. No indeed, Secretary, I will not make you so bold yet.   If you return safe and sound, and in good plight, that is, my lord's brows circled with laurel, and people smell you out to be a Secretary of State, 'tis very probable you may have admittance to my lip, and something else in a lawful way.   [*Calls within*—Walker, Walker !

Walk. These words have comforted my heart ; I'm overjoy'd, trust me now !   Odds so, my lord's upon taking horse.   Ah, ah ! dear Pris.

Pris. Sigh not, man, thou shalt have it ; come, take livery and seisin, and adue.

Walk. Oh, so sweet as the honeycomb !
                                   [*Kisses her.*

Pris. Have a care you do not surfeit with't.
                        [*Calls within*—Walker !

Walk. I must be gone.   Dear Pris, once more !

Pris. Why, law you now, give you an inch and you will take an ell.   I shall be troubled with you——   [*Kisses.*

Walk. No, truly, Pris——   [*Calls within.*

Pris. Why, you are bold indeed !

Walk. Oh, heart ! oh, fates ! why should such lovers part ?   [*Exit Walker.*

Pris. Well, go thy wayes for a modest asse ; thou mightst have had something else, hadst thou press'd me to't.   But the fool will make a fine husband ; when he comes to taste the fruit, he'll so love the tree !   'Tis a sweet thing for a woman of know-

ledge to meet with a man of ignorance, and better
to keep him in't.   My Secretary, I see, never read
Arratine; if he had, he would have been furnish'd
with more audacity.   Lord ! how honour creeps
upon me ; I shall be ladifi'd, there's no doubt on't.
How my ears will be fill'd with madams !   And,
Will your ladyship be pleas'd ?   What will your
honour have to breakfast ?   How do you, madam ?
I am come to give you a visit, madam !   Will you
go to Hide Park to-day, madam ?   How does your
good lord, madam ?   Did you sleep well to-night,
madam ?   Is your dog recover'd of his fit, madam ?
Your faithful servant, madam !   Have you any
service to command me, madam ?—This her highness despises.   I am as proud as she, and methinks
it sounds very well.   Madam !   Why, 'tis a word
of state !

Enter SCULLION-BOY.

Scul. Mrs. Pris, Mrs. Pris ! you must come away
to her highness presently !
Pris. Why, how now, sauce ?
Scul. Sauce ! why, what are you, pray ?   Will
you come away ?   I'le tell her.
Pris. I'le have you boxt anon, sirrah, for this !
                                            [*Exeunt.*

Enter PRENTICES *severally.*

2 *Pren.* Champion, how now, champion ?   What
news, champion ?
1 *Pren.* Nay, what news do you say, then ?
3 *Pren.* Bertlam is gone.
1 *Pren.* The devil and John a Cumber go with

him! Well, I hope General Philagathus will so pay his jacquet!

2 Pren. He will be forc'd to turn it.

1 Pren. That he hath done often enough already.

3 Pren. The rogues were well mounted.

1 Pren. May the horse founder, and the foot die in ditches! My prayers go along 'em.

2 3 Pren. Oh, brave champion!

1 Pren. Come, gentlemen, if you have any chink go along with me; we'll drink Philagathus' health. How they look at one another!

2 3 Pren. Faith, champion——

1 Pren. Speak no more, your countenances betray your meanings; I perceive your masters are not so tender-hearted as mine. He's honest, lives in hope, allows me the merry sice a day to spend till better times come.

2 3 Pren. Thou art happy, champion.

1 Pren. You shall participate of that happiness! 'Twere pitty such proper fellows as we are should part without drinking a health to noble Philagathus his successe.

2 Pren. Well, champion, we'll make you amends.

1 Pren. Let the mends make itself; come away, begon. [*Exeunt.*

Enter WOODFLEET, MRS. CROMWELL, *and* LADY WOODFLEET.

Wood. How say you so, forsooth, mother? as I'm here.

Mrs. Crom. I say thy folly will undo us all.

Wood. I profess, mother, as I'm here, you always harp upon one string. Ne'er stir, as I'm here, and like the cuckoo, have but one note, ne'er stir now.

Mrs. Crom. What ! dost make of me a hooting-stock ?

Wood. No, I profess, not I ; I know my duty, as I'm here.

Mrs. Crom. Thou wouldst fain seem a souldier and a courtier, but thou art neither.

Lady Wood. Good mother, be not so bitter ; he's an honest man.

Mrs. Crom. Hang honesty ! 'tis mere foolery. Thy father had more wit then to be thought one of that needy crue. Could ever man have given the power out of his own hand as he hath done, and to his enemy, a fellow as fierce as *aqua fortis*, and will eat into the very marrow of our families ?

Wood. I profess, mother, you may be mistaken for all this ; he is in some sense but my servant.

Mrs. Crom. And he'll become thy master, to thy shame. Why didst not go thyself ?

Wood. Why ? I profess, whether you believe it or not, mother, I am the greatest man in the nation.

Mrs. Crom. Until a greater come ! How stupid art thou ! Girle, prithee instruct him.

Lady Wood. 'Twould ill become me, sure, to teach my lord. I ne'er was guilty of that crime yet ; he knows his own business best.

Wood. I profess, mother, you are such a strange woman, I know not what to say to you. Had not General Philagathus, like a fool, made this disturbance, I know what I had been this time.

Mrs. Crom. Thou hadst been neither better nor worse then what thou art, the common tavern and town table-talk.

Wood. Why, I profess, mother, you are not so well spoken of neither, for all you look so.

Mrs. Crom. That's 'long of such an idiot as thou art.

Lady Wood. Nay, mother, indeed you do not well. He's my husband; I ought not to suffer this.

Mrs. Crom. Good lord! it seems he plays better at tratrip with thee then thy husband Ireton did. Thou couldst find tongue enough for him, or there's foul lyars if this March-pane fellow did not melt in your mouth in his lifetime.

Lady Wood. I thank you, mother.

Wood. What's that, what's that she says, sweetheart?

Lady Wood. Nothing, my lord, worthy your notice.

Mrs. Crom. Had not a fool rid thee, thou hadst known thy duty better. So much for that! Farewell! [*Exit.*

Lady Wood. Nay, good mother.

Wood. Let her go, sweetheart; the house will be the quieter, I profess.

Lady Wood. She is my mother, my lord.

Wood. And I'm your husband, my lady; as I'm here, I think so. I profess, I know not anybody cares for her company.

Lady Wood. She does not come to trouble you, sir.

Wood. Yes, she does, I profess, and very much. I was just thinking of State affairs, and she has put all out of my head. The Committee have no reason to thank her, to my knowledge.

Lady Wood. Why, my lord?

Wood. Why, the citizens are mad for a free Parliament; the counties are all up; and is it not time to look about us, I profess?

Lady Wood. Indeed, my lord, you say right.

Wood. If a free Parliament sit once, what will

become of us? I profess we must secure ourselves as well as we can. The Rump, as the wicked call it, must and shall come in agen, I profess.

Lady Wood. What will become of your friend, the Lord Bertlam, then?

Wood. I profess, I care not. Your mother takes me for a fool, but let me alone to deal my cards, the Speaker and I are reconciled. But, sweetheart, I profess I must be gone; I say no more. Bertlam, Stoneware, and Lockwhit are knaves, downright knaves! I profess they have fool'd me all this while; it will now turn to 'em, I profess. Let 'em suffer.

Lady Wood. I understood, my lord, they were your friends.

Wood. But I have found 'em out. Say no more; will you go in, sweetheart? I profess, I must be gon.

Lady Wood. I obey you, my lord. [*Exeunt.*

Enter LADY BERTLAM *and* PRISSILLA, *her waiting Gentlewoman.*

Lady Bert. I wonder, Pris, that none of the modern poets have been here with their encomiums since thy lord went?

Pris. It may be Helicon is dry'd up, or their brains are turn'd to addle.

Lady Bert. Well, I'm resolved to make him that brings me the first copy Poet Laureat, provided he brings victory in't. I will dispose of my places myself, and be Lord Steward myself, or it shall cost me a fall. Lockwhit, for all his art, shall never carry it.

Pris. How, her highness become Lord Steward?

Lady Bert. No matter for that, profit and service will come by't. I'le have the ordering of all places both above and below stairs, and so give out to the people.

Pris. And good reason too, bir lady.

Lady Bert. A counsellor! a foolish fellow; at every end he calls me madam!

Pris. Truly, there was one call'd me madam too tother day. Lord, we women are so frail! I thought myself a madam in good earnest.

Lady Bert. Ay, Pris, thou mightst, and be proud on't; but I, I think, am somewhat above that.

Pris. A story, so please your highness.

Lady Bert. I will have eight gentlemen ushers, —that puss Bess had foure; two shall bear up my train.

Pris. Rather foure, and it shall please your highness; that pettyfogger Loethur's wife had one, and, as I'm a Christian, another foolish fellow went bare before her,—no countess could have been better man'd. Well, it will come to my turn shortly; but that the wicked Rump is sat, there lies my fear. Oh, Woodfleet, Woodfleet! thou art stark nought.

Lady Bert. What sayst thou, Pris?

Pris. I was thinking, and it please your highness, what a canary bird Woodfleet was, to settle the Rump, the abominable Rump, and pretend so much love to my lord and master.

Lady Bert. His love is not worth the inquiring after, wench; as for the Rump, I smell 'tis stale already, and must be pepper'd when thy lord returns. Dost think, wench, it shall have a sitting place then? No, I warrant thee. He that jerkt it when he came out of the west, will do the like when he comes out of the north.

Pris. Ay, and it shall please your highness, if he return with victory.

Lady Bert. Ne'er fear it, wench. I have sent for Lilly, and wonder he stays so long; 'tis such a dreaming fellow.

Enter a SERVANT *and* MASTER LILLY.

Serv. Here's Master Lilly, an't please your highness.

Lady Bert. How now, Lilly? hast thou don what I commanded thee?

Lilly. I have examined the Zodiack, searcht the twelve houses, and by my powerful art put the whole regiment of gods and godesses out of order; Saturn and Jupiter are by the ears, and Venus will be rampant, assisted by Mars, the god of battailes.

Pris. This makes for your highness. I love mischief with all my heart!

Lady Bert. How stands my husband's fortune?

Lilly. In the Alnathy of Aries, or as some others have it, Salhay, being the head of Aries.

Lady Bert. Aries! what is that Aries?

Pris. A monster, I warrant it.

Lilly. 'Tis a signe, and signifies a ram.

Lady Bert. You rascal, do you put the horns upon my princely husband?

Pris. It may be a new piece of heraldry.

Lilly. He's subtle, politick, and crafty.

Lady Bert. Thou hitst pretty well there.

Lilly. Then in the Allothanie, or as some have it, Alhurto, being the tail of Aries, I find him eloquent, prodigal in necessity, proud, inconstant, and deceitful.

Lady Bert. Dost thou abuse me, rascal?

Lilly. No such matter.

Pris. Alas ! he means innocently, for these are virtues given to most of the male kind.

Lilly. He's there denoted to be fortunate in warfare.

Lady Bert. Go on, fellow !

Lilly. In Adoldaya, being the head of Taurus.

Lady Bert. Taurus ! what's that ?

Lilly. A bull.

Lady Bert. Dar'st thou horn him again ?

Lilly. 'Tis a signe.

Pris. A very ill signe, the signe of the bull. But he does not mean, and it shall please your highness, the town bull of Ely.

Lilly. Has your lord a mark or mold upon his members ? If he has, he vanquishes his enemies.

Lady Bert. He has that, Pris, I'm sure on't.

Pris. You are best acquainted with his secrets.

Lilly. For Mars being with the moon in the Sextile aspect, encourages men of war, and in the Trine promises success.

Lady Bert. I'le love that Trine while I live for't.

Pris. I wonder where the fellow got all these hard words.

Lilly. Lose not an inch of your state, lest you diminish the lustre of that planet predominates.

[*She struts it.*

Lady Bert. Why, sirrah, you grow saucy. Pris, let the foot-boy pay the fellow for his pains.

Lilly. I hope she does not mean to pay me with kicks. Is she angry ?

Pris. No, no; you have only put her in mind of her majesty, she loves you ne'er the worse for't; you must flatter her.

Lilly. I have been bred to't. I take my leave of your highness.

Lady Bert. But take thy reward with thee. Thou
art sure of what you sayst?

Lilly. As sure as if I had the planets in my hand.
A man can say no more.

Lady Bert. Well, go thy ways, and if thy judgment falter, to second thy gold chain expect a
halter. [*Exit Lilly.*] Pris, what dost thou think
now?

Pris. How can I think amiss? He's a notable
man; I'le get him into the larder one time or other,
and I'le make him show me all.

Lady Bert. Show thee all, wench! out upon't.

Pris. What, the lilly and the rose; I promise
you, for aught I see, the lilly is the best flower in
your garden.

Enter a SERVANT.

Serv. Here's a letter from my lord to your highnesse.

Pris. Hast ne'er a one for me from the Secretary?

Serv. Yes, Mrs. Pris.   [*Exit Servant.*

Pris. So, this fellow is saucy; I must take him
down a button-hole lower. Good news, no doubt
on't; and then we shall have such bonefiring. I'le
read my Switter-com Swatter-com's letter anon.
But her highness begins to look pale upon't; I do
not like this changing countenance.

Lady Bert. Thy lord is murder'd!

Pris. Then my honour goes to the dunghill! A
pox of Lilly and his legion of devils!

Lady Bert. Murdered in his fame, his honour;
the souldiery have forsaken him.

Pris. If that be all, no matter, madam.

Lady Bert. Even call me what thou wilt.

Pris. I should have call'd you highness, I confess, but I hope you are not offended. Lilly is a mere rogue; I'le never endure a lilly hereafter. 'Tis a flattering flower, and stinks abominably.

Lady Bert. He writes me word he'll be in town this night; he's sent for by the Rump.

Pris. Oh, nasty Rump! But an't shall please your highness, shall I seek out for eight proper striplings to man your highness, and four spring-cits to trick up your train; a French taylor, that has a yard thus long; a cook, whose nose will not offend your sawce by dropping in't; a gentleman sewer, that can dance before your dishes; an able carver, to cut up your custards; a taster, that hath a sweet breath and no rotten teeth; a baker, whose hands is not mangy? Who shall be Lord Chamberlain, groom of the stool, your maids of honour, your starcher, your tyrer, yeoman of your cellar, yeoman of your pantrey, yeoman of your pastrey, clerk of your kitchen, clerk of the roles? Lord! I'm even out of breath with reckoning up your servitors.

Lady Bert. How now, audaciousness?

Pris. Why, seriously, I dreamt last night, an't please your highnesse, that we have been but princes in disguise all this while, and that our vizors are now falling off; and who would think that dreams should come to light so?

Lady Bert. Now could I tear my flesh, all my hopes are lost.

Pris. No; you say there's one a coming.

Lady Bert. How? This Woodfleet's wife will o'ertop me!

Pris. Pull her eyes out, and then let a dog lead her.

Lady Bert. Well, I'le do something.

Pris. I'le see your second so good, and 't please your highness.   [*Exit.*

Enter three or four PRENTICES.

1 *Pren.* Hy, boyes! the noble General Philagathus lay at Barnet last night.

2 *Pren.* Say'st thou so, champion?

1 *Pren.* And the pityful, dityful Lambert, one
of Donquixott's lords, is in the Tower. H'as been
a whipster all his lifetime, and now is become a
staid gentleman.

2 *Pren.* Well said, champion!

1 *Pren.* No more of that, if you love me. Noble
Philagathus must be the city's champion; I'le resign
my office, and yet be loyal still.

Omnes. Who will not? who will not?

1 *Pren.* Then you are my boyes again. Do you
not observe how the phanaticks are trotting out of
town? Some of the rogues begin to mutiny.

2 *Pren.* Hang 'em up, then, I cry!

1 *Pren.* So say I, by thousands! Noble Philagathus enters with love, and they go out with
curses; or, like the snuff of a candle, stinkingly.

3 *Pren.* I'm sure they have eaten our masters up.

1 *Pren.* Even to their bowels; that trading is
become a meer skelliton.

2 *Pren.* Now, I hope, we shall see better days.

1 *Pren.* Ne'er fear it, lads. Philagathus is right,
and sound to the very core.

2 *Pren.* What will become of our exchange merchant?

1 *Pren.* What! he that turn'd part of the house
of God into a den of theeves?

3 *Pren.* The very same, the very same.

1 *Pren.* Let him hang himself, and when he is
cold meat, the divel carbanadoe him for a breakfast.
But heark! they are marching out, and [*Drums*

heard within] Philagathus and his honest soldiers are coming in. Oh, let's see um! let's see um!

Omnes. By all means, let's see um.

[*Exit running.*

ACT V.—SCENE I.

Enter MRS. CROMWELL *and the* LADY BERTLAM. *They meet at several doors.*

Mrs. Crom. Bless my eyesight! What, her highnesse without her train! Where is that pretious bird thy husband cag'd? His wings are clipt from flying. Faith, now this comes of treachery! Had he been true to my son Dick, he might have still continued honourable, and thou a lady; and now I know not what to call thee.

Lady Bert. Thy rudeness cannot move me; I impute it to thy want of breeding.

Mrs. Crom. My want of breeding, Mrs. Mincks!

Lady Bert. We cannot expect from the dunghill odorous savours. Were our affections greater than they are, they merit not half the contempt and scorn persues thy wretched family, and the memory of thy abhorred husband.

Mrs. Crom. How durst thou name him but with reverence! he that outdid all histories of kings or Keasors; was his own herald, and could give titles of honor to the meanest peasants — made brewers, draymen, coblers, tinkers, or anybody, lords. Such was his power; no prince e'er did the like. Amongst the rest, that precious piece thy husband was one of his making.

Lady Bert. Would we had never known these painted titles that are so easily washt off!

Enter WOODFLEET.

But yonder comes the cause of all our miseries.

Wood. Ne'er go, yonder's my mother! I profess, as I'm here, I'de rather meet, ne'er stir, a beggar in my dish, so I had, as I'm here.

Mrs. Crom. And art thou there? Nay, ne'er hide thy face for't, though thou mayst be asham'd of all thy actions.

Wood. Why I, forsooth, mother? I profess, ne'er go, not I, mother, as I'm here.

Mrs. Crom. Call me not mother. Thou hast ruin'd my children, and thyself too, like a fool as thou art!

Lady Bert. And me and my husband, like a knave as thou art!

Mrs. Crom. Would ever coxcombe have committed such folly?

Lady Bert. Or ever changling done the like? Jack Adams is a man to thee!

Wood. I profess, indeed, law, you are strange folks; I profess, ne'er go, law. Cannot a man, as I'm here, pass the street, I profess, law?

[*Walks about the stage, they following him.*

Lady Bert. Hang thee, thou'rt good for nothing!

Mrs. Crom. But fleering and fooling.

Lady Bert. And how do you, forsooth, I profess?

Mrs. Crom. And truly, I know what I know, and there's an end.

Lady Bert. Of an old song. Few words are best.

Mrs. Crom. Ne'er go, I'm the greatest man in the nation, I profess, I ne'er stir now. Think you what you will, forsooth, mother, as I'm here.

Wood. I profess, ne'er stir, as I'm here, there's-no end uring it, law now, as I'm here; and there

S

fore farewel, as I'm here, for I'le be gone, ne'er stir
now.   [*Exit running.*

Enter PRENTICES *with clubs.*

2 Pren. Now, champion, what think you of your
General Philagathus?

1 Pren. A rope on't, I know not what to think
on't.   Was ever such a rape committed upon a
poor she city before?   Lay her legs open to the
wide world, for every rogue to peep in her breech.

3 Pren. 'Tis monstrous !

2 Pren. Is this the city's champion?

1 Pren. Well, on my conscience, he's honest for
all this.   The plaguy Rump has done this mischief.
Well, club, stand stiff to thy master; somebody
shall suffer for't.   I say no more.

2 Pren. We shall be coop'd up shortly for hawks-
meat in our cellars, while they possess our shops
and feast upon our mistresses.

1 Pren. Well, I'le warrant the souldiery will be
honest for all this, and then we'll sindge the mag-
gots out of the louzy Rump, or else swindge me.

Enter the 4th PRENTICE.

4 Pren. News, boys ! news !

1 Pren. From whence ?   From Tripulo?

4 Pren. From Guildhall, you knaves.   We shall
have a free Parliament.

Omnes. Hy, hy, hy !   [*They make a shout.*

4 Pren. The General and the city are agreed, and
he has promis'd it.

1 Pren. Oh, noble Philagathus !

2 Pren. Brave Philagathus !

3 Pren. Honorable Philagathus !

4 *Pren.* Renowned Philagathus !

1 *Pren.* Now, you infidels ! what think you now ? Has your fears and jealousies left you, or will you still damn yourselves up with dirty suspicion. You that spoke, even now, you should be coop'd up for hawks-meat shall be cramm'd up for capons, your cellars shall become warehouses, your shops exchanges, and your mistresses persons of honor.

Omnes. And what shall we be ?

1 *Pren.* Squires of the body. Honor sufficient enough for men of our rank, gentlemen.

Omnes. Oh, brave champion !

1 *Pren.* I tell you I will have no more of that. Where is Lilly now ?

2 *Pren.* In one of the twelve houses.

1 *Pren.* We'll fire him out of 'em.

3 *Pren.* How will the man in the moon drink claret then ?

1 *Pren.* Claret is best burnt, sir, by your leave.

3 *Pren.* Ay, but Lilly has eighteen houses.

1 *Pren.* A baker's dozen. We'll fire the odd end first.

Omnes. A match, a match ! we'll do't.

1 *Pren.* But now I think on't, we must have no firing of houses, there's a statute against it. Better once wise than never.

Omnes. Oh, brave Sack !

1 *Pren.* We'll be merry to-night, I'm resolv'd on't, or else never let prentices presume to be honest agen, and therefore follow me. God bless the General !   [*Exeunt.*

Enter WALKER *and* PRISSILLA.

Pris. Now, Secretary, where's your titles now ?

Not so much as a title of 'em remaining, all sunk in the sandbox.

Walk. I'm between Silla and Carybdis, I must confess ; and thou hast gravell'd me, my dear Pris.

Pris. Hang your dog poetry, it made my lord thrive so ill as he did. I think thou didst infect him ; he us'd to have a serene brain, and courage good enough. Sure the viccar of fools was his ghostly father. Be beat without a blow, there's a mystery indeed !

Walk. Truly, Pris, my lord could not help it.

Pris. Not help it ! there's a jest indeed. I'm sure he has helpt himself into prison for't, let who will help him out again. What course wilt thou take now, Secretary ?

Walk. Not horse-coursing, Pris ; I'de have thee know that.

Pris. Why, thou'rt pretty well timber'd for such an imployment. Canst thou make pens ?

Walk. Yes, and ink too, Pris ; I tell you but so.

Pris. There will be a trade indeed for thee.

Walk. Nay, and the worst come to the worst, I can teach to dance.   [*He frisks about.*

Pris. I confess thy sword is alwayes dancing.

Walk. That's the *à la mode* is learnt in France.

Pris. Come, if thou canst dance so well, let's have a frisk, if thou dar'st.

Walk. Truly, Pris, I have not my pumps in my pocket.

Pris. 'Tis well thy mother left thee wit enough for an excuse.   [*He draws.*

Walk. That is not all. Look here, I can fence too !

Pris. What dost thou mean to do ?   [*She starts.*

Walk. Set your right foot forward, keep a close

guard, have an eye to your enemy's point, extend your arm thus. [*She runs, and he follows her.*

Pris. Lord, lord! the man is mad, sure.

Walk. Traverse your ground, sometimes reverse —as thus! Give back then; come on agen, play with his point. If he makes a pass, put it by; make a home-thrust thus, run him through, and he falls, I warrant you. [*She screams.*

Pris. Put up thy fool's bawble there; I profess I'll call my lady else. [*He puts up his sword.*

Walk. Why, did it fright thee, Pris? Seriously, I did but show thee what skill I had at my weapon.

Pris. Thou wouldst make a rare fellow to fence before the bears, if there were any.

Walk. Why, Pris, I dare say I can kill any man living that can't defend himself.

Pris. Ha, ha, ha! I am of thy mind;—that can't defend himself!

Walk. Why, Pris, such as fight must take all advantages.

Pris. And I that do not fight will take the advantage to leave thee and thy foolery. [*Exit.*

Walk. Nay, dear Pris, ne'er go; I'll follow thee. [*Exit.*

Enter PRENTICES *with faggots upon their shoulders; they pass the stage whooping and hollowing.*

Enter again, whooping and hollowing, with rumps of mutton upon spits.

Omnes. Roast the Rump! roast the Rump! [*Exit.*

Enter a BOY *upon a coltstaff carried by two, and others following him, whooping and hollowing.*

1 *Pren.* Silence, silence, I say!

Omnes. Silence, silence there !
1 *Pren.* Gentlemen all, I tell you plain,
My rump does itch, and we shall have rain.
              [Exeunt whooping and hollowing.

*A piece of wood is set forth, painted like a pile of
faggots and fire, and faggots lying by to supply it.*

Enter PRENTICES *and* SOULDIERS.

1 *Pren.* Come, gentlemen, you are welcome. Sit
down, bring some drink there ; 'tis a night of jubile ;
we'll want to drink while the rump roasts.
                  [A form is set forth.

Enter one with drink.

Here's health to your noble General.
   Soul. Thank you, young man.
     *[Racks are set out, one turns the spit with Rump
     on't.*
1 *Pren.* Baste the rump soundly.
2 *Pren.* It bastes itselfe, it has been well fed ; a
dog take it ! But pray give us some drink too, we
are almost dry roasted.

Enter FRENCHMAN.

French. Begarr, dis be very lite night, me can
find my way to my loging, begarr, very well if me
not take a cup too mush by the way. Now, garsoone, what be de matter vitt you ?
   Prentices. Some larshan for the bonfire, monsieur.
   French. Bonfires ! begarr, me tinck de grand
divell be in the bonfires. Here, garsoone, what be
you ? Vill a vou dore larshan to de bonfire ?

Enter MUSICIANS.

Musicians. We are musicians, and will give you a lesson, monsieur.

French. A lesson! dat be very good; begarr, me love itt vitt all mine heart; alle, alle vic moy to de bonfire, begarr, furbone company de souldate [*they go to the bonfire*] dece Angletar, me love dem vitt all mine heart; play a lesson, or, begar, me vil brake a your fiddells.

Omnes. Oh, brave monsieur!

French. Furboone, begarr, now give me de merry song, me give you de larshan.

[*Musicians play a short lesson.*

Souldiers. Have you this song? 'We came from Scotland.'

Musicians. Yes sir.

French. Begarr, me vill have a dat.

Song.

We came from Scotland with a small force,
   With a hey, down, down, a down a!
     But with hearts far truer than steel
       We got by my fay,
       The glory o' th' day,
     Yet no man a hurt did feel.
      [*All sing the tune, and throw their hats about their heads.*

When Bertlam first our army did face,
   Hey, down, down, a down a!
     He look'd as fierce as the devil.
      We feared a rout,
      But he wheeled about,
     The gentleman was so civil.
      [*All sing the tune again.*

Our General marcht with the countrey's love,
  With a hey, down, down, a down a !
  All persons to him did address ;
    Small money we spent,
    For we found as we went
  Good friends, and here find no less.
                            [*Sing all again.*

French. Furboone, begar furboone, done moy de toder cup burn a de Rump.

1 *Pren.* That has been often done in your countrey, monsieur.

French. Begar, me vill dance about de bonfire ; come vit me, men.   [*They dance about the bonfire.*

Omnes. Oh, brave monsieur !

Enter PRISSILLA.

Pris. Let my lady say what she will, I will see the bonfire.

French. Begar, metres, you be a very fine shentile-veman ; begarr, me dance one time vitt you ; nay, begar, you noe serve a me soe.

Pris. I cannot dance, indeed, sir.

French. Begarr, me vill have on touch vitt you, metress.

1 *Pren.* What ! before all this company, monsieur ?

French. Datt me vill, begarr !

Pris. Well, if I must dance, play 'Fortune my Foe.'

1 *Pren.* No, 'Sellinger's Round.'   We are beginning the world again.

French. Me vill have none of dat, me vill have a de corrant of de foot sa saw.   Come, metres, lend a me your hand ; courage, courage, metress !
                            [*Sings a tune, they dance.*

Pris. Well, now, indeed, I must be gone, sir.

French. Begar, me vill see you to your loging! pardon a moy.

Pris. By no means, I shall be knock't o' th' head then.

French. Mee no care for dat, par ma moy, adue! Jee vou remercy pour dis boone company. Adue, petit garsoone.

Omnes. Adue, monsieur!

2 Pren. What are you resolved to do? Every man to his home, or shall we make a night on't?

Omnes. A night on't! a night on't!

1 Pren. Come to the next bonfire.

Omnes. To the next bonfire! to the next bonfire!
[*Exeunt, hooping and hollowing.*

Enter LOCKWHITE, STONEWARE, HUSON, *and* DESBOROUGH.

Des. We have played our cards fair.

Hus. I deny it, we have not played our cards fair.

Stone. Bred, sirs, then yee have plaid them faw, and that's faw play, geod feath, sirs.

Lock. A fool had the shuffling of them, the game had gone better else.

Stone. The faw deel himself was trump, sirs. I think, sirs, wee ha had nee geod luck, sirs, this bout.

Lock. We are lost, sirs; utterly lost!

Hus. No, sir, we are found—caught in a net of our own making.

Des. Thou wouldst give all the shooes in thy shop to be out of't.

Hus. Is there no remedy, my Lord Lockwhite?

Des. No remedy against the king's evil.

Stone. Bred, hees no doctor, sirs ; hees my noble lyer, sirs.

Hus. Who's Keeper of the Great Seal now ?

Des. Where will you find your £1000 per annum now.

Stone. Bred, sirs, doe yee give ? do yee give ? hees gatt nought, sirs, neither of any the gifts I had geen me, geod feath.

Des. Heark you, Mr. Lawyer, have you e'er a *habulus corpulus* to remove us from the storm is coming ?

Hus. With a syssers, razer, or—what a devil do you call it ?

Des. You are politick; will you sell a pennyworth of pollicy, sir ?

Stone. Bred, he had meere need buy some to save his cregg, sirs.

Hus. Come, let's leave the law in the lurch, and every man shift for himself. Adue, Mr. Lawyer.

Des. Adue, Mr. Lawyer.

Stone. Adue, Mr. Lyer.   [*Exeunt.*

Lock. How monstrously have I expos'd myself to th' dirty censure of the basest creatures, things never mentioned but with scorn ; and now I am become the thesis unto theirs ! The very cobler reads a lecture to me, and I'm convinc'd, I should amend my manners, and become loyal dictates long before divinity discovered ! There's no sin like that we know, and that we surfeit in.

Enter WALKER.

Walk. Do you want any pens or ink, pens or ink ? Will you fence, or will you dance ? What pens and ink do you want, gentlemen ?

Enter PRISSILLA *with her basket of oranges and lemons.*

Pris. Fine Civil oranges ! fine lemmons !   Fine Civil oranges ! fine lemmons !   Methinks it sounds very well.   A pox of her tallnesse for me, no matter ; ne'er repine, wench, thy trade's both pleasant and profitable, and if any gentleman take me up, I am still—fine Civil oranges ! fine lemmons

Walk. Pens or ink !   Pens, pens or ink !

Pris. 'Tis he——   Walker !

Walk. Pris ! my dear Pris !

Pris. Why, how now, Secretary?   Thou seest my words are come to pass, I knew what a lord thou wouldst be.   But Fortune's a whore !

Walk. A whip take her !   But shall we meet now, Pris ?

Pris. I think we are met, Walker, although un-happily.

Walk. I mean, upon equal terms.

Stone. Will you buy a geodly ballad, or a Scott spür, sir?   Will ye buy a geodly ballad, or a Scott spur, sirs ? anything to live in this world.   Bred, if I should gang intoll my none countrey, my cregg would be stretcht two inches longer then 'tis.   Will yee buy a geodly ballad, or a Scott spur, sirs ? will a buy a line, a Jack-line, a line, a Jack Bertlam's line ?

Walk. 'Tis the Lord Stoneware !

Pris. No more lord then thyself, Walker.   Let's have some sport with him.   Fine Civil oranges, fine lemmons !   Will your lordship buy any lemmons and oranges ?   Fine Civil oranges, fine lemmons !

Walk. Ink or pens, ink or pens !   Will your lordship buy any ink or pens for the Committee of Safety ?

Stone. Bred a geod, what a whore and a knave is this ?

Enter DESBOROUGH.

Des. Turnips, turnips, turnips hoe ! Did ever lord cry turnips before ? But a pox of lordship; would I had my old farm over my head again. Turnips, turnips, turnips hoe ! Turn up, mistress, and turn up the maid; and who buyes my long turnups, ho !

Pris. He does it rarely well. Fine oranges ! fine Civil oranges ! fine lemmons !

Walk. Ink or pens ! ink or pens for the Lord Desborough !

Stone. Bred, 'tis he indeed ; these are witches, sure. How does your geod lady, sir ?

Des. What, my Lord Stoneware ?

Stone. Ne, bred a geod, I'me ne meere a loord then yer neeneself ; my honoor is in the dust, sir.

Enter one-eyed HUSON.

Hus. Have you any old boots or shoes to mend ? I have helpt to underlay the Government this twenty years, and have been upon the mending hand, but I fear now I shall be brought to my last, and therefore ought to mind my end. Will you buy shoes for brooms, or brooms for shoes ?

Pris. Or a knave for a whip, or a whip for a knave. Fine Civil oranges, fine lemmons !

Walk. Ink or pens ! ink or pens ! How do you, my lord ?

Hus. Dost mock me, fellow ? Who are these ?

Stone. My geod friend !

Des. Brother Huson ! and how, and how ?

Hus. And what, and what? and pox o' that, and
that. Let's imbrace, however.

Enter MRS. CROMWELL, *with* BOYS *after her.*

Mrs. Crom. What kitchen stuffe have you, maids?
Was ever princess brought to such a pass? What
kitchin stuffe have you, maids?
Boy. Gammer Cromwell, our maid calls you.
Mrs. Crom. Where, you rascall?
Boy. In my——
Mrs. Crom. You rogue, do you abuse me? I'll
claw your eyes out.
[*Flings down her tub and runs after him.—Exit.*

Enter again presently, and takes up her tub.

Mrs. Crom. Oh, Dick! Dick! did ever I think
to come to this! What kitchin stuffe have you,
maids? have you any kitchin stuffe, maids?
Pris. Fine Civil oranges, fine lemmons! Will
your ladyship buy any oranges and lemmons?
Mrs. Crom. Dost thou mock me, bagage? I'll be
at thee presently.
Walk. No, indeed, she does not; 'tis Pris, my
Lady Bertlam's woman, and I am Walker, her
secretary.
Mrs. Crom. How! thou hast walkt fair indeed.
Where is her highnesse now?
Pris. They say she intends to cry fresh cheese
and cream.
Mrs. Crom. She has brought her hogs to a fair
market.
Hus. And so we have all, methinks.
Mrs. Crom. What, art thou there too?

Stone. Bred, an I'se here ta, and my geod Loord Desborough ; bred a geod, heere's eene a jolly company.

Mrs. Crom. It somewhat palliates my miserie, that in afflictions you like sharers be.

Pris. Come, let's mind our business, words are but wind. Fine Civil oranges, fine lemmons ! [*Exit.*

Walk. Ink or pens, ink or pens ! Will you buy any ink or pens ? [*Exit.*

Stone. Will yee buy a geodly ballad, or a Scott spurr ! Will yee buy a Jack-line, a Jack Bertlam's line, or a line for a Jack a Bertlam. [*Exit.*

Des. Turnips, turnips, turnips, hoe ! Turn up, mistress ; and turn up, maid ; and turn up, my cousin, and be not afraid of a long, long red turn-up, ho ! [*Exit.*

Hus. Boots or shoes, boots or shoes to mend ! [*Exit.*

Mrs. Crom. What kitchin stuffe have you, maids ? what kitchin stuffe have you, maids ? [*Exit.*

Enter LOCKWHITE.

Lock. I am a poor lawyer, gentlemen, and can show you *legerdemain* for your money ; no *hocus pocus* like me. I have two hands, neither of them disabled from taking fees. Have you any causes to split ? for that's my doom ; my bag is a receptacle for them. I am for that cause brings me most profit, be it good or be it bad ; but, indeed, have been better experienced in the bad, and now would fain follow the good cause, and turn honest. But a man shall hardly grow rich then, you'll say, and then 'twill vex a man.

Howe'er, I'll try't ; for, to my grief, I find
Riches ill got do scatter with the wind.

Have you any work for a poor housell lawyer ?
for a poor, honest lawyer. I am your next man,
gentleman.

Ambition and base avarice, adue !
Howe'er your glory's seen, they are not true.

EPILOGUE.

'Tis done ; and now to censure. But be just,
Th' Author's name's committed to your trust.
You have here in a mirrour seen the crimes
Of the late pageantry changeling times.
Let me survey your brows ;—they are serene,
Not clouded, or disturb'd with what y'ave seen !
None whose grand guilt appears toucht to the quick
And in revenge would 'gainst their mirrour kick.
Nor in a corner can I one descry
Sneaking, that dare give Bellarmine the lie ;
So that we do conclude the Author's fear
Is now remov'd ; there's no phanatick here.
You are a glorious presence, clear as day,
And innocent as buds that sprout in May.
'Tis you must gild our hemisphere, and give
A life to us who willingly would live.
Then, if you please to grant us our request,
Signe us your servants, and we'll do our best.

GREAT obscurity exists as to the subsequent career of Major-General Lambert, who was upon the 14th June 1662 convicted of high treason with Sir Henry Vane, and sentenced to death with him, but who was banished to the island of Jersey, "where he remained till his death, which happened about thirty years after," whilst Sir Henry was executed on Tower Hill. What became of Lady Lambert has not been ascertained.

In the last edition of Grainger there is this entry : "Lambert" sitting "painting. Se ipse pinxit. J. Smith, fecit." I was credibly informed by one of the family residing in Oxfordshire, and who is in possession of the original pictures, that it is General Lambert. It certainly is not Lambert the landscape painter, as classed in Bromley. Then follows this *notandum:* "Major-General Lambert took up his pencil for his amusement, after Cromwell had wrested his sword from his hand. He painted flowers, which he was fond of cultivating. He is supposed to have learned his art of Baptist Gaspara."* That the General was a cultivator of flowers is undoubted ; but if the assertion of his being a painter is correct, it is the only instance of any of Cromwell's generals having a taste for the fine arts.

This much is obvious, that the fall of Lambert removed one obstacle in the path of Monk, who had, in his progress south, begun to ascertain the state of opinion in the north of England, and the general feeling in that part of the country as to the position of the self-constituted rulers of the land, which was anything but favourable, and that the general feeling was for a *free* Parliament. At Leicester, in his march to London, he was met by two spies of the Rump, specially sent to dissuade him from encouraging in any way the general desire for a free Parliament. These worthy representatives of their tyrannical masters were deceived by Monk, who, to use a common Scottish adage, "was not so green as cabbage like," and the result of their communings was to obtain from the Rumpers an order for the removal of the soldiers in London, in order that there might be no collision between

* London, 1824, vol. iv. p. 72.

T

them and the army from Scotland to support the rulers that were, and to oppose the machinations of the factious portion of the citizens. This requisition was without hesitation acceded to, and the troops from the north quietly took the places previously occupied by those of the south.

In this manner Monk entered London at the end of January, and what followed can best be described by two contemporary writers, evidently unknown to each other, but both concurring in almost every particular. The two authorities referred to are John Aubrey, Esq., a well-known antiquary, who was in London when Monk arrived, and whose biographical accounts of men of eminence of his time were made for the use of Anthony-a-Wood, and have been printed from the original MSS. in the valuable collection of letters in the Bodleian Library, in three volumes, 1813, 8vo. The first extract is from the " Life of Monk."

"OLIVER, PROTECTOR, had a great mind to have him home, and sent him a fine complementall letter, that he desired him to come into England to advise with him. He sent his Highnesse word that if he pleased he would come and wait upon him at the head of 10,000 men. So that designe was spoyled. Anno 1659-60, Feb. 10th (as I remember), he came into London with his army about one o'clock P.M., he being then sent for by the Parliament to disband Lambert's armie. Shortly after he was sent for to the Parliament House, where in the House a chaire was sett for him, but he would not in modesty sitt downe in it. The Parliament (Rumpe) made him odious to the citie purposely, by pulling down and burning their gates (which I myself sawe). The Rumpers invited him to a great dinner, Februar, shortly after, from whence it was never intended that he should have returned. * The members stayed till 1, 2, 3, 4 o'clock ; but at last his Excellency sent them word that he could not come. I believe he suspected some treachery."†

Further on Aubrey continues : "Thredneedle Street was all day long and late at night crammed with multitudes crying out *A Free Parliament! a Free Parliament!* that the air rang with their noises. One day, viz. February 1,

---

* In a note Aubrey says, "Of this I am assured by one of that Parliament."

† The Rumpe of "a house" was the wooden invention of General Browne (a woodmonger).—AUBREY. *Letters from Bodleian Library*; vol. iii. London, 8vo, p. 154.

he coming out on horseback, they were so violent that he was almost afrayd of himselfe, and so to satisfy them (as they use to do importunate children), *Pray be quiet, you shall have a free Parliament.* This about seven, or rather eight, as I remember, at night, immediately a loud holla and shout was given, all the bells in the city ringing, and the whole city looked as if it had been in a flame by the bonfires, which were prodigiously great and frequent, and ran like a train over the city, and I sawe some balconies that began to be kindled. They made little gibbets and roasted rumps of mutton. Nay, I saw some very good rumpes of beaf. Health to King Charles II. was drank in the streets, by bonfires, even on their knees; and this humour ran by the next night to Salisbury, where was the like joy; and so to Chalke, where they made a great bonfire on the top of the hill; and from thence to Blandford and Shaftesbury, and so to the Land's End; and perhaps it was so over all England. So that the return of His Most Gracious Majesty was by the hand of God."

Next comes the statement of Pepys, whose *Diary* is *omni exceptione major.* Vol. i. p. 24.—"Met Monk coming out of the chamber where he had been with the Lord Mayor and aldermen; but such a shout I never heard in all my life, crying out, 'God bless your Excellence!' Here I met with Mr. Lock, and took him to an ale-house; and when we were come together, he told us the substance of the letter that went from Monk to the Parliament, wherein, after complaints that he and his officers were put upon such offices against the city as they could not do with any content or honour, it stated that there are many members of the House that were of the late tyrannical Committee of Safety; that Lambert and Vane are now in town, contrary to the vote of Parliament; that many in the House do press for new oaths to be put upon men, whereas we have more cause to be sorry for the many oaths that we have already taken and broken; that the late petition of the fanatique people, presented by Barebones, for the imposing of an oath upon all sorts of people, was received by the House with thanks; that therefore he did desire that all writs for filling up of the House be issued by Friday next, and that in the meantime he would retire into the city, and only leave them guards for the security of the House and Council. The occasion of this was the order that he had last night to go into the city and disarm them, and take away their charter, whereby he and his officers said that the House had had a mind to put them upon things that should make them odious, and so it would be in their power to do what they would with them.   We were told that the Parliament had sent Scott and Robinson* to Monk this afternoon, but he would not hear them ; and that the mayor and aldermen had offered their own houses for himself and his officers, and that his soldiers would lack for nothing.   And, indeed, I saw many people give the soldiers drink and money, and all along the streets cried, 'God bless them !' and extraordinary good words.   Hence we went to a merchant's house hard by, where I saw Sir Nich. Crisp, and so we went to the Star Tavern (Monk being then at Benson's).   In Cheapside there was a great many bonfires, and Bow bell and all the bells in all the churches as we went home were a-ringing.   Hence we went homewards, it being about ten at night.   But the common joy that was everywhere to be seen ! the number of bonfires ! there being fourteen between St. Dunstan's and Temple Bar, and at Strand-bridge I could at one time tell thirty-one fires ; in King Street seven or eight ; and all along burning and roasting and drinking for rumps, there being rumps tied upon sticks and carried up and down.   The butchers at the Maypole in the Strand rang a peal with their knives when they were going to sacrifice their rumps.   On Ludgate Hill there was one turning of the spit that had a rump tied upon it, and another basting of it.   Indeed, it was past imagination both the greatness and the suddenness of it.   At one end of the street you would think there was a whole lane of fire, and so hot that we were fain to keep on the farther side."

It must have been in February or March 1659–60 that the comedy was originally performed, and it could not have been brought out at a more suitable time than when the London citizens, liberated from the tyranny of their rulers, were giving such decisive evidence of their joy.   The exhibition of Fleetwood, Lambert, their wives, and the leading members of the Rump, on the stage, could not fail to ensure the success of the piece, and materially aid the Royalist party.

* These were the same individuals that had been sent to Monk at Leicester. Scott was originally an attorney, and had accumulated considerable wealth. He was executed after the Restoration as a regicide. Robinson appears to have escaped.

THE CHARACTER OF THE RUMP.

LONDON :

PRINTED IN THE YEAR THAT THE SAINTS ARE
DISAPPOINTED, 1660.

THE CHARACTER OF THE RUMP.

A RUMP is the hinder part of the many-headed beast, the back-door of the devil's arse a peake, tyranny and rebellion ending in a stink, the State's incubus, a crab Commonwealth with the but-end formost; 'tis a town-ditch swelling above the walls, a sink taking possession of the whole house, the humours left behind after the substance of the body politic is purg'd away by the devil's potions, the tumour of the breech, *Caninus apetitus in ano*, the epilogue grown greater than the play, the close of the will crept into the place of *in nomine Dei, Amen*, the whore of Babylon with her arse upwards ;—'tis like a comet which is all tail, and portends no lesse mischief, or you may call it the tail of the great dragon, and 'tis a thumper, for the devil's tail in Chaucer, being stuck in this, would look but like a maggot in a tub of tallow, and yet he saith—

> " That certainly Sathanas hath such a tail,
> Broader than of a pinnace is the sail."

If you would reach me the equator, or rather one of the tropiques, I would give a shrewd guesse at its abominable bignesse. But 'tis best measured with the sword, as there is one hath done it to my hands—*Saint George* kill'd the dragon, but *George Monck* kill'd the dragon's tail. 'Tis pity to blurr this sheet with its prodigious nature, unlesse we mean to make it a winding-sheet for their Rump-

ships, but that is needlesse; for they have another
scene to act, under the gallowes, it being just
they should corrupt the aire being dead, that made
it their businesse to oppresse the earth whilest they
were living. Its mother is rebellion, and the devil
its reported father; but the truth is, it owes its
first being to the Pope, who that time made the
devil a cuckold; folly and self-interest were its
nurses, but the noble General *Brown* was its god-
father. 'Tis observ'd that *Pride* first rais'd them,
and pride it was that gave them their first fall;
when *Noll*, like an expert mountebank, gave them
a glister of opium, which made the Speaker dumb,
and (oh, wonder!) kept Sir *Arthur's* everlasting
wag-tail'd tongue quiet, and put them all into a
sleep, which would have lasted till doomsday if
the rustling of a *Lamb-beard* had not awakened
them. But they have had a nap since, and besides
that, the symptomes of death are now upon them;
for by the violence of a *Scotch* poticn they are
become stark mad, and every day are about to
destroy themselves. The only cordial which is left
them is the hopes of a Commonwealth, and there
can be no restorative but an army of sectaries.
Their physic hitherto hath bin only purging, but
because the matter of the disease is a masse of
earth (King's and other's lands) lying upon their
consciences, the noble *Monck* is providing them
a vomit, which, with an *aymulett* of hemp to be
tied about their necks, will render them perfectly
cured. An ingenious person hath observed, that
Scot is the Rump's man Thomas, and they might
have said to him when he was so busy with the
General—

"Peace for the Lord's sake, Thomas, lest Monck take us,
    And drag us out as Hercules did Cacus."

But *John Milton* is their goose-quill champion, who had need of a help meet to establish any thing, for he has a Ramshead, and is good only at Batteries, an old heretick both in religion and manners, that by his will would shake off his governours, as he doth his wives, foure in a fourt-night. The sunbeams of his scandalous papers against the late King's book is the parent that begot his late new Commonwealth; and because he, like a parasite as he is, by flattering the then tyrannical power, hath run himself into the bryers, the man will be angry if the rest of the nation will not bear him company, and suffer themselves to be decoyed into the same condition. He is so much an enemy to usual practices, that I believe when he is condemned to travel to *Tyburn* in a cart, he will petition for the favour to be the first man that ever was driven thither in a wheel-barrow. And now, *John*, you must stand close and draw in your elbows, that *Needham*, the Common-wealth's Didaper, may have room to stand by you. This is a Mercury with a winged conscience, the skip-jack of all fortunes, that, like a shuttle-cock, drive him which way you will, falls still with the cork end forwards; the Rump's trumpeter, being he that first found out the way to make a fart sound in paper; a rare fellow at funerall orations, witness his eloquent shreds in praise of that devil incarnate, King-killing *Bradshaw;* a brazen face that dares lay his excrements under the nose of the whole world, and hath less wit than the country-man, who, putting down his breeches in the open streets, turned his buttocks to the com-pany, because they were not so well known as his face. He was one of the spokes of *Harrington's Rota*, till he was turned out for cracking. As for

Harrington, he's but a demy-semy in the Rump's musick, and should bee good at the cymball, for he is all for wheeling instruments, and, having a good invention, may in time finde out the way to make a Consort of Grindstones. He hath oceans in his head, which, if he take not heed, will deluge his other parts. He is no common man, for such he sayes can onely feele and not see, but the next summer he will see his errours first, and then feele the smart of them. Would any man in his witts (think he) renounc't his own present interest and possession, to be at the curtesy of others for another portion or inheritance. The people of England have lived happily even to the envy of others under Regall Government; they knew their own rights and native priviledges. Shall they surrender these, and cancel their present happinesse which they are sure of, for the expectance of a better condition at the will and pleasure of new masters, upon the onely security of Mr. Harrington's romantick Commonwealth? That the new senators will do all they can to keep the people in slavery, and to support their owne authority, is strongly to be presumed from the fresh example of the late monopolizers at *Westminster;* and if they should doe so, what better remedy have the free-borne people of England, than Mr. Harrington had against him that say'd his *Oceana* was a strumpet? He may know that if there were any inconvenience (as no Government is perfect), yet it is prudence rather to suffer a stone ill-placed in the foundation (though it be an eye-sore) to lye unmoved, than, by endeavouring to pluck it out, endanger the whole building. How many new lawes have been made in this nation, with full and deliberate advise of the three estates for the benefit of the Common-

wealth, when yet time and experience, the touch-
stones of truth, have found them inconvenient
afterwards, and given occasion of their repeale in
subsequent Parliaments! Have not many men
applauded themselves with the beautifull figure of
a house drawne in paper, when the materiall building framed after the modell hath deluded their
hopes, and given repentance instead of satisfaction?
Surely Mr. Harrington did not copy any of his
lines out of the book of fate; therefore there is no
necessity but that it may be subject to the inci-
dents of other projects, whereof not one in a
thousand but have engaged the untakers in infinit
more troubles and vexations than were at first
foreseen.   I shall say no more of him, but desire
him to recant in time, least he be estemed hereafter but the Rump of a Polititian.   The Rump
had no mouth but that of their Speaker, which is
not very big, but hath spoke a horrible deale of
treason in his dayes.   Its arms have extended
through the whole three nations, and at last
whipt their own politick breech; but I think it
wants the propagating part ever since Noll
eunuch't it, so that no Rump can be borne such.
They must be framed by art, and the receipt of
their composition you will find in the following
lines, copied from Sir Arthur Haslerigg's own
manuscript :—

> " Hew out a statue from Mount Caucasus,
>   Big as the Colosse in the Isle of Rhodes ;
>   Then adde a brazen face and iron hands,
>   A poisonous viper's heart and leathern lungs,
>   A tongue of bell-mettal, and ostrich stomack
>   To digest iron.   Let his leggs and feet
>   Be made of quicksilver half fixt, and when
>   His outward members are by curious art
>   Fram'd out in such dreadful proportions,

Then let the Furies, in hell's dark alembeck,
With damned chymistry extract the spirits
Of secret treason, cursed sacriledge,
Black murder and false-hearted perjury,
Pride, hatred, lust, and swinish luxury,
Fraud, drunkennesse, oppression, and the rest
Of the black progeny of vice ; and with
The quintessence of these, being sublimated
Unto the height of wickedness, inform
The ugly mass with a more ugly soul.
And that the monster may not want a name,
Say he's a Rumper, and we'll say the same."

According to Aubrey, Charles the First " loved "
the company of Harrington, "only he could not
endure to hear of a Commonwealth ; and Mr.
Harrington passionately loved His Majestie." He
was on the scaffold with the King when he was
beheaded; " and I have oftentimes heard him speak
of King Charles I. with the greatest zeal and passion, and that his death gave him so greate griefe
that he contracted a disease by it." His Majesty
presented him and " Herbert the traveller," who
was also present on the scaffold, with watches.*

We omitted to notice that Mrs. Behn, in 1682,
produced at the Duke's Theatre *The Roundhead ;
or, The Good Old Cause*—a comedy, in which she has
made great use of *The Rump.* The prologue is
" spoken by the ghost of Huson, ascending from
Hell drest as a cobler." The epilogue, by Lady
Desbro. It is like most of the writer's plays,
very amusing.

* See *Letters in Bodleian Library, etc.,* vol. iii. p. 370, for
further particulars as to the author of the *Oceana.*

LONDON'S GLORY,

REPRESENTED BY

TIME, TRUTH, AND FAME,

AT THE MAGNIFICENT TRIUMPHS AND ENTERTAINMENT OF HIS
MOST SACRED MAJESTY

CHARLES II.,

THE DUKE OF GLOUCESTER, THE TWO HOUSES OF
PARLIAMENT, PRIVY COUNCIL, JUDGES, ETC.

*At Guildhall, on Thursday, being the 5th day of July 1660, and in the
12th year of his Majesty's most happy reign.*

TOGETHER WITH THE ORDER AND MANAGEMENT OF THE WHOLE
DAY'S BUSINESS.

Published according to Order.

SIR THOMAS ALEYN, KNIGHT,

LORD MAYOR OF THE CITY OF LONDON.

MY LORD,—I had the honour to serve you in the celebration of your Companies' love, the 29th of October last, and from thence derive a boldness to present you with the epitome of this day's business. My lord, as your loyalty hath been great, your joy cannot be little, nor your happiness less, that the hand of Providence in the time of your magistracy should restore our most gracious and undoubted Sovereign to his just (though long deprived) rights. This being committed to chronicle, must necessarily render you eminent to posterity, and make your honour firm, which before was subject to be blown away by the breath of malice and detraction. Pardon the presumption (my lord) if I subscribe myself, the humblest of your servants,

J. TATHAM.

TO THE READER.

READER,—I have omitted some passages, in regard they might have prov'd too tedious, and my time was limited. If it want illustration, excuse the surprisall, which, as it was sudden, took me unprepared. But I confess I am highly obliged to a person of worth for his notes, of whom I likewise beg pardon if I have digress'd in any thing.

TIME'S SPEECH.

MOST SACRED SIR,

[*Kneels.*

Time, on his bended knee, your pardon craves,
Having been made a property to slaves,
A stalking horse unto their horrid crimes:
Yet when things went not well the fault was Time's.
My fore-top held by violence, not right,
Dy'd the sun's cheeks with blood, defil'd the light:
That all men thought they eas'd their misery
If they could but securely rail on me.
These clamours troubled Time, who streight grew sick
With discontents, as touch'd unto the quick;
And so far spent 'twas thought he could not mend,
Rather grow worse and worse; all wish'd his end.
Nay, was concluded dead, and, worst of all,
With many a curse they peal'd his funeral.
Now see the change: since your arrival here
Time is reviv'd, and nothing thought too dear
That is consum'd upon him; ne'er was he
So lov'd and pray'd for since his infancy.
Such is the vertual fervour of your beams,
That not obliquely but directly streams
Upon your subjects; so the glorious sun
Gives growth to th' infant plants he smiles upon.
Welcome, great Sir, unto your people's love,
Who breathe their very souls forth as you move.
Their long and tedious suff'rings do express,
'Till now they ne'er had sense of blessedness.
The cheer'd-up citizens cease to complain,
Having receiv'd their cordial Soveraign.
Among the rest the Skinners' Company
Crowd to express their sense of loyalty.
And those born deaf and dumb, and can but see,
Make their hands speak *Long live your Majesty*;
Whose royal presence cures the wounded State,
Re-gilds Time's coat, and gives a turn to Fate.

TRUTH'S SPEECH.

MOST GRACIOUS SOVERAIGN,

[*Kneels.*

Bound by allegiance, Truth, daughter to Time
(Long since abus'd), welcomes you to this clime,
Your native soyle, to which you have been long
A stranger.   Now Truth should not want a tongue;
Although she hath been murder'd by report,
She's now camp-royal and attends your court;
And as, in rules of strict divinity,
He that desires the Judge's clemency
Must first condemn himself, and so prepare
His way for pardon, 'tis your kingdome's care;
Who do confess, whilst other nations strove
Which should be happiest in your princely love,
Were so insensible of that blest heat,
A pulse they wanted loyalty to beat;
With penitential tears they meet your palme,
Shewing a loyal tempest in a calme.
Then from your rayes of majesty they do
Derive such joy speaks no less wonder too.
Children that hardly heard of such a thing
Now frequently do cry *God bless the King;*
Nay, though their damned sires instructed them
To hate the cask'net, yet they'll love the gem.
Such is your radices that you refine
Sublunar things to species more divine.
You have new coyn'd all hearts, and there imprest
Your image, which gives vigour to the rest
Of their late stupid faculties, that now
They'll pass for current, and true subjects grow.
Th' untainted Clothiers' Company, by me
Their instrument, pray for your Majesty:
May you live long and happy, and encrease
For ever crown the harvest of your peace,
Since graciously you have deceiv'd our fears,
Instead of wars brought musick of the spheres.

U

Fame's Speech.

Most Mighty Sir,

[*Kneels.*

Fame, that ne'er left you at the worst essay,
Welcomes you home, and glorifies this day.
You whose blest innocence and matchless mind
Could ne'er be stain'd or any wayes confin'd,
Has stood the shock of Fortune's utmost hate,
And yet your courage did outdare your fate,
That even those fiends (for sure none else could be
Your enemies) admir'd your constancy,
Commending that they most did envy; so
Against their wills your fame did greater grow.
And when those miscreants 'gainst you did prepare,
And thought you sure, your wisdom broke the snare.
'Twas strange that through the cloud none could descry
A spark of that fulness of majesty.
But Heav'n, that orders all things as it list,
Shut up their eyes in an Egyptian mist.
You have past many labyrinths, are return'd
Now to your people, who long time have mourn'd
The want of your warm beams; they have not known
A sommer since your father left his throne,
That like th' benum'd Muscovians they now run,
With eager haste, to meet their rising sun;
And if the rout in uproar chance to be,
It can't be judg'd but loyal mutiny;
Since that you do their golden times revive,
They to express a joyful salve strive.
Blest Prince, thrice welcome is the general cry,
And in that speaks the Grocers' Company,
To which the present Mayor a brother is,
Whose loyalty finds happiness in this,
This royal change. Fame now shall spread his wing,
And of your after glories further sing;
Since in your self you are a history,
A volume bound up for eternity.

The Order and Management of the Whole Day's Business.

The chamber windows and penthouses to be covered with tapistrie, or such hangings as may glorifie the day.

The streets, from the south end of the Old Jury to Temple Bar, are railed on both sides the way where conveniency will permit; the several Companies in their livery gowns and hoods, with banners and streamers, lane the streets, in expectation of his Majestie's approach, from the Great Conduit to Temple Bar.

The Lord Mayor, Aldermen, and their retinue, are all mounted and divided into two bodies; several choice persons out of the several liveries in plush coats and gold chains ride also.

The gentlemen of the artillery compleatly armed.

Threescore and twelve of the Sheriff's officers mounted in scarlet cloaks, and javelins in their hands, divided into a van and rear-guard from and to Whitehall.

The main body is ranked out two by two, consisting of the two city marshals and their twelve attendants; eight waits in scarlet-coloured jackets, with the citie's badge on their sleeves, and cloaks with silver lace; one quartermaster, Mr.   , carrying the great banner of England; after him 26 gentlemen of the black robe, that is to say, beginning with the two secondaries, and ending with the common serjeants.

Then the city waits in their gowns and silver chains, one quartermaster, one conductor; the common-hunt carrying the King's great banner, and the water bailiff on the left hand of him, carrying the citie's banner; after them the town clerk, and Mr. Chamberlain, the common cryer and sword-bearer; after them the Lord Mayor and Court of Aldermen.

Then six trumpets and one kettledrum, one quartermaster, one conducter, Mr. Bromley carrying the banner with the crest of the King's arms, Mr. Burt on the left hand of him carrying the citie's pendent, and in the reer of them one carries a pendent with the Grocers' arms; in the reer of him 32 gentlemen of the said

Company ; and then follows 298 gentlemen of the other 11 Companies, placed according to their degree : between each of the said Companies is ordered 4 trumpets, one of them carrying a pendent with their arms.

Note that the Grocers, Skinners, Merchant-Taylors, and Cloth-Workers have each of them 52 select gentlemen to ride, the rest of the Companies but 24.

Then of the other 12 Companies, consisting of 156 gentlemen, besides 28 trumpets, 12 pendant-bearers, that is to say, one pendant-bearer and two trumpets between Company and Company, only the head of the Dyers' Company have 6 trumpets, and being the first of that division have a quartermaster, Mr. Alexander carrying the Scottish banner, and Mr. Knight carrying a pendant therein.

Then ten other of the Companies, of which the Sadlers' being chief, have 6 trumpets, the other nine Companies but two a piece. To this division is appointed 10 pendant-bearers, and one quartermaster, Mr. Bancroft carrying the Irish banner, Mr. Blinkensop carrying a pendant with the citie's arms, and 164 gentlemen in plush coats following.

The seventh division consists of the Sheriff's officers aforesaid, with 6 trumpets in the front of them.

The eighth is the gentlemen of the artillery-ground, who fall in the reer of the Sheriff's officers.

The several bodies being drawn out, the officers of the Poultrey lead the van after them.

The gentlemen of the artillery after them.

The divisions of the black robe after them.

The Lord Mayor and aldermen's servitors.

After them the three divisions of citizens in plush coats, &c., beginning with the Grocers' Company, and so follow in order ; the officers of Wood Street counter being the reer-guard.

In this order and equipage the whole body moves through the Old Jury, Cheapside, Paul's Churchyard,

Ludgate, and so to Whitehall, the gentlemen of the artillery ground guarding one side of the way, and the gentlemen of the long robe the other, through which the Lord Mayor and aldermen with their retinue pass to Whitehall; the elder aldermen face about, and the chamberlain, town clerk, sword - bearer, common cryer, common hunt, water-bailiff, &c., march up to the head of the youngest aldermen, and there place themselves.

The gentlemen of the artillery, and poultrey counter, poultrey officers quit their ground, and fall in the reer of the Wood Street officers, &c.

His Majesty, attended with the Lords of the Upper House, the Commons in Parliament, Lords of his Majestie's most honourable Privy Councel, barons, viscounts, earls, marquisses, and dukes, the Lord Mayor, Lord Chamberlain, Lord Chancellor, the Lord Treasurer, the highly accomplish'd princes the Dukes of York and Glocester, takes his way for Guildhall, and at Fleet Street Conduit makes a stand, where he is received by a person representing Time in a very glorious pageant, who addresseth himself to his Majesty on his knee in the manner aforesaid.

And so his Majesty, the two dukes, and the rest of the noble retinue and gentlemen, pass on to Paul's Churchyard, where they are intertained by another pageant, very much amplified and adorned, in which is seated Truth, who maketh her address as aforesaid.

Another pageant presents its self at Foster Lane, being a large and goodly fabrick, a trumpetter placed on the top, where it was intended Fame should speak; but at the Great Conduit in Cheapside, Fame presents her speech.

At Paul's Chain is another pageant in the nature of a droll, where is presented the figure of Industry, and the Carders and Spinners, in relation to the Clothiers' Company.

At Cheapside Crosse another droll, where Pretty and the tumblers play their tricks.

A lane made from the north-west corner of the Little Conduit toward the Great Conduit as aforesaid, through which the whole body pass, consisting of the gentlemen

of the black robe and aldermen, into Guildhall yard.
The Sheriff's officers dismount at the north end of St.
Lawrence Lane, delivering their horses to be convey'd
towards Wood Street, in order to his Majestie's retreat
after dinner, and themselves betake them to their several
services in the hall.

The Peers and Commons dismount at Guildhall gate,
and by the conductors are directed to their several
roomes for entertainment. Their coaches are driven
through Aldermanbury, Cripplegate, White Cross Street,
Finsbury, &c., in regard of their number.

The Lord Mayor, Lord Chamberlain, Lord Chancellor,
Lord High Steward, Lord Treasurer, the two Dukes, and
his Majesty ride up to the porch of the hall before they
light.

Carpets are spread from the hall door to the retiring
room for his Majesty to tread upon, where the conductors make a lane to pass.

The Master of the Horse and Captain of the Guard
also ride into Guildhall yard, and dispose of themselves,
&c.

Note that the secretaries, clerks of the Council, clerks
to both Houses, the Gentlemen of the Bedchamber, the
Masters of Requests, the Master of the Ceremonies,
Yeoman of the Mouth, the sewer, the carver, and the
butler to his Majesty, are admitted into the hall, and no
other.

The new Council Chamber in Guildhall is appointed
for his Majestie's presence chamber and banquetting
room.

The old Council Chamber, Orphan's Court and Lobby,
ornamented accordingly, is ordered for reception of the
Lords of the Council, Judges, and other nobility.

The Mayor's Court for entertainment of the House of
Commons.

In the Great Hall.   [*His Majestie's Table.*]

The hasting towards the west is appointed for his
Majesty and his royal brothers to dine at, where a chair
of state and other ornaments answerable are placed.

The part of the hall lying between the eastside of Little Ease and his Majesty's hasting eastward, appointed for the House of Peers, Lords of the Council, and Judges, to dine at, &c.

At the west part of Little Ease in Guildhall (ornamented accordingly) the House of Commons are to dine.

Attendants upon his Majestie and his royal brothers as to their table.

Eight stewards, consisting of 4 aldermen and 4 common council men.

2 comptrollers.
2 ushers.   *His Majestie's Table.*
2 butlers.
2 masters of the revels, in velvet coats.

Attendants on the House of Peers.

Eight stewards, whereof 4 aldermen and 4 common council men.

2 comptrollers.
2 ushers.   *The House of Peers' Table.*
2 butlers.
1 master of the revels.

The House of Commons' Table.

The like number of persons (except masters of the revels) like habited.

Gentlemen entertained in Blackwell Hall.

6 stewards.
3 comptrollers.
2 ushers.
2 butlers.

Notice given that his Majesty and the rest are in their several retiring rooms, every officer, according to his condition and quality, imploys himself, the conductors placing the servitors (being clad in plush) side by side from each dresser to their several tables, on which they are to attend.

At the sound of the loud musick the whole service is immediately set on each table.

The Lord Mayor's and Sheriff's officers are divided into parties, and placed as servitors to each table.

Note that all the servitors wear his Majestie's colours on their arms.

His Majesty during dinner time hath several musical compliances, both instrumental and vocal.

That ended, his Majesty and the rest retiring, is presented with a banquet.

After which, his Majesty being ready to depart, the gentlemen of the artillery, &c., placed from the south end of the Old Jury to the west end of Cheapside, with trophies and trumpets, receive his Majesty, being plac'd on the left hand the street, the several Companies on the right.

The Lord Mayor, aldermen, and whole body attending his Majesty to Whitehall, the Lord Mayor hath the honour to wait on him into the Presence Chamber. In the interim the gentlemen of the artillery and the rest prepare for their retreat, expecting his Lordship's return, which being discovered, a volley is given, and every man departeth to his [home].